PAPA DON'T
PREACH

ALSO BY THOMAS LONG

A Thug's Life
Cash Rules

Anthologies:
Around the Way Girls 2
Around the Way Girls 3

PAPA DON'T PREACH

Thomas Long

www.urbanbooks.net

LON

Urban Books
10 Brennan Place
Deer Park, NY 11729

ISBN-13: 978-1-893196-65-0
ISBN-10: 1-893196-65-8

First Printing May 2007
Printed in the United States of America

10   9   8   7   6   5   4   3   2   1

This is a work of fiction. Any references or similarities to actual events, real people, living, or dead, or to real locales are intended to give the novel a sense of reality. Any similarity to other names, characters, places, and incidents is entirely coincidental.

Submit Wholesale Orders to:
Kensington Publishing Corp.
C/O Penguin Group (USA) Inc.
Attention: Order Processing
405 Murray Hill Parkway
East Rutherford, NJ 07073-2316
Phone: 1-800-526-0275
Fax: 1-800-227-9604

Acknowledgements

The past year has been a good year for ya boy. I got this new joint that you're about to read and I think it's my most in depth work ever. I hope you feelin' it too. If not, it's too late now cause you already spent $15 to buy it (LOL—just joking). On the real, I appreciate all of my readers 100 percent. I got a movie coming out in '07 called **"4 Life"** that's based on my first book **"A Thug's Life"**. The cast for this movie is outta this world. I got another flick coming out soon afterwards based on **"Cash Rules"**, my second novel, that's gonna be even sicker. I couldn't ask for much more than that because I would be being greedy. I'm not gonna bore you to death with ten pages of acknowledgements like this is the sleeve of a rap album or something (LOL). Nah, on the real, I just wanna send a shout out to the following:

Jihad, K. Elliott, K'wan—it's been real from the start so let's keep it that way my niggas; My Bmore nigga Tony Austin, President of Russell Simmons Music Group and founder of Watch Me Now Films—from the gym to the big screen you making ya boy's dreams come true. You just don't know what you done started. I appreciate ya vision for **"4 Life"** in bringing it into fruition. You told me that you was gonna make it happen and you did. Ain't many niggas that keep it real like dat. You're a trailblazer. The movie came out phenomenal. Now, let's do it again and get this money, my nigga!; #96 from the Baltimore Ravens, Adalius Thomas, co-owner of Watch Me Now Films—can we get another Super Bowl up in Bmore or what? Nah, 4 real, I appreciate you and Tony for believing in my talent; my nigga Hak (the director of "4 Life")—you're a star on the rise in Hollywood. All them phone calls and ya insight on scriptwriting is invaluable. I hope we get to work together again in the future; Tyrone Dixon (producer of "4 Life")—thanks for ya words of wisdom and encouragement. You done lit a fire in me to start banging out some hot scripts!; Wood Harris (Dayvon)—to be a superstar actor and all that, you're one down to Earth cat! I had you in mind to play the lead from the jump. You made Dayvon come to life exactly how I envisioned; the beautiful Elise Neal (Jare) and Sundy Carter (Sasha)—the experience meeting you two queens was brief but a true pleasure. Thanks for lending your talent to this project. It's because of you two that every brother in the hood is gonna wanna see **"4Life"** (lol); Page Kennedy (Ty)—a raw talent—there ain't much more to say than that; JD Williams (Pooh)—you did ya thing, son!; my nigga Michael K. Ross—we gonna definitely chop it up in LA. You one live cat fa sho!; Karron—another Morganite; the DP for **4 Life**—Tommy Maddox—you're a genius man! My man Darryl Walthol—good lookin' out!; the lovely La Dawn Black from 92Q—thanks for having me on ya show back in the day. Sorry, it took me so long to shout you out. I wish you much success with ya writing; last but not least to Carl Weber and Urban Books for opening the door for me to do what I do.

1

Mickey's Bar and Lounge, a cozy little spot located in the downtown area, was the place to be on a Friday night in Baltimore. It was where a select group of young Black professionals went after work to have a drink and mingle. Some of the finest brothers and sisters in the city could be found there dressed in the hottest gear. The bar area in the front of the lounge was where everybody stopped first to get something to sip on and to socialize. The medium-sized dance floor in the rear area stayed packed with partygoers dancing to the slamming sounds of DJ Precise, who played the latest R&B songs and mixed in a nice blend of house music. Mickey's had a standing-room capacity of about one hundred people, but the crowd usually exceeded that.

Nigel and his two partners in crime, Pretty Ricky and Fats, sat in an old Ford Taurus parked up the street from Mickey's. They scoped out the line of partygoers entering the club and licked their chops, thinking about the potential to score big if they robbed the place. The size of the crowd that entered Mickey's guaranteed them that there was a lot of money to be snatched if they pulled the job off. They noticed that there were only two bouncers searching people as they entered the club. With security so light, this job was too good to be passed up.

"Aaah, that was some good shit right there. I feel like I'm floating on cloud nine right now," Nigel said ecstatically as he inhaled the fumes of cocaine smoke coming through the tiny holes in the aluminum foil that covered his medicine bottle. The medicine bottle served as his homemade crack pipe. He waited about a minute before he took another pull.

"Stop hoggin' the pipe, Nigel," Ricky shouted. "We tryin' ta beam up to Scotty too!"

Nigel passed the makeshift pipe.

Pretty Ricky took the pipe, placed a small rock-shaped piece of cocaine into the hole in the side of the bottle, and lit fire to it with his cigarette lighter. As the fumes entered his lungs, he relaxed his head up against the headrest on the back seat. He let the high soak in and enjoyed the buzz.

Pretty Ricky got his name because he used to be considered somewhat of a ladies' man. In his better days, he resembled Billy Dee Williams, with his dark, wavy hair and golden-brown complexion. Today, he was hardly a pretty nigga, because his yellow, stained teeth and acne-filled face made him look like a creature from a horror film.

"Y'all niggas look higher than a muthafucka. Y'all should be ashamed of ya selves. You know that shit ain't no good for you. Nancy Reagan told us all to 'just say no' and look at you two fools," Fats joked. "You're setting a bad example for the youth of America."

"Nigga, shut the fuck up and hit this shit. You talk too damn much. You keep smoking these rocks and that big-ass head of yours might just get smaller and not weigh you down as much." Nigel said with a slight chuckle. Pretty Ricky laughed as well.

Fats, real name Theodore Wilson, got his nickname because everybody used to tease him about having such a slim
body and a large head. His huge cranium weighed so heavily
on his skinny neck that it looked like it would cause him to
tilt over at any moment when he walked down the street. The
weight loss from his drug use only made his physical defect
stand out that much more. He was used to being teased about
his large head and paid their jibes no mind.

Not wanting to be left out of the party, Fats took the pipe
outta Pretty Ricky's hand to get his chance to beam up to
Scotty. They all took turns passing the pipe back and forth to
each other until every single rock was gone. They waited for
their high to die down some before they decided the time
was right for them to make a move.

It was around one-thirty in the morning when they sprung
into action. The club was about to close down at two. Most of
the people inside were too intoxicated to be alert for what
was about to go down. The element of surprise is a bitch.

Shotgun in hand, Nigel approached the doorway of
Mickey's Bar and Lounge looking like a black panther ready
to attack his prey. Pretty Ricky and Fats were right by his side
and equally strapped with some heavy artillery. They all wore
masks to conceal their identities. When they opened the door
of the club, they were greeted by two buffed bouncers. Nigel
and his crew came in the door with their weapons aimed,
cocked and ready to squeeze. The two muscle-bound buf-
foons were caught off guard and looked terrified.

Nigel pointed his shotgun at one of the security guards.
"You make a fuckin' sound and I'ma splatter ya brains all over
the wall!"

The two security guards' muscles and brawn were no
match for the steel that was in the hands of the three masked
gunmen. They walked backward into the lounge with their
hands in the air, escorted by Nigel and his team.

The DJ caught a glimpse of the two security guards being escorted into the lounge against their will by the three armed men and instantly cut the music off. The people in the crowd turned around to see why the music had stopped. When the patrons saw the three armed Black men dressed in all black and wearing masks, they all began to panic. A few of the ladies screamed in fear, as pandemonium filled the room.

Nigel cocked the double-barreled shotgun that he held in his hands once, to let everybody in the place know that he meant business, and fired one shot in the air. As the crowd ran for cover, he and his comrades made their way to the center of the lounge.

"A'ight, y'all know what time it is. This is a stick-up!" Nigel yelled at the crowd of stunned partygoers.

"That's right," Pretty Ricky added. "The first muthafucka that moves up in here is gonna know what it feels like to taste some hot-ass lead."

Everybody in the club hit the floor.

"Please, don't shoot," the bartender pleaded. "We don't want any trouble. You can have all of the money out of the cash register. Here, it's all yours." He took all of the money out of the register and attempted to come from behind the bar to hand it to Fats.

Fats knocked the money out of his hand and pistol-whipped him upside his head. "Didn't we say nobody move up in this muthafucka!" Blood began to ooze from the gash that opened up over the bartender's right eye.

Nigel barked at the bartender, "We're running this show, you lil' faggot. You don't tell us what we can have. We're calling the shots. Now, we want everything in that register and in the pockets of every one of you muthafuckas up in here before we leave. Now, get ya ass over here and pick this money up off the floor!"

The bartender got down on the floor and did as he was instructed, holding his hand over his eye to try to stop the flow of blood. Fats took the wad of money from him and put it into the large cloth bag that he removed from his shoulder.

"We want everybody up in here to strip down to your drawers. Next, I want all of your wallets and pocketbooks placed in this bag that my friend here has in his hand. Take off all of them jewels as well. We ain't got all day. We're giving you five minutes to do as you've been told or else this gun in my hand is gonna get to spittin' some rounds," Pretty Ricky promised the petrified bar patrons. As wired as he was from the coke, he was insane enough to deliver on his promise.

All of the patrons began to disrobe quickly, fast, and in a hurry. A few of the male patrons wore a look of emasculation on their faces, not being able to defend themselves from being robbed, while the females in the lounge stood in their bras and panties and attempted to cover their private areas as much as possible. Within minutes, all of their valuables were thrown into Fats bag.

Once that was done, Nigel instructed everybody to lie down on the floor face-down. "We'd like to thank you all for your cooperation. It was a pleasure robbing ya asses blind. If anybody attempts to get up before we make it outta the door, I promise you that your death will make the eleven o'clock news with the gaping hole this shotgun in my hand will put in ya body. I want everybody to count to one hundred while my associates and I exit the premises. Everybody, have a good night," Nigel said, a sinister grin on his face.

The rambling sound of the petrified patrons counting to one hundred was all that could be heard throughout the lounge as Nigel and his goons made their exit. They ran back to the car, excited to have pulled the job off without a glitch. They got away with over ten G's in cash and goods for less than ten minutes of "work." With money to get high for at least a week, they were in crack fiends' heaven.

2

"Watch it, nigga!" Debbie said. "Slow ya ass down. That shit hurts. You're about to tear my walls apart, fool."

Nigel didn't realize the amount of pain that his intense thrusts were causing Debbie, and in all honesty, he really didn't care. He was high outta his mind, and all he was concerned with was bustin' a nut.

"Shut up, trick, and take this dick. That's what you're here for—to get high and get fucked. Let me do my thing without interrupting me." Nigel kept pounding on her just as intensely.

"Beat da thing up, Nigel. When you're done I want another turn with that ho," Fats yelled from the bed next to Nigel. He was getting busy with Pinky, another "strawberry" they'd picked up off the strip.

Pretty Ricky was in the adjoining room getting some brains from another tramp named Princess, as he sat on the edge of the bed still doting on his crack pipe.

Nigel and his crew booked two adjoining rooms at the

Town House Motel on Reisterstown Road to trick away the money they'd made from their caper. They'd scooped the girls up from on Garrison and Liberty Heights, an area of Baltimore City known for prostitution.

Debbie was the best-looking one out of the trio. She had long flowing hair that hung from her petite body and a flat chest with nipples the size of quarters, but her plump little ass made her worth fucking. Pinky was an albino chick that looked pale enough to be Casper the Friendly Ghost. She didn't have all of the battle scars of a full-fledged "rock star" because her ass was still fatter than a ghetto rat and her humongous breasts weren't sagging yet. Princess's name didn't fit her in any way, shape or form. Her face looked like a mule's ass. She had a crooked buck-toothed smile and could suck a dick for two hours straight without losing a stroke. That talent was good enough to get any woman in the hood some action.

The three men took turns fucking all three of them for the past five days. The females didn't mind being passed around like a bad cold, as long as there was free rock to smoke.

"There it is, bitch. Take that all over ya nasty ass!" Nigel yelled as he ejaculated on Debbie's neck and rolled over onto the bed.

She quickly wiped away the semen with her hand and attempted to get up off the bed and run into the bedroom, but Fats grabbed her arm. He'd already finished getting his thing off with Pinky, who'd gone into the other room to join Pretty Ricky and Princess for a threesome, and was ready for another turn with her.

"Where are you going at, girl? Bring that phat ass over to daddy. Let me see that thing jiggle one more time." Fats stood in the center of the floor, his semi-erect penis in his hand.

"Well, hurry up and do what you gotta do. Y'all niggas outta coke, so it's almost time for us to be up outta here."

Debbie laid out motionless on the bed as Fats mounted her and pumped as hard as he could in and out of her dry vagina until he reached his climax. It took him all of three minutes to reach his peak.

Nigel watched from other bed as he continued getting high. "Hey, Ricky, your boy Fats is a two-minute brother. He done smoked all that coke, and all he can do is stay in the pussy for three minutes. That's a damn shame."

Pretty Ricky could be heard laughing through the open door between the two rooms.

"Fuck you, nigga. I've been fucking for five days. My shit is tired."

"Well, since you're done, can you drop us back off on the strip?" Debbie started to gather up her tattered clothing and headed toward that bathroom to do a quick wash-up in the sink and to get dressed. "Y'all ain't got no more shit, and we need to be on the block so we can make some money." She yelled into the other room to tell Pinky and Princess that it was time to bounce. "Yeah, I need to get home anyway. We done had our fun with y'all tired asses."

"Fellas, let's get rid of these hoes and be up outta here," Nigel said, physically exhausted from the activities of the last few days.

In no time flat, they were all dressed and ready to leave. They all piled into Nigel's car. One by one, he dropped them all off at their destinations, and then headed home to his wife Lorraine and his son JR around four in the afternoon.

Nigel thought about what awaited him when he reached his house. He knew that he was in for some shit from Lorraine and her big mouth since he hadn't been home in almost a week. He'd been down this same road so many times before over the last few years that it was nothing new. Nonetheless, he wasn't looking forward to dealing with the hassle.

As he made his way toward his house on Woodland Avenue, he spoke to a couple of his neighbors posted up on the end of the block. He walked slowly to the house, making sure not to slip and fall on the cracked wooden steps. His plan to go into the house and get some shuteye wasn't gonna happen without a fight. He heard Lorraine's mouth as soon as his key turned in the lock and opened the door.

"Nigga, where the fuck have you been? You've been gone all of this time and I didn't know if you were dead or alive. This shit is gonna stop!" Lorraine said, with both hands on her thin hips. Her druggin' had robbed her of her once shapely figure.

Nigel knew just how to shut her up. "Look, woman, I ain't up for ya shit right now. I'm tired, and I wanna get some rest. You ain't the least bit concerned about me. Take this money and get the fuck outta my face. That's all you really want anyway." He handed her a fistful of wrinkled dollars totaling close to four hundred dollars. He made sure that he kept some of his loot to bring home to her. He had to have something to give her for being gone for so long. Nigel was the kind of addict that, no matter how much money he blew getting high, made sure that he kept a roof over his head. The bills had to be paid—all twenty-two dollars of the rent for their Section 8 home and whatever the electricity bill came to each month. He knew that the rest of the money that he gave her was going straight into a crack pipe.

"You ain't all that your damn self, Nigel. Is this all the money that you got for me after being gone all of those days? I bet you blew the rest of ya money out there on some two-bit hoes that you picked up off the streets, didn't you?"

"I'm a grown-ass man and I can do what the fuck I want. I didn't ask you about who you've been trickin' with while I was gone to get ya blast. I know you had some nigga up in here diggin' you out. I ain't a fool by a long shot, but that's your business. You can fuck whoever you want to, as long as I don't come home and catch no nigga up in here. If I do, then you know that's your ass. As long as my son has food to eat, then we have no problems. What I just gave you is enough money for you to smoke ya brains out for a good while. Don't forget to take some of it and pay the turn-off notice that we got from Baltimore Gas and Electric. And you better have this filthy-ass house clean before I wake up, you un-grateful bitch." Nigel looked around the messy house, trash and debris scattered everywhere, and shook his head in dis-gust.

"Yeah, whatever you say, nigga. What's good for you is good for me as well. You're out there fuckin' around on me. I got needs too. Ya son is upstairs sleep. He's been asking for you. He wanted to know when his Daddy was coming home. I shoulda told him, 'Never.'"

"Don't play with me, woman. You keep running ya mouth and I'ma close it for you."

Lorraine knew that tone too well. She knew that when Nigel was pissed off enough, he would lay hands on her without the least bit of guilt or remorse. He went upside her head more than enough times. She would start the arguments with her mouth, and he would end them with an open-hand smack to her jaw, an everyday occurrence in the Hawkins household.

Nigel walked past Lorraine and up the squeaky stairs. He looked into JR's room and saw him sleeping peacefully. Nigel looked on with pride at his son, who'd inherited his father's grey eyes, his grandfather's chubby cheeks, and his mother's smile and nose. Nigel went into the room to kiss him on his forehead, waking him up outta his sleep.

"I was looking for you, Daddy." JR rubbed his eyes. "Mommy wouldn't tell me where you were. Where have you been at?"

"Daddy had to take care of some business, lil' man. I had to work to get some money together to pay the bills." Nigel picked JR up outta the bed and cradled him in his arms. He tickled his ribs playfully.

JR giggled. "Daddy, can I ask you a question?"

"Yeah, you can ask me whatever you want to, son. Nothing is off-limits to my lil' man."

"Are you sure? I don't want you to get mad at me."

"Son, you're a Hawkins man. You can ask me whatever you want. I promise I won't get upset."

"Well, the other night while you were gone, Mommy thought I was 'sleep, but I wasn't and I snuck outta my room to get something to drink. Mommy was in the living room alone, and I saw her crawling around like a dog. She was talking to herself saying that she was looking for rocks or something. She started picking balls of lint off the couch. She looked crazy, Daddy. What was she doing?" JR had a look of confusion on his face.

"Your mother wasn't doing anything, JR." Nigel forced a smile. "She was just playing around. It's nothing for you to be worried about."

Nigel chuckled inside because he knew what was really going on with Lorraine. He'd been on the same geek trip himself many times. Smoking that shit made his mind play tricks on him in the same manner. When the crack was cooked up right, it got him higher than a muthafucka. On a regular basis he'd found himself crawling around looking for some more shit when there was no more to be found. If he saw a ball of lint on the couch or the ground, he would pick it up and think it was a crack rock. When it came to crack cocaine, there was never enough of that shit to satisfy the jones that it gave to a hype. In fact a basehead could pass out from exhaustion before losing the desire to chase that high.

"Daddy, I'm hungry." JR rubbed his belly and lay across his father's lap.

"Your mother didn't feed you?"

"Nah. I'm starving. I haven't eaten since yesterday. When I asked Mommy to fix me something to eat, she beat me and told me to lie down and take a nap." JR lifted up his shirt to show his father the bruises on his back from the belt that Lorraine used on him.

"Is that right? She beat you like this? I can't have nobody beating on my lil' man. Right now I want you to run downstairs and tell your mother that I said for her to fix you something to eat. If she says no, then I will deal with her." *That bitch is just trifling. She can't even feed her own son, but I bet she made sure that she had some rock to smoke.*

"Okay, Daddy. I heard you two down there arguing. I wish you wouldn't fight each other so much. I want us to be a happy family. I love you, Daddy." JR gave his father a big hug.

"I love you too, baby boy." Nigel got a warm feeling inside from his son's affectionate words. In his heart he wanted to give JR a better life, but he was too caught up in his addiction to change their reality. His love for crack was stronger than the bond he had with his son, or any other human being. If Nigel had to make a choice between getting high or saving somebody's life, he would choose the drug without a second thought, and that person would be one dead soul.

JR slid off the bed and ran down the stairs to relay his father's message to his mother. Nigel waited a few minutes for him to return, but he didn't. That meant that Lorraine did as she was told and fixed JR something to eat.

Nigel went to the bathroom to take a leak. He pissed like a racehorse because he'd been holding it the whole ride home. After he finished relieving himself, he took a washcloth from the towel rack to wash his crusty face. Nigel barely recognized his image in the mirror. His once firmly built two-hundred-plus-pound frame had wilted to a measly bag of bones, and it all seemed to happen overnight. His cheeks

were so sunk in that he looked like a walking skeleton, and
his collarbone stuck out through the top of the filthy Russell
sweatshirt that he'd been wearing for the past five days. His
black Nike sneakers were battered and torn from the countless hours he'd spent roaming the streets of Baltimore at
night, and the whites of his eyes were bloodshot-red, due to a
lack of sleep. They damn near looked like they wanted to pop
outta his head, because they were so dilated. The odor that
permeated from his body was so repulsive that it would make
a skunk run and hide for cover. He was so ashy that his dark
skin looked pale white. He was in serious need of a bath and
a bottle of Lubriderm lotion.

Nigel Hawkins tried everything imaginable to convince
himself that his life wasn't as fucked up as it really was, but
nothing worked. He was once one of the smoothest hustlers
that the streets of Baltimore had ever molded and shaped.
Today, he was a crackhead, robbing and stealing whatever he
could to support his habit.

Nigel's marriage wasn't based on love; it was a situation of
convenience. Crack cocaine and his son were the only bonds
that he and his wife shared. He was caught up in his own
ghetto soap opera that had more twists and turns than a
Stephen King novel.

His father, Augustus Hawkins, married the love of his life,
Aileen, when he was twenty-two, and the couple had three
sons, Albert, Franklin, and Nigel. An old-school gangster with
Mafia ties who was heavily involved in the numbers racket
and ran a string of whorehouses throughout the city, Augustus had spent several small stints in prison throughout Nigel's
childhood, and taught him everything he knew about the
streets.

Aileen was a beautiful woman who came from a modest
Christian family. She was instantly swept off her feet by the
suave, fast-talking Augustus. She didn't approve of her hus-

band's choice of profession, but her humane spirit allowed her to see the good in him when no one else could. To her, Augustus wasn't the ruthless criminal that others made him out to be. In her eyes, he was a good father who did what he had to do to provide for his family. All of the diamonds and fancy fur coats that he bought her also blinded her to the wrongfulness of his illicit activities.

Aileen went against her family's wishes and married Augustus. While he was out in the streets making money to take care of the financial needs of the family, she stayed at home to rear the children, and had no problem being a housewife or being subservient to her man.

Nigel was his father's pride and joy. Augustus showed favoritism to Nigel over his older siblings, causing the older Hawkins boys to be caught up in conflict with Nigel throughout their adolescent years and into adulthood. While his older brothers chose to get an education and pursue legitimate careers, Nigel wanted to be just like his father, a hard-core thug.

His father would share stories with him about his exploits in the streets, and he soaked them up like a sponge. When his father talked about his time in jail, Nigel became fascinated with the jail tales and would eagerly wait for his father to share new ones with him. His father drilled it into his head that going to the big house was a part of any true OG's initiation into street life. When Nigel's father told him, "You gotta respect any man strong enough to do a bid in jail," Nigel knew that, if he ever wanted to earn his stripes in the hood, one day the penitentiary had to be his home for a spell.

Nigel constantly got into fights throughout school and ran with a rough crowd. He was suspended from school more times than he had fingers and toes. He bullied the other kids by taking their lunch money or whatever material thing they had that he wanted. He was so bad that his teachers didn't know what to do with him. His mother would punish him whenever he got in trouble in school, but Nigel always ran to his father to get his punishment lifted.

He got locked up for everything from truancy to stealing candy from the corner store and was sent to juvenile hall many times in his teenage years.

His father condoned his deviant behavior and saw it as a part of his rite of passage to manhood. Feeling no real connection to his older two sons, Augustus was proud to see one of his offspring follow in his footsteps and be an outlaw.

Nigel's life was shaken up at fourteen when his father was murdered in a dispute over a winning lottery ticket. From his bedroom window, he watched a man stab his father three times in the chest. When the police failed to arrest the man responsible, Nigel hunted the man down and killed him in cold blood exactly two years after his father's death, shooting him six times at point-blank range and leaving his body to rot in a cold alley. Because there were no witnesses, he was never arrested for the crime.

Nigel felt empowered by the ability to take a human life with a small piece of steel. It was at this point in his life that he dropped out of school and plunged full steam ahead into a life of crime, immersing himself in the culture of Baltimore's underworld of thieves and evildoers.

Nigel tried every hustle imaginable to make money. He boosted clothes, but grew tired of that hustle when he saw the amount of work and risk involved. He tried running numbers, but that just wasn't his bag. He found his niche when he discovered how persuasive he could be with the young ladies. Throughout school, he was always able to convince some young, naive girl to buy him anything he wanted. He was also adept at talking them right outta their panties without spending a dime. Consequently, he decided to try his hand at being a pimp. He was an instant success.

By the time he was eighteen, he had a stable of ten loyal

girls out on the track of Pennsylvania Avenue working for him, and bringing him all of their earnings at the end of the night.

Over the years, the angry little kid with a mean streak had grown into a tall, dark, and handsome stud with an alluring personality and a candid wit about him. He was the reincarnation of his father. He was constantly reminded of this fact by the older heads in his Sandtown neighborhood who were around in his father's heyday. Nigel felt a sense of pride being compared to his father. He was wiser than the average young thug his age because his father had schooled him well in how to conduct himself like a true gangster. He drove the baddest Cadillac that General Motors ever made and wore the finest clothing and jewelry that the American dollar could purchase. He had a fleet of the finest women of every different flavor eager for him to be their pimp. They all instantly fell in love with the sharply dressed brother with the silvery tongue who promised them a world of riches and security.

Although the money was good to him, Nigel soon grew tired of the pimp game. Dealing with so many unstable females who had countless personal issues was more of hassle than it was worth. He needed a new hustle.

His childhood friend, Polo, turned him on to the drug game. When he saw how easy the drug game was and how much more of a profit he could make selling drugs, there was no stopping him. With the help of his two best friends, Pretty Ricky and Fats, he quickly lined up a steady flow of customers and started copping major weight from Polo to supply their needs. Pretty soon, his clientele was so large in the Greenmount Avenue and Eager Street section of the city, he started making money hand over fist. It was coming faster than he could spend it all. His success as both a pimp and a drug dealer would have made his father proud to call him his son.

As much as Nigel was respected for his intelligence, he was feared for his brutal temper. He was a fair businessman, but if you rubbed him the wrong way or tried to cheat him out of some money, then you had better be prepared to pay with your life. Nobody had ever gotten away with stealing anything from him and lived to tell about it. Nigel Hawkins was no joke and every shyster with a scam knew to steer clear of his path. He could slice a muthafucka up something terrible with a razor, and he had an itchy trigger finger. It was better to be his friend than his enemy. Once you had Nigel for an enemy, you had an enemy for life that wouldn't rest until he got his revenge.

Nigel's aura of invincibility changed when he met the woman of his dreams, Lorraine Miller. Their interaction would forever alter the course of his life and become the driving force in his downward spiral to his current state of being. Lorraine Miller was the one woman that every hustler in the city of Baltimore wanted to bag. She could have easily been a runway model with her stunning looks, but she was too caught up in the fast life to pursue that dream. She loved to party all the time and loved to be in the company of any man that was loose with spending his money on her. She was a statuesque beauty with her auburn red colored hair cascading down her back, and her backside was so plump that it told a story with every movement of her butt cheeks. She had long, slender, shapely legs and innocent, light brown eyes that made her the perfect candidate to be any player's top armpiece.

At first Lorraine used to be Polo's woman, but once Nigel laid eyes on her, he had to have her. He didn't care if he had to step on his friend to get what he wanted. Lorraine was equally taken in by him as well and wound up breaking things off with Polo to get with Nigel.

Polo was heated with Nigel, but he was no fool. He didn't want any part of a beef with a lunatic like Nigel. Polo was a hustler all about making money, and the murder game wasn't a part of his repertoire. He knew that if he got into it with Nigel, their confrontation would only wind up in bloodshed. Polo never forgot about his betrayal, but kept his resentment to himself. In fact, he still did business with Nigel because he was a good earner.

When Lorraine and Nigel hooked up, he became the envy of all his so-called competition. The fact that everybody knew she used to be Polo's girl only enhanced his standing as a bona fide gangster nigga not to be crossed.

Nigel had been with a lot of women in his twenty-something years on the Earth, but he had never been with a woman of Lorraine's caliber. She had a fire and flair in her personality that made him a sucker for her love. He spoiled her to no end with anything material that she wanted. Nigel damn near broke his neck to please her, but it was never enough. Lorraine would still ask for more than he gave. Whenever he did something that she didn't like, she would curse him out on the drop of a dime and look so sexy doing it that it was hard for him to get mad at her for having such a salty mouth. Lorraine had Nigel wrapped around her finger and used her wiles and charm to make him submit to her every whim and desire.

Lorraine loved to party hard seven days a week. She loved the excitement and the status that came along with being the woman of one of Baltimore's most notorious gangsters. Of course, along with the fast life and partying always came the allure of the drug culture. Lorraine developed a fascination with "nose candy," otherwise known as cocaine, the wonder drug of the early eighties, because of the intense euphoria of the upper high that it gave her. Since being turned on to it by her uncle, Lorraine couldn't go out to a club without first powdering up her nose with some of the best coca that Nigel sold to his loyal customers. Nigel would sniff a line or two here and there just to take the edge off his hectic life, but it never became a problem for him until Lorraine turned him on to smoking crack. She nagged him constantly to try it out with her, telling him that it would enhance their sex drives and make their sex life more uninhibited.

Nigel eventually gave in to her request. Once he tried smoking the glass dick, it became his best friend. He turned his two homeys, Pretty Ricky and Fats, on to the pipe, and they became caught up in the same madness with him and Lorraine. The four of them spent days on end sitting at their dining room table taking turns geekin' out on the hard white powder.

Smoking crack unleashed every demon that existed within Nigel's soul. He became increasingly paranoid. His already short-fused temper became easier to fuel to the point of rage, and he became physically abusive to Lorraine whenever they ran out of coke to smoke or she ran her mouth too much. He got into fights whenever he went out to a party. He also became less and less on point with handling his business. The more Nigel and his crew used their own product, the less money they were able to make, and after he came up short on a couple of packages, Polo eventually cut off his supply.

With his status much higher in the game now, Polo surrounded himself with a pack of killer goons to do his dirty work if Nigel wanted beef with him. He was happy to cut his old friend off after his earlier betrayal.

Without his own stash of cocaine to use, Nigel was forced to cop from other local dealers. Having to delve into unfamiliar neighborhoods to buy drugs exposed him to countless arrests on CDS possession charges. He went in and out of jail, serving anywhere from thirty days to six months at a time in the city jail over the next few years, bringing his childhood ambition of going to prison to fruition.

With his back against the wall and a thousand-dollar-a-week crack habit, Nigel took to using the gun to extract money to feed his habit. He embarked on a crime spree to jack anybody that had something worth stealing. It was nothing for him run up on some rich White dude, stick his loaded .38 in his mouth, and tell him to ante up all of his belongings. His victims were usually too petrified to resist. Most of the time, he got away with just enough money for him and Lorraine to get high for that day.

Tired of nickel-and-dime scores, he decided that it was time for him to step his game up. He moved on to doing B&E's with Pretty Ricky and Fats. They didn't give a damn if somebody was home or not when they broke into their house. If it was something up in there that they thought had value, they went up in there to snatch it all. If anybody inside resisted, then committing murder was never out of the question if the situation called for such actions. The trio then moved on to hitting up corner liquor stores and gas stations. The job they'd done at Mickey's was the biggest one they'd ever pulled off.

Nigel lay asleep in his bed in an unconscious state. His body tried to make up for all of the rest it missed out on over the last few days. You could have dropped a brick on his head and he wouldn't have woken up. He rested until nightfall came. To an addict, nighttime, the cloak of darkness, was the best time to maneuver.

Once he wiped the crust outta his eyes, it was time to go back out on the hunt. Nigel's jones had kicked in and he wanted to get high. The crack pipe was calling him. The money he'd made off his last job was gone. It was time for somebody else to come up off some loot. He threw on a pair of wrinkled jeans and a sweatshirt and headed over to Pretty Ricky's house, to set up their next caper.

3

On his way over to Pretty Ricky's house, Nigel decided to stop by and see his mother, who he hadn't seen in about two weeks. She lived a few blocks down the street from Pretty Ricky on Orleans Street. Genuine concern for her well-being wasn't the reason he wanted to make a surprise visit. He had no money left and knew that he could hit her up for at least thirty dollars to get him a blast to get him out the gate. All he had to do was come up with a good lie. His mother, one of his biggest enablers, never turned him away whenever he came around begging for cash.

Nigel had bought his mother the house that she lived in, back when things were good for him in the drug game. Even though it was in the hood, the house looked like one of those mid-six-figure homes in the suburbs and was paid for in full. All she had to pay were the utility bills, which were taken care of by the Social Security check she received each month. Nigel bought his mother the finest furniture that his money could buy and made sure that his mother had the best, just like his father would have wanted her to have. He parked his car in front of her house and knocked on the door.

Aileen Hawkins came to the door dressed in a long velour robe. She was a heavyset woman with streaks of grey streaming through her hair. Most of them probably came from worrying about her wayward son. She looked through the peephole to see who it was, and once she saw that it was Nigel, she let him in.

"What you want, boy? Why are you stopping by here so late? It's nine o'clock in the evening. You know I'm usually in the bed right now. You need some money? You look a mess," she said, a look of disgust on her face as she got a glimpse of his raggedy clothing. "Come on in here." The man that stood before her wasn't the same man she knew several years back that was always draped in expensive suits and flashy jewelry. He used to wear the finest colognes, but now he smelled like raw sewage. She was thoroughly disappointed at how much Nigel had let himself go. Nonetheless, she still loved him unconditionally.

"Dag, Ma! Why you gotta be so hard on me? I'm still ya baby boy, ain't I? You know I love you and you're my favorite girl," Nigel said playfully as he entered the house. He attempted to hug her and kiss her on the cheek, but she extended her arms to push him away, the pungent odor from his body irritating her nose.

"Nigel, you need a bath. You smell like a trash can. I don't want that scent all over me!" Mrs. Hawkins fanned her hand in front of her nose, trying not to puke from the foul aroma. They walked into the living room and both took a seat on the couch.

"Stop playing, Ma," he said, feeling dejected by his mother's comments. "I don't smell that bad. You don't have to treat me like that. Times are hard for me, Ma. I just stopped by to see how you're doing. Is everything all right?"

"I'm fine, child. Albert and Franklin stop by here every day to check on me." Mrs. Hawkins reflected on his many faults once again and wished that Nigel would have done more with his life than become a degenerate bum. "How come you couldn't find anything better to do with your life than become a hoodlum?"

"I'm not a hoodlum, Ma. I'm the man that Daddy made me to be. I was never cut out to be no square nine-to-five type of working cat. I know I hit a rough patch, but I'ma get back on top real soon." Nigel hated it when his mother tried to compare him to his brothers. (Albert was a lawyer, and Franklin worked for the city as a social worker.)

"You ain't nothing like your daddy. He stayed sharply dressed and always kept money in his pockets. Even though he made his money out in the streets, he carried himself with dignity and pride. That's why people respected him. I know that he's turning in his grave to see you living the way you are. You let yourself get all messed up with them drugs. I pray for you every day that the Lord will come and deliver you from this evil that has a hold on your soul. I got a good mind to take my grandbaby away from you and that trifling woman of yours. Lord knows, he don't need to be around such foolishness."

Mrs. Hawkins never liked Lorraine from the first time she met her. She didn't like the control she exerted over her son and had pleaded with him not to marry her, but Nigel didn't listen. Judging by the way Nigel's life went downhill since they got involved with each other, she realized her suspicions were well founded.

"My son ain't going anywhere, Momma. He's staying with me. I can take care of him just fine!" Nigel exclaimed loudly. He wanted to curse his mother out for bringing up his father, the last person that he ever wanted to disappoint, but he held back the foul words he wanted to spew and just let her say her piece.

"You better lower ya tone in this house. I'm still ya mother. Show me some respect, or so help me God, I'm gonna forget that I'm the God-fearing woman that I am and slap the taste outta ya mouth."

"I'm sorry, Momma. I apologize." Nigel knew that he had to get back into her good graces if he wanted to get some money outta her. Plus, she was still his mother and she deserved his respect.

"Now let's get down to the nitty-gritty. Why don't you tell me what's the real that reason you stopped by here?" Mrs. Hawkins knew her son better than anybody. She carried him in her womb for nine months. A mother's intuition never goes away no matter how old her child gets.

"Well, Mama, I need some money for gas for the week. I'm trying to get me a job. You want me to get myself together, but I can't do that until I find work. Can you lend me some money just this one last time?" He asked with such sincerity, you would have never known he'd just told a bald-faced lie. Nigel had mastered the ability to look a person dead in the eyes and tell them a lie without feeling the least bit of guilt. As long as he got what he wanted from them, he didn't give a damn about their feelings.

"Lend you some money? Boy, you know you ain't never gonna pay me back. You might as well ask me, 'Can I have some money?' Here, take this and get up outta my face." Mrs. Hawkins reached into her robe and pulled two twenty-dollar bills outta her bra.

"Thanks, Mama. I swear I'ma get me a job and show you that I can be a responsible man."

Getting a job was hardly in Nigel's plans. When his mother gave him forty dollars instead of thirty, he was elated. Now he could cop more crack than he had initially intended. He told her, "I love you, Mama," and raced out the front door.

She just shook her head in shame. She knew what he

planned to do with the money, but she would rather give it to him than have him commit a crime to support his habit.

Nigel was gonna use the money she gave him to get high, and would still break the law to get more drugs once it was gone. He jumped in his car and sped off. He hit a right at the corner and went about three blocks north before he reached his destination. There was a group of young thugs posted up on the corner hustlin'. He parked his car right in front of them and blew his horn one time, and one of the boys ran over to the car.

"Hey, my man, what y'all got out here today?" Nigel asked the kid, who looked no older than fourteen. In the streets, that was old enough to pitch, and old enough to count money.

"We got that suicide out here today, unc. You better get it while it's hot."

Nigel smiled because the streets were buzzing about the suicide crack rock on the East side. He'd heard that it was so banging that when you smoked it you would think that you died and went to heaven. He had to try it to see if it was the real deal.

"Let me get four dimes, lil' homey," Nigel told him.

"Look, you damn crackhead," the young boy shouted, "I ain't ya lil' homey. We ain't friends, nigga. Where's ya money at?"

"You better watch ya mouth, son. I ain't one of ya lil' friends. I'll kick ya monkey ass," Nigel shouted through the passenger window.

The young boy stepped back and lifted his shirt to reveal his shiny .38 revolver.

Nigel wanted to get outta the car and put some work in on the young boy for being disrespectful to him, but he played it cool. Getting a hold of the four vials of crack that he was about to cop was more important than his pride.

"You got it this time, young'un." Nigel handed the boy his money through the window.

The boy snatched the money outta his hand. "I ain't think you wanted no drama, old-timer." The boy yelled to one of the other workers, "Hey, yo, let me get four!"

In no time, the other young soldier came back with four vials of crack and handed it to Nigel, who took the vials and was on his way. *I'ma have to ride back through here and stick these little muthafuckas up for disrespecting me*, Nigel thought.

He pulled his car into an alley and checked around to make sure that there were no cops around. Next, he pulled out his crack pipe and proceeded to inhale the poison into his lungs. His lips felt numb from the effects of the cocaine smoke. He got a burning sensation in his chest, and his heartbeat rapidly increased. The rush that he got from the high made him feel like Superman. He smoked every drop of the crack before he got to Pretty Ricky's house because he didn't want to have to share his shit with his cronies.

When he reached Pretty Ricky's house, he noticed him sitting on his front steps alone, and Fats was nowhere in sight. "What up, chief? You ready to ride tonight?" Nigel's eyes were as big as silver dollars as he stepped outta the car.

"Oh, you know I'm ready to get down, but I got some bad news for you." Pretty Ricky took a big pull on the Newport cigarette that hung from his mouth and flicked the ashes on the ground. Pretty Ricky took one look at Nigel and knew that he was high. As bad as he was fiendin', he was upset that his man didn't share his high with him.

"What's that?" Nigel lit up a cigarette and inhaled.

"Man, Bones came through a little while ago and told me that Fats got knocked off around his way trying to cop. His old lady was with him, and they got busted together. It happened not too long after you dropped him off earlier. You know he was on probation for them pills he got caught with last year. He ain't got no money for bail. His PO is definitely gonna violate him this time. Shit, I was surprised he was still on the streets for this long with all of the dirty urines that he gave up over at the Parole and Probation spot on Guilford Avenue. When I was on paper, my PO violated me because my piss came up dirty just once. Since Fats is down, I guess it's just me and you tonight, homes." Pretty Ricky hung his head low.

"Damn, that's fucked up. How much time you think he's looking at?"

"Well, he had two more years on probation, and the judge will probably give him all of that to serve." Pretty Ricky took another pull of his Newport and flicked the butt into the street.

"I'ma miss his big-headed behind while he's gone," Nigel said. "You know we gotta make sure that we keep some money on his books." What Nigel just said sounded good when it came outta his mouth, but he knew damn well in his heart that any money that he came across would go straight into a crack pipe to support his habit. Fats would have to survive the best he could on this bit.

Pretty Ricky was sad to hear that his main man got locked up, but his need to get that next high made his suffering short-lived. It was time for him to get on again. "That goes without saying. So, what we got planned for tonight?"

"I was thinking about hittin' up the Diamond Liquor Lounge down in south Baltimore tonight," Nigel said. "I scoped it out last week. They make good money up in there. The owner is some old White dude and he works in there alone. It should be an easy in-and-out job."

"A'ight, then let's do this. I'ma run up in the crib real quick and grab my strap and then we can hit the road," Pretty Ricky, excited that he was about to score, raced toward his house.

"Hurry up, nigga!" Nigel yelled with a sense of urgency. The buzz that he got from his last blast had worn off and he was getting agitated.

Pretty Ricky came back outta the house in record time, and they were out on the trail.

When they reached downtown Baltimore, Nigel made a left at the light on Lombard Street and parked his car on the corner. He shut off the engine and turned off the lights. They both grabbed their guns and tucked them in their dips. They didn't wear their masks because Nigel figured that the old man would be too shook up to remember what they looked like after he saw two big guns shoved in his face. It was almost midnight, and not a soul was out on the street. The store would be closing shortly.

As they approached the door of the liquor store, they saw two customers in the store at the counter engaged in a conversation with the owner. They entered the liquor store cautiously. The two men at the counter appeared to be drunk, from the tone of their voices and their slurred speech.

One of the drunks pleaded with the storeowner, "Come on, man, let us get a pint of Blood on the arm. We'll pay you back next week. If you won't give it to us for free, then let us sweep the front of your store in the morning to earn it."

"If you don't have any money, then I can't do a thing for you. It's as simple as that. I can't stand when you bums come up in here and beg for my goods. I worked hard to build this store up from the ground, and nobody ever gave me a damn thing. You both need to get off your lazy behinds and get a job," the owner barked at the two helpless souls. Just then he saw Nigel and Pretty Ricky approach the counter, pistols in hand.

"We don't want any trouble, old man. Just give us the money in the register, and we can be on our way." Nigel's tone was calm, but forceful. He pointed his gat at the owner's forehead, and Pretty Ricky aimed his at the two drunken customers.

"I'm not giving you shit. You punks wanna come up in here and try to rob me for my hard-earned money? You'll have to get it in blood," the owner said defiantly. He had more balls than Nigel could have imagined.

"Hey, can't we all just get along?" one of the drunken men pleaded. "We just wanna get something to sip on and be on our way. Please, put those guns away."

Nigel kicked the man in the chest, knocking him to the ground, and the other drunk leaned down to check on his associate. In the short moment that Nigel took his eyes off the owner, the old man reached under the counter and pulled out a loaded .45 revolver and squeezed the trigger, letting off two shots. One of them landed in Pretty Ricky's midsection, and he tripped backward and landed on his backside.

Nigel returned fire. "Take that, you old son of a bitch!" He hit the owner twice in the chest, and the old man fell to the ground, covered in blood. In the midst of the commotion, the two drunks managed to run out of the store undetected. Nigel reached into the cash register, and took out all of the money, and put it into his pocket.

"I'm hit, man!" Pretty Ricky said frantically. "This shit is burning like hell!" He held his bloody hand over his wound as the blood flowed at a steady stream.

"I'ma get you outta here, man. Don't worry!" Nigel retrieved Pretty Ricky's gun from off the ground and placed it in his dip. He wrapped Pretty Ricky's arm around his neck and carried his injured friend to the car. He opened the car door, leaned the driver's seat forward, and laid him across the back seat.

"You gotta get me to a hospital, Nigel. I'm losing too much blood," Pretty Ricky said faintly, his wound slowly sapping his strength.

"Just hold on for me, daddy. I'ma get you there as fast as I can."

"I'm feeling weak. I know you can't stay with me at the hospital because the cops are gonna wanna question me about how I got shot. Just dump me in the lobby and get up outta there as fast as possible. At least one of us can make it up outta this thing in the clear."

"I'm on it, man, I'm on it!" Nigel put the pedal to the metal en route to the hospital.

"How much money did we get for this job?"

"We ain't get shit. I wasn't thinking about the money after I saw you were hit. All I was worried about was gettin' you outta there. How the hell are you gonna ask me some shit like that when you're about to bleed to death in my back seat?" Nigel thought that Pretty Ricky was too distracted from being shot to see him reach into the register and take the money. The addict in him didn't wanna share the loot. He wanted it all for himself so that he could get high alone.

"I don't know, man. I'm feeling delirious right now. I was trying to take my mind off the pain that I'm feeling." Pretty Ricky winced in pain when he attempted to chuckle. He knew that Nigel had lied because he saw him take the money out of the register, and decided not to say anything about it right now. He was just testing his hand to see what his response would be and planned to bring it up again at a later date if he survived his wounds.

Nigel kept talking to Pretty Ricky in an effort to keep him awake.

Ten minutes later, Nigel screeched on the brakes when he reached Maryland General Hospital. He got out of the car and left it running, flipped up the front seat, and attempted to help Pretty Ricky to his feet. He almost fell into the back seat when he tried to lift him up. Nigel regained his footing and assisted Pretty Ricky in reaching the emergency room and dumped his limp body in the entrance doorway.

"Somebody, get a doctor," Nigel yelled. "My friend's been shot!"

Several people in the emergency room turned around when they heard the commotion.

Nigel darted back out the door and raced to the car. He jumped back in the driver's seat and sped off. He had to get rid of the guns in a hurry because he wanted no connection between him and the crime scene. He planned to dump them down the sewer somewhere on the other side of town. He also had to clean all of the blood off his back seat. However, before he did anything else, he needed something to calm his nerves. His best friend, the crack pipe, knew just how to soothe his tension. It was calling his name loud and clear.

4

Nigel dumped the guns from the robbery down a sewer somewhere in East Baltimore. There was no way in hell the cops would ever think to look for them clear across town. He spent the night in his car parked in an alley off Pennsylvania Avenue. When he awoke, his nerves were a wreck as he drove home. He couldn't enjoy his high the night before like he wanted to because he had a lot of shit on his mind. He was pissed that the robbery went bad. All he got outta the deal was a measly two hundred dollars. That was all the money in the store's cash register and he'd just spent it up gettin' high. He was back right to where he first started—broke, busted, and disgusted. His miscalculation of the amount of money that was in the store should have been a warning sign to him that he was slippin', but he didn't have time to think about his mistakes. His mind was focused on his next victim because he had a monkey on his back to feed with an appetite the size of King Kong. It wouldn't rest until it was fed.

Nigel was mad that Pretty Ricky caught a hot one in the process of the robbery. He hoped and prayed that he would be all right. He wasn't worried about him snitching to the police because he knew that Pretty Ricky was a soldier. He knew that he'd hit the storeowner with two point-blank shots but wasn't sure if he was dead. He also thought about the two drunken customers that snuck out of the store. In the midst of trying to get away and helping his wounded comrade, dealing with them had slipped his mind. It was in his best interest that the owner didn't survive and that the two drunkards were too intoxicated to remember what he or Pretty Ricky looked like. If by chance they did, their testimony would send both of them off to the big house for a long stretch. *Damn, we should've worn our masks*, Nigel thought in hindsight.

He puffed on a Newport to calm his nerves, blowing circles of smoke out of the driver's side window. The soulful sounds of the O'Jays song, "For the Love of Money," played on the broken-down car radio, the knobs having fallen off long ago. He could relate to every word of the song. They echoed his real life thoughts about his jacked-up life, being poor and in the hood. He would do anything to get money. The interior of the car was raggedy with its torn up cloth seats and broken door handles. The front passenger window only rolled down a third of the way. It was hotter than hell in there in the summer time because he had no AC in the car. The oil hadn't been changed in at least six months, and the transmission was slipping. It might have been a hooptie, but it was his ride. It got him wherever he needed to go, and that was all that mattered. As long as he could put the key in the ignition and it started, he was all good. He'd planned to drive his car until it died out on him.

It was almost six o'clock in the morning when he reached his block. The streets were empty. Even the drug dealers and the fiends weren't out yet. There was a deafening silence in the air that should have been cause for alarm. Whenever it was this quiet in the hood, something just wasn't right. Nonetheless, Nigel put the key in the door and went inside of his house. He flipped the light switch by the door, but nothing happened. He went into the living room and attempted to turn the light on by the couch. He turned the knob on the lamp and got the same thing. No light. He went into the kitchen and looked in the refrigerator. The light inside of there was out as well. There was only one conclusion to be reached—The Baltimore Gas and Electric Company had shut the power off. *Ain't this about a bitch? I gave that woman the money to pay the electric bill. She must have smoked that shit up. I can't believe this. I'ma beat her ass for lettin' this happen.*

"Lorraine, where the fuck are you at, woman? I know ya ass can hear me. I'm on my way up there now. How in the hell did you let the lights get cut off?" Nigel made his way up the stairs and down the hall toward his bedroom. He got no response. When he reached his bedroom, he noticed that it was empty. Lorraine was nowhere insight. He walked down the hall to JR's room and saw him laid out across his bed. "JR, where's your mother?"

"She told me she was going to the store last night. I've been here by myself, Daddy. At first, I was watching TV until the lights went out. Then I couldn't sleep because I was too scared to close my eyes. I didn't know where you or Mommy was at," JR said, bags under his eyes from a lack of rest.

"It's all right, lil' buddy. I'm here now. Everything's gonna be all right." Nigel's rage continued to grow and grow. Lorraine was gonna feel every ounce of his wrath for leaving their son alone in the house. Anything could have happened to him. She would receive a serious beat-down for her neglect once he laid eyes on her again.

"Daddy, how come you have blood on your shirt? You got cut?"

Nigel had totally forgotten about the shooting, and that he had Pretty Ricky's blood all over his shirt. "Oh, Uncle Ricky cut himself. I got his blood on me, trying to help him out." Nigel lifted his shirt over his head, took it off, and threw it onto the floor.

"I hope that he's all right."

"Yeah, he's fine. I'ma take you over to Grandma Aileen's house so you can get something to eat and get some rest."

"Okay, Daddy."

Nigel looked inside of JR's beat-up wooden dresser to find him some clothes to wear. He pulled out a couple of pairs of underwear and socks. He also found him a few pairs of jeans with shirts to match. He put JR's clothes in a bag, picked up his bloody shirt off the floor, and went into his room to change his clothes. He threw the bloody shirt in a bag and planned to dispose of it as soon as possible.

Once he finished changing his clothes and gathered up JR's things, the two of them exited out of the front door and jumped in the car. JR rode shotgun as they maneuvered down the road and fell asleep along the way. Nigel had to carry him in the house when they got to their destination. Nigel knew that his mother would be pissed that he was knocking at her door for the second time in two days. Still, he banged on the door so loud that all of the neighborhood could hear.

It took Mrs. Hawkins about five minutes to respond. JR had begun to get heavy in his arms by the time she opened the door.

They walked in the house, and Nigel laid JR across the couch.

"Boy, why are you knocking at my door like you done lost ya mind?" his mother said angrily. "Why do you have my grandbaby with you? Did you and that woman have a fight? That boy needs to be in school. Lord knows, I don't know what I'm going to do with you."

"Momma, I'm sorry for waking you up, but this was an emergency. I gave Lorraine the money to pay the electric bill, but she didn't do it. They cut our lights off. She left JR in the house by himself. That's why he's not in school. I swear I'ma divorce her as soon as I save up enough money. You just watch. You were right about her, Momma. She ain't been nothing but trouble for me. I should've listened to you when you told me not to marry her."

"Aaah, boy, you need to hush ya mouth. You ain't no bargain as a parent either. This boy has the worst of both worlds with you two. And you were gonna marry that woman whether I said something to you or not. You are just that bull-headed and stubborn," his mother joked.

Nigel had to smile at her comment. She had him pegged to a *T*. "You're right, Momma. You always are. I need to ask you for another favor. I know I just got some money from you yesterday, but this is an emergency. I don't know where my wife is and when she's coming back. Can JR stay here with you for a couple of days until I get the money together to pay the electricity bill? I don't want him staying in our house with no power."

"Of course, he can stay here with me. The two of you make no sense. You call yourself parents, but neither one of you are responsible enough to take care of yourselves, let alone this child here. Take him upstairs and put him in the back room so he can get some rest."

"Thank you, Momma. I appreciate everything that you do for me." Nigel lifted his son off of the couch, carried him up the stairs, and placed him in the bed.

JR woke up just as his father was about to leave the room. His eyes were half-open as he spoke. "Daddy, are we at Grandma's house?"

"Yeah, baby boy. You're gonna stay here with ya Grandma

Aileen for a couple of days until I get things straight at home."
Nigel walked back over to the bed and sat down on the edge.

"Why can't you stay here with me? I hate it when you go
away. You and Mommy always leave me by myself." JR got
out from under the cover and laid himself across his father's
lap. His eyes were full of tears as he threw a temper tantrum.
Like any male child, he yearned for the attention of his father.
He wanted him to teach all of the things that a father should
teach his son, but most of the time Nigel was like a mirage—
unreal and only around for a short spell.

"It's gonna be all right, Junior. Daddy has to take care of
business. You'll understand things better when you become a
man. Today is Friday, so you'll only miss one day of school. I'll
be back to get you on Sunday, I promise. Now, wipe those
tears away. Hawkins men don't cry," Nigel said sternly. "That's
for punks."

"Okay, Daddy. I ain't no punk." JR pounded on his bird
chest with his fists to add emphasis to his statement. "One day
I'ma be a gangster like you and Grandpa." JR wiped away the
moisture that ran down his cheeks.

Nigel had told him some of the same stories that his father
instilled in his brain as a child, adding in some of his own ad-
ventures as well. He'd told him all of the good things about
the street life, but left out the bad parts, like going to jail and
getting strung out on drugs, and JR soaked up the tales with
the same enthusiasm that Nigel did when his father used to
school him.

JR loved spending time with his grandmother. She spoiled
him to death. No matter how angry she was at Nigel for what
he had done with his life, Mrs. Hawkins could never turn her
favorite grandson away. She had other grandkids from her other
two sons, but she had an extra-special place in her heart for
JR, because she knew that Albert and Franklin could take

care of themselves and their children. With two messed-up parents like Nigel and Lorraine, JR needed the extra love, affection, and compassion to overcome the insane world he was subjected to under their care.

"That's my boy. Now get back in the bed and get some rest. Grandma is gonna make you some pancakes when you wake up," Nigel said.

JR jumped up and down on the bed. He loved his grandmother's pancakes. "Okay, Daddy. I hope Sunday comes real quick, so you can come back to get me." JR crawled back under the cover.

Nigel kissed him on the cheek. "I love you, baby boy," he said and went back downstairs to join his mother in the living room.

"Thank you, Momma. You are the best. Anything that you need me to do, I will do. As a matter of fact, when I come back to get JR on Sunday, I'm gonna cut the grass for you and clean up the yard. Before I go though, Momma, I need one more favor. I burned up the gas that I bought for the car when I was riding around town looking for Lorraine. I still need to get gas to make it through the weekend. This is the last time I'ma ask you for anything. Can I borrow another forty dollars?" Nigel knew that he was pushing his luck, but the worst she could do was say no.

"Nigel, you are a nuisance. You're gonna send me to the poorhouse. Wait right here until I come back." Mrs. Hawkins went up to her room and came back down the stairs a few minutes later with the money.

Nigel's face lit up when he saw the cash. His mother came through for him once again. He got butterflies in his stomach. Just the thought of being able to cop gave him a rush that was better than having an orgasm. He kissed his mother on the cheek and jetted out the front door on a mission.

5

After he left his mother's home, Nigel drove back over to Pretty Ricky's house. The tires on his car screeched as he turned the corner sharply. He parked his ride in the first spot that he could find. As he approached the house, he saw Peaches, Ricky's older sister, up on the porch. Nigel observed her for a minute before he spoke. She had a cigarette in her mouth and a beer can in her hand. She started her morning with the same routine every day—a bag of dope and a six-pack of beer. Her frail body was covered with track marks on her arms and legs from shooting heroin for so long. There wasn't a vein on her body that she hadn't used to inject dope into her system. Her doctor had told her recently that she had cirrhosis of the liver from drinking so much alcohol. She was a junkie from the old school when there was good dope out on the streets of Baltimore and not the watered-down shit they sold today. She was leaned up against a pole on the porch, bent halfway over in a dope nod. It looked like her face was about to hit the ground, but every time she got close to doing so, she managed to pull herself back up. The cigarette in her mouth was full of ashes that needed to be plucked.

"Peaches, wake ya ass up, girl!" Nigel yelled, startling her.

She rose to an upright position, and some of the beer in her hand spilled onto the porch. "Nigel, what's up, baby? You scared me. You made me spill some of my shit." She drew closer. "You want a beer or something?"

Nigel opened the front gate and joined her on the porch. "Nah, I'm good, Peaches. I just came to holla at you about something for a minute," Nigel said calmly. "It's about ya brother."

"His ass ain't come home last night. What has he gotten himself into this time?" Peaches scratched her abscess-filled arms, and pus began to ooze from her sores.

"I know he didn't come home. He was with me. We tried to make a move last night and shit just went wrong. It's kinda bad. He got shot."

"My brother got shot? What the hell do you mean?" she asked hysterically. Her brother was all she had left in the world since their parents died. She accidentally dropped her can of beer.

"Calm down, Peaches. Don't be so loud. I think that he's gonna be okay. I dropped him off at the hospital last night. He was conscious and talking when I left him there. The doctors are gonna take good care of him." Nigel grabbed her to calm her down. "There's no need for you to worry."

"What hospital is he in? How the hell did it happen? Why did you leave him there by himself?" Peaches was irate.

"He's at University Hospital. Why the hell do you think I left him? We just tried to jack somebody. I wasn't gonna stay around and wait for the police to get there to answer any questions."

"Well, take me over there so I can check on him."

"That was exactly what I had in mind. Let's go," Nigel said.

Peaches ran into the house to get her keys. She locked the front door, and they were on their way.

"Hey, Nigel, how much money did y'all get from the robbery? I know y'all made out with something. Why don't you hit me off with twenty dollars outta my brother's share so I can get my morning shot?"

"We ain't get shit, baby girl. When I saw that ya brother was shot, my main concern was us getting outta there safely. I had to put two shells in the storeowner. If I had some money, you know I would hit you off. I'm assed out right now." Nigel would be damned if he shared the forty dollars in his pocket with her. He'd worked too hard to weasel that loot away from his mother.

"That's fucked up. My brother gets shot and y'all niggas is about to go to jail. For all of that, y'all ain't get no money for ya troubles? If you ask me, y'all need to give up the robbery game because y'all are just not that good at it," Peaches said jokingly.

"Fuck you, Peaches. That's some jacked-up shit to say to me. How many times have we taken care of you when you were ill? Any time we score, we make sure that you get ya shot, don't we?"

"Aah, nigga, stop crying. I'm just fucking with you. I know you would look out for me if you had some money. A sista just need a lil' taste to get me going. I ain't tryin' to be ill out here. After I check up on my brother, I'ma have to turn me a coupla tricks to get my blast."

Nigel glanced at her and just shook his head. *Ain't no trick in his right mind gonna pay a penny to fuck your funky, tired ass.*

While they were driving down the road, Nigel was so caught up in their conversation that he ran right through a red light. A police car pulled up behind him out of nowhere and threw on its flashing lights. The police officer motioned for him to pull his car over. Nigel put on his right-turn signal and pulled over to the side of the road.

"Oh, shit. What the fuck are we gonna do?" Peaches went into panic mode, moving around nervously in the passenger seat.

Dealing with the police in any capacity was cause for alarm for a dope fiend. If you weren't breaking the law, there was a chance that they could plant some shit on you to give them a reason to lock you up. Once they ran you down to the precinct, they would throw all kinds of shit at you to try and make you become an informant out on the streets. There was a thin line between criminals and law enforcement in Baltimore City.

"Calm ya ass, down. We ain't did shit but run a red light. All he's gonna do is give us a ticket and we'll be on our way. Ya ass ain't ridin' dirty, are you?"

"Nah, I ain't got no dope on me. I just told you that I need you to help me out with a few dollars to get my morning shot. Anyway, if I was dirty, I would've told you that before I got in ya ride."

"Then just sit back, relax, and let me handle this thing here," Nigel said confidently.

Nigel saw the officer in his mirror talking into his radio.

A few minutes later, the officer got out of his car and walked toward Nigel's vehicle. The officer unlatched the clasp on his gun holster, just in case he needed to reach for his steel. When he got to the car, he tapped on the glass to get Nigel's attention.

Nigel rolled his window down.

"Do you know why I pulled you over?" the officer asked, a tall, thin Caucasian male with a Southern accent.

"No, sir, I don't know why you pulled me over. I was doing the speed limit," Nigel responded calmly.

"Well, you just cruised through the red light without stopping. You could have caused an accident. Somebody could've gotten hurt. Can I have ya license and registration please?"

"Not a problem. I'm sorry about that. Here you go, officer." Nigel handed his license and registration to the officer. Lucky for him, he'd swindled his mother out of some money a few months back to renew the tags on his car.

The officer glanced into the back of the vehicle. "Sir, why is there blood on your back seat?"

"There is? Where? There must be some kinda mistake." Nigel turned around to look at the back seat. He'd forgotten to clean it up the night before. He felt like a fool for doing such a dumb thing. He put both of his hands over his face to hide his humiliation.

"Sir, I'm gonna need you and the young lady to step outta the car and get down on the ground now!" The officer reached for his walkie-talkie and called for backup.

"I ain't gonna be able to do that, officer!" Nigel turned the key in the ignition and sped off.

The officer jumped into his car in hot pursuit and turned on his flashing lights.

Peaches yelled, "Nigel, what the hell are you doing? That's the fucking police! You can't outrun them! Pull this car over and let me out!"

"Hell, nah! Them muthafuckas are gonna have to earn their money. They ain't gonna take me down without a fight!"

Nigel weaved through the city streets, almost causing a dozen accidents with his reckless driving. He ran traffic lights, stop signs, and almost hit a few pedestrians throughout the chase as Peaches repeatedly pleaded with him to pull over.

Pretty soon, there were several other police cars in on the chase.

Nigel turned down an alley and no longer saw police cars behind him. "Now that's what I'm talking about, baby girl!

That's some driving right there! The rollers ain't got shit on me!" Nigel pounded on his chest. He continued to drive down the long, narrow alley and quickly realized that shit wasn't as sweet as he thought it was.

As he was about to exit the alley, a police car cut him off. He put the car in reverse and tried to back down the alley and was met by another police car. They had him cornered. He had nowhere to run or hide. He was trapped.

"Damn, Nigel! What the fuck have you gotten me into?"

"Bitch, shut the fuck up! I didn't plan for this shit to go down like this." Nigel had a look of sheer rage on his face. He mumbled every curse word he could think of under his breath, mad at himself and the rest of the world.

"We want both of you to open the car doors and come out with ya hands raised in the air. Next, we want you both to lay face down on the ground," one of the pursuing officers yelled through a megaphone.

Nigel and Peaches stepped out of the car, got down on the ground, and placed their hands behind their heads, their faces up against the stale concrete. It was smart of them to do exactly what the officer said to do because Baltimore City cops had no problem shooting a Black person in the back for not obeying a direct command.

However, Nigel had to be a "Billy bad ass." When the officer attempted to put the handcuffs on his wrists, he resisted. He flipped over and kicked the officer in the groin, and the officer fell to the ground in pain.

The other officers quickly came to their partner's aid.

"Ooooh, you little dirty motherfucker. You wanna be a tough guy, huh? Well take this, you little prick!" One officer took his billy club and smashed Nigel in the chest.

"That ain't hurt. Is that all that you got?" Nigel asked boldly.

The officers answered his question as three of them proceeded to pound on Nigel relentlessly, blows coming at him from every angle. Blood began to run from his mouth and forehead. He tried his best to fight back, but he was overwhelmed.

Peaches pleaded, "Y'all ain't got to beat on him like that. This doesn't make any sense. Please stop hitting him!"

"Shut up, you little junkie whore. He should've kept his mouth closed and went down peacefully. You keep running ya mouth and you're next," one of the female officers said.

Seeing that it was a no-win situation, Peaches put her face back down on the ground and remained silent.

When the officers decided that Nigel had enough, they handcuffed both of them and stuffed them in the back of separate squad cars. His car was later towed away by a Baltimore City police tow truck.

The last twenty-four hours were pure hell for Nigel. With all of the dirt he did in his life, this was the first time he got knocked off on a humble, a routine traffic stop turning into a multiple-car police chase. Plus, he got his ass kicked. Nigel wanted to get high to escape from the world, but that was outta the question. Now in police custody, he just hoped he could find an easy way out of his mess. And it was just Peaches's misfortune to get caught up in Nigel's and her brother's drama.

6

"Nigel Hawkins! Nigel Hawkins! You've got a visitor!" the officer yelled into the cell. The officer repeated Nigel's name several more times before he awoke from his sleep.

Nigel thought he was dreaming when he heard his name called. He lifted his bruised and battered carcass off of the bed and rose to his feet. He grabbed a hold of his ribs with his left hand. A sharp pain shot through his left side when he tried to stand up. He took his right hand and placed it on his forehead. His entire face was black and blue, thanks to Baltimore's finest. The ass-whipping that he got when he was arrested had continued when he reached the precinct. Police officers hated to have to chase a suspect. When they did, they made him pay for every second of their time they had to waste in pursuit of him.

Nigel used his one phone call to call his brother Albert. Even though he couldn't stand his brother, he knew that he was a good attorney. Despite their differences, Nigel was confident that he would represent him. He had represented him on several occasions in the past in his legal dilemmas, and he knew that his mother would force Albert to help him out because they were family.

The officer escorted Nigel down the hall and into the interrogation room, and seated him in the middle of the room at a small table, a bright white light shining down on him from above.

Albert sat in a chair next to him.

Albert looked nothing like his younger brother. While Nigel and Franklin inherited their father's height and good looks, Albert was short and stocky and two shades lighter than Nigel, with dark brown eyes. He took after his mother's side of the family with his high cheekbones and pointy nose.

What he lacked in looks, he made up for in the brains department. He was a straight-A student throughout high school. He graduated at the top of his law school class at the University of Maryland and was operating his own law practice specializing in both criminal and civil law. He drove a Porsche and lived in a spacious estate in Harford County. He had a wife and three beautiful children, two girls and a boy. He had done pretty well for himself.

His dislike for Nigel was evident from the time he walked in the room. Having a crackhead for a brother did nothing to elevate his social status among his colleagues. In fact, he always told his friends that he only had one brother, Franklin. As far as he was concerned, Nigel was non-existent.

"What's up, big bro? It's good to see you," Nigel said sarcastically. He shared an equal level of dislike for Albert and used to gloat in his and Franklin's faces when they were kids that he was their father's favorite. Albert and Franklin used to beat him up when he was little, but that all changed once Nigel got older and added on some weight and height. Neither one of them stood a chance in a fight with him today. When he was on top of his hustle game, he would rub it in their faces that their nine-to-five jobs could never afford them the life of luxury that he lived. Now that the tables had turned, he was the one that was jealous of both his brothers' success in life.

"Hello, Nigel. I see that you have gotten yourself into another fine mess. When are you gonna get tired of breaking our mother's heart?" Albert asked in a proper tone.

Nigel laughed in his face. Whenever he ran into either Albert or Franklin at his mother's house, they were on his case about him going to church and getting his life right with God. Whenever they came at him with their religious talk, Nigel would storm outta his mother's house, but not before lacing them up with a slew of profane words.

"Don't you have any soul, bro? You sound just like one of them crackers. Momma is fine. She doesn't have to worry about me. I can take care of myself."

"You are hardly funny. If you could take care of yourself, you wouldn't be living like a vagabond out in the streets. You better remember that you need my help. I'm only here because I know that Momma would give me hell if I didn't represent you. She's your saving grace. I'm not gettin' paid to defend you. You keep running ya mouth and I'll walk right out that door," Albert said bluntly.

"A'ight. You're right, bro. I didn't mean what I said. You got me. I'm at your mercy. So what's the deal? Are we gonna sue these bastards for whipping my ass or what?" Nigel snickered inside. *You little nerdy muthafucka. You wouldn't last a day in the joint before somebody made you their bitch.*

"Are we gonna sue the police department? You must be crazy. That should be the last thing on your mind. You're facing some serious charges here, Nigel. They've got you for resisting arrest and assaulting a police officer. I know that you did something to provoke them to hit you. I'm here to try and make a deal for you." Albert shook his head from side to side. He couldn't believe how ignorant Nigel was to the law, as many times as he'd been arrested.

"Make a deal? Shit, Nigel Hawkins don't take no deals. It's just like you to take the White man's side against your own flesh and blood. You uppity Black folks are all the same, always bending over backward to please them crackers. It's my word against that cop's. Baltimore City officers have a history of using excessive force. Look at my face. You only cop a plea when ya back is against the wall. Didn't you learn that in law school, mister big-shot attorney?"

Albert took a deep breath and exhaled. He wanted to curse Nigel out, but he did his best to remain professional in the face of his brother's ignorance. Before Albert could respond, they were joined in the room by a police officer.

"Hello, gentlemen. I'm Detective Nathan Jakes. So, you're the notorious Nigel Hawkins, the son of Augustus Hawkins? My father was a cop before me. He had several run-ins with your father. I see you're just as much of a prick as he was." Detective Jakes was a husky White male with huge forearms. He stood over six feet tall and walked with a limp. He'd taken a bullet in his left kneecap several years ago that limited his mobility. Jakes had been on the force for eight years before he'd made detective. He had a reputation for being on the take and bending the law to make his cases stick in court.

"Excuse me, Officer," Albert chimed in, "but your comments about my father are unnecessary. Can we just stick to the matter at hand?"

"You two are brothers? Damn, I would have never guessed that in a million years. I apologize if I offended you." Detective Jakes looked back and forth at Nigel and Albert but failed to see any resemblance between the two of them.

"Yeah, let's stick to the facts. You pigs whipped my ass and got me in this joint all over a traffic stop. What kind of bullshit are y'all trying to pull?"

"If that were only the case, we would have let your ass go a long time ago. You've got some bigger charges to answer to, Nigel. So, why did you pull off when the officer asked you about the blood on the back seat of your car? Do you have anything to hide?" Jakes's statement caught Albert by surprise.

Nigel sat silently, but the look on his face said it all—He was in deep shit.

"Nobody mentioned anything to me about any blood on the back seat of his car. Would you care to elaborate on this, Officer?"

"Certainly. I planned on doing so. There was a robbery at the Diamond Lounge on Lombard Street the other day. The owner of the store, Mr. Edgar Rosenberg, was shot twice, but he survived. Luckily, the bullets went right through him. Also, a Mr. Richard Allen, aka Pretty Ricky, was dropped off at the emergency room at University Hospital in a car that matched your brother's vehicle. He suffered a gunshot wound to the abdomen. The doctors were able to remove the bullet, and he's expected to recover." Detective Jakes looked at Nigel. "Mr. Rosenberg ID'd photos of you and Mr. Allen out of a police mug shot book as the robbers. He admitted to shooting Mr. Allen in self-defense, but he says that you're the one that shot him. We have several detectives waiting now to get the okay from Mr. Allen's doctor to question him. I'm sure that once the lab finishes testing the blood on your back seat, it will show that it's a perfect match for your Mr. Allen's blood type. That evidence will place you both together at the time of shooting. Do you deny these allegations?" Detective Jakes took a seat and anxiously awaited Nigel's response. He knew from his many years on the force that some criminals would deny their crimes even when the evidence was stacked against them. Nigel appeared to one of those criminals in his eyes.

"I ain't shoot nobody! That man is lying! I was at home

with my wife last night." Nigel felt relieved to know that Pretty Ricky was all right, and pissed that the storeowner had lived. *I should have emptied the whole chamber in his ass.*

"Oh, the story gets better. We also have two men—Mr. Kenneth Duncan and Mr. Charles Booth—that have also placed you both at the scene of the crime. They say that they were in the store when the robbery occurred. In the midst of the shoot-out, they managed to get out of the store. We also questioned the young lady that was in the car with you. She admitted to us that you told her that her brother got shot last night in the commission of a robbery. Mr. Hawkins, I think it would be wise for you to confess to the crime. Make this easy on yourself. If you don't, with ya jacket, charges of attempted murder and armed robbery will send ya ass out to the state pen for at least twenty years." Officer Jakes knew that this was an open-and-shut case and just wanted to make Nigel squirm a little, for amusement.

"Fuck you, pig. I ain't confessing to a goddamn thing. You can take that badge of yours and shove it up your ass!" Nigel shouted. He lunged toward Jakes in an effort to choke him, but Jakes moved before he got a hold of him. Albert jumped up and got between them before the situation escalated any further.

Detective Jakes drew his weapon, and Nigel backed down, reluctantly taking his seat.

"Officer, I need a moment to talk with my client in private, if you don't mind," Albert requested. He saw that the job that was before him was much more difficult than he at first had envisioned. With three eyewitnesses, not even Harry Houdini could escape that type of evidence.

"Not a problem, counselor. Take all the time you need. Your brother will have nothing but time to kill pretty soon." Detective Jakes smiled confidently and left them behind to pick up the pieces of the bombshell he'd just dropped.

"Nigel, what the hell have you gone and done now with your ghetto self? Is any of the story he just told true?" Albert asked in his most proper voice.

"Yeah, I did that shit, but they ain't got no weapons to prove that I shot anybody. I got rid of them things after shit went down," Nigel confessed proudly. As far as he was concerned, the storeowner got what he deserved for not doing as he was told. Had he not drawn his gun, then he would not have gotten shot.

"You are in deep shit this time. We need to work on getting you a deal. You will definitely be going to prison for this one. Mother is gonna be so upset." He had handled similar cases throughout this career, and the outcome was usually the same when the police had such overwhelming evidence.

"Make a deal for what? All they have is three muthafuckas that claim I robbed that store. They have no weapon or any physical evidence to tie me to the robbery. That blood on my back seat don't mean a damn thing. All it means is that I saw Ricky last night and took him to the hospital after he got shot. The worst thing that they can pin on me is that I lied about being with Ricky at all last night. That's a minor charge. They might be able to place Ricky at the scene of the crime, but my fingerprints ain't on shit. I made sure that I wore gloves. All you need to do is destroy those three witnesses credibility in court and I will walk outta there a free man. Ricky ain't gonna rat me out because he's a soldier."

Albert stared off into space in utter amazement and thought that despite all of his street knowledge, Nigel lacked plain old-fashioned common sense.

"If things were only that easy, Nigel. With your record and history of violence, it's not the credibility of the witnesses that will be on the line, but it will be your black behind. They've got enough circumstantial evidence to get a conviction easily. There is no defense that I could mount for you.

Not only that, you're a Black man in America, so you're already guilty until proven innocent in the court's eyes. While you think that I might have forgotten that I was Black, you need to remind yourself that you are Black and will always get the short end of the stick in these situations. I'm good at what I do, but I'm not good enough to make a miracle. That honor belongs to God."

"So what are we gonna do then? I ain't trying to do no twenty years in jail," Nigel stated nervously. For the first time he showed some signs of realizing that he was in deep trouble. The little stints in jail that he had done in the past were nothing compared to what lay ahead for him.

"I'm gonna talk to the DA and see what I can work out. Whatever deal I am able to negotiate, it would be in your best interest to take it immediately. I would also suggest that you go back to your cell and pray because you're gonna need God's mercy to get any leniency in this matter. That's my best advice as your attorney and brother." Albert adjusted his glasses and cleared his throat.

"I ain't tryin' to hear that shit. God can't do nothing for me now. I might need to get another attorney. I need Warren Brown up in this bitch and not some holy-rolling tight-suit like you. *C.O.*, take me back to my cell!" Nigel yelled.

The *C.O.* came in the room to escort Nigel back to his cell.

As Nigel left out of the room, he put his head down and walked past Albert without saying another word. He mumbled to himself that Peaches was gonna pay for snitching on him. He was irritated because he wanted to get beamed up. Life always went better when he had coke up in his system. He believed that it made his thought process clearer. Without it, he was like a sheep lost in the wilderness.

He needed guidance in his life, but he was too far-gone to accept good advice from any man at this point.

7

More than enough time had passed since the last time JR saw his father or mother. He cried himself to sleep many nights at his grandmother's house. He thought constantly about his father's promise the last time they were together to come pick him up. That day came and went with no signs of Nigel anywhere. He was heartbroken at Nigel not keeping his word for the umpteenth time. The love that he felt for him started to turn into deep resentment. He felt unloved and unwanted. He wanted a man around to teach him how to play basketball and baseball. He yearned to spend time with his father, like some of the boys in his class got a chance to do, and was envious whenever the other boys in his class talked about what they did with their father over the weekend. He was a lonely seven-year-old child.

Nobody had heard a word from Lorraine since she'd left him in the house alone. She could be anywhere at this point. JR didn't care where she was or if she ever returned. She treated him so badly that he was glad to be out of her presence. She went through mood swings when her drug supply ran out and took her frustration out on JR on a regular basis. He recalled coming home from school to beatings with an extension cord almost every other day. His only crime was being a child in the care of a drug-addicted parent. Lorraine usually whipped JR when Nigel wasn't around, because she knew that Nigel would tear fire outta her ass if he saw her whip him. Whenever JR was lucky enough to see Nigel, he wouldn't hesitate to tell him how bad Lorraine treated him. Nigel would respond by beating the living shit outta Lorraine for her actions. JR would sit and watch his father strike his mother and loved it when his father came to his rescue. It made him feel like he mattered to Nigel.

Not only did he not miss the beatings that his mother administered, JR also hated the fact that she had other men in the house when his father wasn't around. Lorraine entertained a host of male associates whenever Nigel was gone on one of his drug binges. She didn't care who the man was. If he had money she could use to get high, then she was down to spread her legs and share her goods long enough for him to bust a nut. She figured that since Nigel wasn't around to supply her habit, then she had to use whatever means necessary to get her next blast. Pussy never lost its market value. If a woman was down to kick it out, there was always some man around to spend his cash to get a taste, regardless of what the woman looked like.

JR was too young to understand the perils of addiction and the insane behavior that it entailed. All he saw was his mother messing around on his father, and he resented her for what she did. He wasted no time telling Nigel about each and every encounter, hoping she incurred his wrath. However, it also meant that an ass-whipping awaited him when Lorraine found out that he was the one who told Nigel about her indiscretions.

When JR first asked his grandmother where his father

was, she gave him an answer that didn't satisfy him. She told him that his father was out of town on business. That lie didn't last long, as JR continued to ask probing questions. JR was a little smarter than the average child, and he began to put the pieces to the puzzle together for himself. He reached the conclusion that his father must have gotten arrested and sent to jail. He witnessed this script play out many times before. In his young life, he saw his father taken off to jail by the police on numerous occasions.

His grandmother finally broke down and confirmed his suspicions about his father's whereabouts. She figured that there was no sense in deceiving him any longer because, after she talked to Albert about Nigel's legal situation, she knew that he would be locked up for the rest of JR's childhood and early adult years. With Lorraine AWOL, the responsibility of raising JR would fall into her lap. She thought that her days of child rearing were far behind her, but as was usually the case in the hood, Grandma always had to step up to the plate and play mother and father to her children's kids when they got themselves caught up in the legal system. Nigel's fate would soon be determined at his upcoming court date.

On this particular day, JR was in the backyard playing with Jeremy and Peter, his cousins. Jeremy was Franklin's youngest son. He was the same age as JR, but much taller. You could tell that he was gonna be at least six feet tall when he grew up. Peter, Albert's oldest son, was three years older. He looked just like his father and inherited his diminutive stature. The three of them were playing a game of basketball, using a milk crate hung up on a telephone pole as a makeshift basketball hoop. They took turns taking shots at the basket.

"You can't guard me, boy. I'ma break ya ankles with this crossover like I was Michael Jordan," Jeremy bragged to JR as he drove to the hoop. True to his word, he shook JR right outta his drawers as he dribbled right past him. When he was going up for the shot, JR came from behind him and pushed him hard in the back, and Jeremy fell to the ground and scraped his knee up against the concrete. He began to cry.

"Dag, JR! Why did you have to foul him like that?" Peter asked angrily. He went over to look at Jeremy's wound to see how bad it was. It was a minor scrape, but blood flowed from it steadily.

"Shut up, punk. This is street ball. You ain't out in the county where y'all live at with them little White kids. If you come down the lane here, you should expect to get fouled. He needs to stop crying like a little girl." JR poked out his chest.

Jeremy rose to his feet. Shaking off his pain, he walked toward JR with his fists balled up, ready to scrap. "You better watch ya mouth before I hit you in it," Jeremy said, standing face to face with JR, and holding a huge size advantage.

But JR was his father's son and a born fighter. Before Jeremy knew what hit him, JR struck him in the stomach with a sharp right-handed blow. Jeremy doubled over and fell to his knees. JR followed his right up with a quick left that landed on the bridge of Jeremy's nose. Blood trickled down his nostrils. He turned toward Peter, hoping that he would join in on the fracas, but Peter didn't want any trouble and helped Jeremy to his feet.

"Y'all are some punks just like your fathers. My daddy was right about that, fo' sho'. Neither one of y'all would last a minute out in these streets," JR said, taunting his cousins. His father was always open in sharing with JR his dislike for his brothers and felt the same way about their children.

"Yeah, well at least my father has a job and isn't a crackhead like your father. I hope he never gets outta jail for as long as you live," Peter said.

That sparked a fuse in JR, who became possessed by a power far greater than himself. He went into attack mode. He rushed toward the two boys and knocked them both to the ground. He let both of his hands go in a windmill-like motion, all of his blows connecting with some part of each of their bodies. Peter and Jeremy covered up to try and block the blows.

In the midst of the commotion, Franklin happened to be in the kitchen window and saw the fight. He ran down the steps and out into the alley to break up the fight.

Franklin pulled JR off of his cousins. "What's going on out here?"

"Uncle Franklin, he's an animal. We were out here playing basketball, and he pushed Jeremy down on the ground for no reason. He started everything. JR ain't nothing but a trouble-maker!" Peter ran over and stood next to Franklin.

"You shouldn't have said nothing about my father," JR shouted. "You run your mouth to me and I'ma close it for you." JR's fists were still balled up, and he was ready to go some more.

"All right, that's enough. You're all cousins and shouldn't be fighting each other. JR you act just like ya father, all wild and crazy. He was the same way when he was your age. You don't make any sense to be acting this way. Go on in the house!" Franklin allowed his personal feelings toward Nigel to influence the way that he treated JR. Instead of stepping up to the plate to be a male role model for his nephew, he treated him like an outcast.

JR pouted. "You always wanna take their side in everything. I wish my Daddy was here so he could whip ya butt."

"Well, ya father is not here, so take your smart behind in that house. Don't talk back to your elders. If you say another word, I'ma give you a reason to cry." Franklin pushed JR toward the steps.

JR walked up the steps and into the back door. "Wait till I

get bigger," he mumbled under his breath. "I'ma see how tough you are then when I beat ya ass."

"What did you say?" Franklin asked.

"Nothing." JR went up the stairs to his grandmother's room, and his facial expression of anger turned to one of a helpless victim in an instant. He knew that once he shed a few tears and gave her his twisted version of what happened between him and his cousins, they would be the ones in trouble. He loved to play her against them. As far as Aileen Hawkins was concerned, her favorite grandson could do no wrong. Franklin would also get a few choice words from her for talking to him so mean. JR learned at a young age how to use his grandmother's favoritism to his advantage. Before he entered her room, he made sure his eyes were watery.

"What's wrong with Grandma's baby? Why are you crying, JR? Tell me, what's wrong." Mrs. Hawkins grabbed JR up into her arms and cradled his head up against her chest.

"Grandma, Peter and Jeremy were picking on me. They called me a dirty bum and said my father was a crackhead. I got mad, and we started to fight. Uncle Franklin came and broke it up and he said that I was a no-good troublemaker like my father. They hurt my feelings, Grandma. I wish they would like me. I didn't do anything to anybody. I just want to be normal like everybody else." JR's words were somewhat muffled by his stuffy nose and the glob of spit that was lodged in his throat from his crying, as he laid on his sympathy routine extra thick.

"My baby ain't no troublemaker. Wipe them tears away, JR. Grandma loves you. You're special to me, and that's all that matters. I'ma have a talk with all of them and tell them to leave you alone. If you stop crying, I'ma take you out and buy you something real nice at the mall."

"Okay, grandma, I'll stop crying." JR smiled and wiped his

eyes. His act worked like a charm. Grandma Hawkins always had his back, no matter what he did. She believed that he was right, even when all of the evidence showed his faults.

Even though he had the love of his grandmother, this still wasn't enough for JR. He wanted to be with his father. The fight with his cousins was only the beginning of his acting-out antics. Many more similar violent outbursts would follow soon afterwards for JR in school, and with other neighborhood kids. His anger and frustration over his father's absence from his life had come to the surface and had him headed for trouble.

8

Over five months passed since the last time that Nigel got high. He awoke out of his sleep many nights in a cold sweat as a result of his vivid drug dreams and went through the mood swings and feelings of depression that came along with not having any cocaine in his system. The littlest thing would set him off. His bad temper got him into several physical altercations with other inmates while he was being held at the city jail until his trial date. Nonetheless, he was able to weather the storm and survive the ordeal that an addict had to go through when caught up in the legal system.

It wasn't like drugs weren't plentiful in jail. In fact, they were just as available in the joint as they were on any corner in any hood in Baltimore City. He simply didn't have the money to cop, and his mind was too distracted by his legal dilemma. Being drug-free, Nigel ate more and slowly began to put on weight. In no time at all, he was back up to his former walk-around weight of two hundred pounds. His skin began to clear up, and you could now see the whites of his eyes, which used to be bloodshot red from so many sleepless nights of smoking coke. He was beginning to look like his old handsome self.

While sitting in jail waiting for his court date, Nigel had a lot of time to think about his choices in life. He questioned how he was able to rise to the top of the street game so fast yet fall from the top twice as fast. He remembered how much respect he got when his shit was tight and how he had been reduced to being talked to "greasy" by the young hustlers on the block when he went to cop. He thought about all of the material things that he'd lost because of his cocaine use and how he let drugs take him away from his son. He wished that he'd never let Lorraine pressure him into smoking the pipe. Had he not started getting high, he still would've had all of his material possessions. In his eyes, Lorraine was the root of all of his problems.

Today would be the day that his fate would be decided. When he walked into the courtroom dressed in the gray suit that his mother had bought him, he appeared firm and resolute in his manner as the officer escorted him to his seat next to Albert. He glanced across the courtroom to find his mother and son, who were seated in the middle of the right side of the courtroom along with Franklin. He flashed a smile in their direction, as if to say that he was gonna be all right.

Lorraine was absent, as expected. She had yet to show her face or make an effort to claim her child.

Nigel waited patiently for the judge to call his case. After about an hour, it was his turn to bat.

"Nigel Hawkins, would you please rise before this court," Judge Hicks said in a bold James Earl Jones-like voice.

Nigel stood up, as did Albert.

"It is my understanding that the State has reached a plea bargain in this case. Is that correct?" Judge Hicks looked in the direction of DA Shirley Epstein.

"That's correct, Your Honor," DA Epstein replied. "We've

reached an agreement with the defendant. In exchange for his pleading guilty to the charges of armed robbery and illegal possession of a firearm, the State agrees to drop the charge of attempted murder against him. He has agreed to accept a sentence of twenty years in prison, with the chance of parole in fifteen years."

"Counselor, is this what your client has agreed to?" Judge Hicks asked Albert.

"Yes, it is, Your Honor."

"Very well," Judge Hicks said. "Let's make this official. To the charges of armed robbery and illegal possession of a firearm, how does the defendant wish to plead?"

"I wish to enter a plea of guilty, Your Honor," Nigel replied without hesitation. He'd opted to not have a jury trial after he had a chance to clear his head from the haze of the drugs and saw his legal situation a little clearer, choosing instead to take the deal that Albert had negotiated with the district attorney. Had he chosen to take the case to trial, if he was found guilty, he was likely to face a sentence of life with no parole, given his lengthy arrest record. The plea bargain assured him that he would see the streets again, albeit after a long hiatus.

As for Pretty Ricky, he also took a deal and was sentenced to ten years for his role in the robbery. The State dropped the handgun charge against him in exchange for his plea bargain.

"Would you like to say anything to the court before I impose my sentence?" the judge asked.

"No, Your Honor," Nigel responded calmly. "I just want to get this over and done with so I can start serving my time. There's no sense delaying this situation any longer."

"Very well. It's the court's decision to accept the DA's recommendation of a sentence of twenty years for your guilty plea to the charges mentioned. Mr. Hawkins, it is my sincerest hope that you take this time in prison to think about all of the lives you've harmed with your actions. Looking at your long history of crime, you have a lot of atoning to do to society. You have been a menace in this city for your entire adult life. I see that you have a young son, and I pray that he doesn't follow the same path as you did. God bless his soul. Bailiff, take this man away."

Nigel looked up to see JR staring at him with tears in his eyes, as the bailiff escorted him out of the courtroom. He wanted to reach out and pick him up, but his arms were handcuffed behind his back.

"Get your hands off of my father," JR yelled. "You ain't taking him nowhere!" JR got up outta his seat and tried to run toward the bailiff, but Franklin and Mrs. Hawkins restrained him, his little body unable to break free from their grip.

Nigel was led out of the courtroom to his new home, the Maryland State Penitentiary.

JR was left behind in his grandmother's care. He would be a grown man when Nigel returned to the streets.

Seeing so much of his evil ways in him, Nigel just hoped that JR would live long enough to grow up before the streets ate him alive first.

9

With nothing but free time on his hands, it didn't take Nigel long to fall back into his old ways. Now five years into his bid, all of the reflective thoughts he'd had before his day in court about the mistakes he'd made in his life were now a distant memory. During that period of time, he'd promised his mother that he was going to use his time in jail to get himself together and be a better son to her when he returned to society. He'd also pledged to maintain a relationship with his son while locked up, if she agreed to bring JR to see him for visits.

However, once he was settled in and adapted to prison life, he was back into the swing of things, getting high on a regular basis. All of that positive talk was just that—idle chatter with no substance. It took him all of eighteen months to return to being the same old crackhead he was out on the streets.

Mrs. Hawkins brought JR out to the jail to see him twice a month so that they could spend time together. Today would be his second visit with his son for the month. Until recently, JR used to look forward to trips out to the jail to see his father. At first, they used to have meaningful conversations about what was going on in his life, but lately Nigel had been acting distant whenever he would visit.

Today appeared to be another one of those days. Nigel was in an irritable mood already, because he didn't have his morning blast up in him. Nonetheless, he gathered himself together to make it down to the visiting room when the CO came to get him.

When Nigel reached the visiting room, he handed the CO at the desk his pass and scanned the room to find him mother and son. He spotted them in the corner seated by the vending machine. He noticed how big JR had become since he came to jail. He was almost the same height as he was, with a stocky build. He was now twelve years old and on his way to becoming a man.

Nigel walked over to them, a mean scowl on his face. It was clear that his mind was elsewhere. He would rather be up in his cell, smoking crack, than sitting in the visiting room engaged in a stupid conversation. He approached their table with major attitude.

"Hey, Pops." JR attempted to embrace his father. "What's going on?"

Nigel pushed his arms away and sat down. "Come on, boy, I ain't in the mood for none of that mushy stuff. What's up, Mommy? Is this boy giving you any more problems?"

Mrs. Hawkins looked on in disbelief. "Nigel, what is wrong with you? Why did you just brush JR off like that? You look crazy, your hair is not combed, you've got that scraggly-looking beard. Are you using drugs again?"

Upset after his attempt to show affection was rebuffed, JR stared at Nigel awaiting his response.

"Nah, I ain't getting high. Why a man gotta be on drugs because he ain't shave and what not? I just had a rough night last night, that's all. Boy, why you staring at me all crazy? Is there something on your mind? Don't think that because you done got all big that I can't whip ya behind."

"Daddy, what is wrong with you? I ain't do nothing, and you pushing up on me all crazy and what not. I think Grandma is right. You must be on drugs again."

Out of nowhere, Nigel hauled off and slapped JR across the face.

JR held his bruised cheek in awe and became filled with rage and hate toward Nigel. A tear formed in the corner of his eye. He couldn't believe that his father had just hit him.

The CO's noticed the commotion and ran over to address the issue. They quickly grabbed Nigel to take him back to his cell.

"Boy, don't ever come out your mouth wrong to me," Nigel yelled as the CO's dragged him away. "I'm your father, remember that."

"You ain't my father. You ain't nothing to me!" JR shouted.

Nigel heard him faintly as he was being escorted down the hall.

Mrs. Hawkins embraced JR in an effort to console him. "Your father is sick, JR. He didn't mean it. He needs help. It's the drugs, it's not him," she said as they exited the visiting room.

JR paid her words no mind. The man he once loved and admired had rejected him, treating him like a total stranger. "Well, I hope those drugs kill him."

Mrs. Hawkins knew that JR didn't mean what he said, but was just talking out of hurt and frustration. "Lord, I need you know more than ever before," she prayed. "Please guide me and tell me what to do." Mrs. Hawkins held out hope that Nigel would change, but after this display, it was clear to her that he was caught up in the insanity of his addiction. Her burdens seemed too heavy for her to carry right now. She had a son held hostage by drugs, and a grandson consumed with hatred. She didn't know what to do. She needed God's watchful eye and strength to guide her through this crucial time.

10

When Nigel reached his cell, he was regretful about the way he'd just acted. He loved JR more than he loved himself, but his frustration and craving for cocaine had him losing his mind. He wished that he could take back what he just did, but it was too late. What was done was done. He needed to escape from reality. He anxiously awaited his cell-mate's return to their cell. He would have the medicine he needed to feel right. He was sure that the coke would make all of his feelings of guilt subside.

Nigel's cellmate, Rodney Briggs, was the perfect friend to have to aid him along in his addiction. Rodney and Nigel hit it off right from the start when Nigel was transferred from the city jail to the state penitentiary. Baltimore was a small city and they happened to know some of the same people out on the streets.

Rodney had heard a lot of things about Nigel's reputation in the streets from his older brother, Carmine, who was in the game around the same time as Nigel. His brother had a great deal of admiration and respect for Nigel when he used to handle his business like a true G. Due to his brother's reputation as a drug kingpin out on the streets, Rodney had access to whatever he wanted in the joint. In turn, anything Nigel wanted, be it drugs, cigarettes, or anything he desired from the prison commissary, Rodney was able to get for him. He looked out for him as a sign of respect for a dude that he considered to be an OG in the game. If his brother held Nigel in high regard, then he felt that it was his responsibility to show him his proper respect, regardless of how far he had fallen off.

Twenty-five-year-old Rodney looked at least ten years older and was street-smart way beyond his years. He had a tall, frail frame and wore his hair cut close. Sniffin' dope was his bag, and his skin had a dirty brown hue to it from the effects of his heroin use. He looked at the IV drug user as the worst of all junkies and swore to himself that he would never let his dope habit get so bad that he would start shootin' up.

Rodney was serving a life sentence on murder and kidnapping charges. He had kidnapped the sister of a drug dealer by the name of Freddy "Black" Cole and held her hostage for a $250,000 ransom. When Black refused to pay the ransom, he killed his sister and left her body in the abandoned house where he'd held her captive. The police found her decomposed body after about a week, and Rodney was arrested when the police discovered his fingerprints at the scene of the crime. Several witnesses also came forth stating that he had bragged about the killing to them. He was already two years into his bid and fully institutionalized into prison life by the time Nigel Hawkins came into his life.

"What's up, dog? What you working with today?" Nigel asked Rodney. "I got it bad. Did you come up on something out on the yard?"

"Yeah, I got five joints for you and five for me, homes. That should hold us down for a minute. You I know I couldn't get on without looking out for my road dog." Rodney slid Nigel the crack rocks crumpled up in a piece of paper.

Nigel took one of the crack rocks, placed it in his stem, and inhaled the fumes until there was none left.

"Who'd you get this from? Bo and them boys? This some good rock right here, Rod," Nigel stated, half-choking on the smoke that filled his lungs.

"Yeah, them niggas just got the shipment in yesterday. My brother be hittin' Bo's connection on the outside off with work for dirt-cheap. Bo had one of his bitches bring it in here. He got a thing worked out with that CO nigga, Patterson, that works the day shift. You want some of this boy to chase that rock with, big homey?"

Rodney took two hits of heroin up each nostril and leaned back on his bunk. He had a silly grin on his face, and his eyes were closed. The dope had kicked in, and he wanted to savor the moment.

"Nah, that ain't my bag, young'un. That dope be having a nigga noddin' out and sitting around looking stupid as a muthafucka like you do right now." Nigel watched Rodney slump over on his bunk. He took another pull on the crack pipe.

Rodney slid into a serious nod for a minute before he spoke.

"Suit yourself. That's more for me, but I'ma tell you one thing. When I was on the streets, I used to sniff a pill of this shit and fuck my girl all night long. Them bitches love that dope dick, Nigel." Rodney wiped drool from his mouth.

The two of them would shoot the shit like this every day all day.

"Young'un, you're still wet behind the ears. Five minutes in the pussy and your ass is bustin' off in a bitch," Nigel joked. "You ain't even got to front for me."

Rodney shot back, "Yeah, a'ight. Whatever you say, old-timer. Some dope probably wouldn't do anything for a nigga your age. You probably need a pump to get ya shit up for a bitch. My girl used to say old niggas like you had the worms. Is that true?"

"Shut up, nigga. Ask ya mama if I can get it up. You're blowing my high with ya simple ass." Nigel took another hit off the pipe.

If anybody else had made a "ya-mama" joke, Rodney would have been on their ass like white on rice, but since Nigel was his right-hand man, he could get away with it.

"Hey, Rod, you know what, man? This jail shit is for the birds. The White man got shit set up for us niggas to fail. He brings drugs into this country to get us high, but then he locks us up when we go rob a muthafucka to support our habit. Or he keeps us poor in the hood and expects us not to sell drugs after he shows us how much money we can make off of the shit. This is a fucked-up world that we live in, man." Nigel had a serious look on his face. His eyes were buggy and made him look like a beetle, and his heart was racing a thousand beats per minute. The cocaine had him wired.

Whenever he got high, Nigel always wanted to have an intellectual conversation about something going on in the world. He would rant and rave about the president and the poor way he ran the country, or he would go on and on about how all of the people in the church were hypocrites who were going to hell. Under the influence, his mind told him that his conversation was about some profound shit, but in reality, there was no logic to be found in his foolishness, something that Rodney pointed out to him on a daily basis.

"Nigel, you're a crazy nigga. You don't know what the fuck you're talking about. That coke got you thinkin' you're an Einstein-type o' nigga that can figure out the mysteries of the world. That's why I don't fuck with that shit. It fucks with ya brain. Ain't nobody make me sell no drugs or kill that bitch. I could have gotten a job and been a white-collar muthafucka, but I knew that wasn't me. From the time I was a lil' nigga, I knew that I wanted to sell drugs and live the fast life. Once I saw how my brother and his crew was gettin' it in, I wanted to be down. You know you did too, once you saw how sweet the money was out in them streets. We can't even front about that. I loved the money, the bitches, the fast cars, and all of that shit. I loved bustin' my gun and puttin' a cap in a nigga. The only things I didn't like about the game was that I got caught, and this monkey on my back. Once I started fuckin' with that dope, things got all fucked-up for me. I should've listened to my brother when he told me to never get high on my own supply. It was downhill for me from the first time I tried that shit."

Rodney's blunt honesty was one of his better traits, and he never made any excuses for being in the predicament of being a lifer with no chance at parole. He knew that his heroin habit had him licked and planned to die a dope fiend.

"Yeah, you right. I loved all of that shit too. I couldn't live my life any other way. I ain't never gonna be no square. Why do you think we liked that shit so much, though, man?" Nigel asked.

"It's just our nature, man. Some niggas were born to be doctors and lawyers, and others of us were born to be thugs. God made us all different and to serve different purposes in the world. If there were no thugs like us to commit crimes, then there would be no need for lawyers to exist. There would be no judges, prosecutors, or any of these crooked-ass CO's. The same thing is true for doctors, because if nobody got sick or shot and had to go to the hospital, then they wouldn't have a job. To exist, they all need thugs like me and you. We're all connected in this world." Rodney had confidence in his belief of an interdependent society.

Since he'd been locked up, Rodney spent a lot of time in the prison library reading books about philosophy, sociology, psychology, theology, or any other "ology" that sparked his interest. It was a shame that he didn't share the same passion for education while he was on the streets.

"Yeah, that makes a lot of sense. You're a smart lil' nigga, Rod. I'ma call ya ass the professor from now on. Nah, fuck that. You're the reincarnation of George Jackson and Huey Newton," Nigel said jokingly.

"Just because I'm a thug nigga don't mean that I ain't got no brains, ya heard? Some of the best minds in the history of the United States came through its jails and institutions. Look at Al Capone, look at John Gotti, look at Larry Hoover. It takes a lot of smarts and wisdom to run a large-scale criminal organization like all of them did. They are just as smart as any of these CEO's of any of the Fortune 500 companies."

Nigel nodded in agreement then said, "You know what, man? I think I just fucked things up with my lil' man. I ain't have no coke up in me, and I just snapped out on him in the visiting room." Nigel pulled out a recent picture of JR out of a book and just stared at it as he talked.

"Don't even sweat that shit, homes. He'll get over it eventually. If he don't, then fuck it. Ain't shit you can do about it in here anyway."

"Yeah, I guess you're right," Nigel responded, still getting high. His regret was sincere because, in spite of all his craziness, his love for JR was genuine. He held on to the faint hope that one day JR would see that it was the drugs and not him that had changed him as a person.

"It is what it is. We do shit under the influence and then regret it later. You should just be lucky that you got ya moms around to take care of ya seed. I don't know who's taking care of the five lil' niggas that I left out on them streets. All of my baby mamas is crazy. Both of my peoples are dead. They died out there chasing the dragon. They both OD'd on some bad shit. My brother and I basically had to raise ourselves. I don't know where none of my baby mamas is at right now. My kids could be anywhere on this here earth. It's just another generation of Black children that will be out there to raise themselves. This world is fucked-up." Rodney wore a serious look on his face as he sunk deeper into his thoughts.

"Yeah, it is, but what can a nigga do?"

"I guess that's the price that we pay to play the game. Ain't no sense crying about that shit now. Man up, nigga. I know that I'm in here for life. I can't change nothing out in the world from in here. Whatever is gonna happen with my kids is gonna happen. Their fate is in God's hands. You sure you don't wanna try some of this heroin, man? Come on, take one toot up each nostril at least once with me so you can see how it feels. This boy will take all of your worries away."

"A'ight, nigga, give me that shit," Nigel said, his defenses worn down by the "truth" that Rodney just hit him with about his inability to control life outside of the cell that he now called his home. There was nothing that he could do for JR behind bars. His addiction played with his mind and convinced him that JR didn't need him in his life to be a father figure.

Feeling defeated and throwing his own pity party, Nigel inhaled one line of heroin up each nostril.

A few minutes later, his head was in the toilet as he threw up.

Rodney looked on at him and smiled. The same thing had happened to him the first time that he'd tried dope. He knew the feeling all too well and had been chasing it unsuccessfully ever since.

"How do you do this shit, man? Coke ain't never made me throw up like that." Nigel gathered himself together and lay back on his bunk to recuperate.

"That's how it is the first time," Rodney told him. "Now lay back and relax. Once that shit finish sinking into your soul, you're gonna see what the hell I was talking about when I said that heroin is the truth."

A few minutes later, the heroin had spread throughout Nigel's bloodstream. His eyes were shut, and he had a smile on his face as bright as the sun. Engulfed in the feeling of tranquility that heroin delivered to its victims, he felt like he was in heaven, the bad memory of vomiting erased from his mind.

"Damn, Rod, you ain't never lied. That boy got me feeling mellow as a muthafucka. That coke be having my heart racing, but the dope just made me calm down. Let me get some more of that shit," Nigel said, his tone sluggish. He sat bent over on his bunk, his head about to fall into his lap, as he waited for Rodney to break him off a few more lines.

Rodney obliged him and shared the remainder of his stash with him.

Rodney was right when he told Nigel that heroin would make him feel good in the beginning, but once it became a habit, his body would never be the same without it in his system. Being ill was a feeling that no junkie wanted to feel. It was the closest thing to death that a person could experience without actually dying. It was so bad that a heroin addict would do whatever was necessary to take that pain away. Nigel was a demon with his crack habit alone, and now that he'd added heroin into the mix, Rodney had no idea what kind of fire he had just ignited. They both nodded out into a state of unconsciousness, as the heroin did its job in blocking out the outside world.

11

"JR, it's time for dinner, boy," Mrs. Hawkins yelled from the bottom of the stairs. "You and Raynard, come on down here and get something to eat!"

Raynard was JR's best friend, who lived around the corner and attended the same school as JR. He always came over on Sundays to get some of Mrs. Hawkins's finger-lickin'-good grub.

"Okay, Grandma, we'll be down in a few minutes," JR replied.

JR was now sixteen years old going on twenty-one. He was tall like his father with big hands. His height made him appear to be older than he really was, not to mention he used to lift weights in his grandmother's basement to keep his muscles toned. He inherited his father's talent for being a ladies' man. Even though he was only a sophomore in high school, he was able to get play from the upper-class females. He dressed fly, always smelled good, and his charm and good looks made him appealing to their eyes despite his age. The older dudes in school were jealous of the attention that he got, but never stepped to him. JR had a reputation for knockin' niggas out. He was nice with his hands and even more dangerous with the loaded .357 that he kept on him at all times.

JR and Raynard were making a name for themselves out in the streets. JR was known around his neighborhood as a hothead, quick to pop that steel on a nigga if he even looked at him wrong. The only person that had the balls to fight him was Raynard, who was just as evil and as good a fighter.

They got into it one day on the basketball court when JR fouled Raynard hard coming down the lane. They went at it fair and square and fought to a draw. JR respected Raynard for having the balls to stand up to him when all of the other cats on the court let him get away with whatever he wanted to without the slightest protest. Their mutual respect for each other led to them becoming the best of friends.

All of the bitterness and feelings of anger and loneliness from the betrayal he'd felt from his parents fueled his aggressive behavior out in the streets. Since the day he'd cried in the visiting room the last time he saw his father, JR swore that he would never shed a tear over anyone. The only person that he truly loved and trusted was his grandmother, who held him down no matter the situation. She was his heart.

The two boys were in JR's bedroom vialing up two ounces of crack cocaine. Before they got down to business, JR made sure that his bedroom door was locked. He didn't want his nosy grandmother to accidentally walk in on them while they doing their thing. If she knew he had drugs in her house, she would have hit the roof. It would have broken her heart to see that he was caught up in the same madness that took away her baby boy, Nigel.

Since his father was locked up, Mrs. Hawkins had spoiled JR rotten. She would spend her last penny and even get money from her other two sons to make sure that JR had all of the new designer clothes and video games that the other kids had. She never wanted him to feel as though he wasn't as good as they were because his parents weren't around. But, despite all of her sacrifices to make sure that he always had the best, it just wasn't enough. He was his father's son, and he had to answer the call of the streets.

What Mrs. Hawkins didn't realize was that her spoiling JR with so many material possessions only gave him added incentive to want to acquire things in life the fast way. Without her making him earn the things that he received, he saw no need to work hard for anything that he wanted. And his father had already whet his appetite, from the time he was a toddler, about the riches that the streets had to offer.

Her good intentions were easily misconstrued and made JR feel a sense of entitlement to the finer things in life without having to pay a price for them.

Once Raynard's father started frontin' them coke to sell, the allure of the fast money from selling drugs had him out on the block grindin' until the wee hours of the night. Their reputation on the streets rapidly grew.

JR and Raynard were like stars in the hood. All of the girls wanted to give them some play because of the amount of dough they were clockin'.

JR's grandmother had no clue that he was selling drugs, because he hid most of his clothes and jewelry that he bought over at Raynard's house. He had been saving his money up to buy himself a Benz. He would have to find somewhere to hide that as well, so his grandmother wouldn't see him sittin' so fat.

Raynard, busy talking on the phone to Latrice, his main squeeze, took his mouth away from his cell phone, and said to JR, who was vialing up, "Yo, we better hurry up. That's the second time she done called us to eat. If we don't go downstairs now, she's gonna come up here and wanna know what we're doing." Raynard had been over to Mrs. Hawkins's house enough times to know her ways.

Raynard stood about 5 feet 8 inches tall and weighed 170 pounds. He wore his hair in a faded Caesar, like the rapper Nas, his head full of waves. He had a thin mustache and beard and was as much of a playa as JR. That was why they got along so well. They were two young brothers on a mission to get all the money and pussy they could before they died. Money, cars, and hoes were all these young G's knew and cared about, and nothing else mattered.

"I know, nigga. I'm almost done. I got like ten more vials to fill, and we can bounce. If ya ass was helping me out instead of flapping ya gums on the phone, we would be done by now. I can't wait to get down there and chow down on that fried chicken and macaroni and cheese that Mama Hawkins done whipped together. I'm hungrier than a muthafucka," JR said, measuring out the remaining crack rocks and placing them into the vials carefully.

"Shut up, Latrice," Raynard said. "Hold on for a minute. Don't you hear me over here talking to JR? Yeah, I'm hungry too, dog. A brother needs to eat before he hits the block. I need my energy if I gotta deal with these fiends. Oh yeah, don't be hatin', nigga, because you ain't as smooth with the ladies as I am. Nah, on the real, once we knock this package off, we can go see my pops. He said that he might front us even more coke, depending on how fast we get rid of this work. I don't know about you, but I'm trying to move them kilos like Nino Brown, baby!"

"That sounds like a plan to me. I'm done vialing up. Let's go get some grub, and then we can hit the strip." JR placed all of the vials inside of a large brown paper bag and put the paper bag inside of his knapsack, as well as his .357. He hid the knapsack under his bed and planned to come back to retrieve it once they'd finished eating. He reached under his bed and retrieved a pair of new Air Jordan's and slid them onto his feet. He threw on his Yankees fitted hat and was ready to roll.

"A'ight, Latrice, I'ma see you tomorrow. I gotta bounce," Raynard said, following JR down the stairs.

When they reached the dining room, Mrs. Hawkins had two man-sized plates on the tables waiting for them. Their eager eyes were wide open and eager with anticipation to feast on the meal before them as they both sat down at the table to eat.

"The food is probably cold now. What were y'all two doing up there in that room all of that time?" Mrs. Hawkins asked.

"We weren't doing anything, Grandma. We were just playing video games and talking about school." JR hated lying to his grandmother, but he had no choice. If he told her the truth, it would've only caused her pain and disappointment. Also, he never wanted to fall out of her good graces.

"Raynard, my baby brings home good grades from school. How are you doing in your classes?" Mrs. Hawkins asked as she ate her meal.

"I'm doing real well in school, ma'am. I don't get all A's like JR, but I'm a B-student in most of my classes. JR helps me with my homework when I need it."

Between Raynard and JR, the goody-two-shoes BS flowed thickly in the room. They both hooked school on the regular and got by in their classes because of sheer natural ability and not from hard work or studying. It was easy for them to miss a day in class and still be able to keep up with the rest of the class. Any assignments that they did miss, they could easily con some young girl in their class to do for them for a small fee. They'd learned early on how to "win" in the Baltimore City Public School System.

"Go get some rest, Grandma," JR said after they were through eating. "Raynard and I will wash the dishes. Then we're gonna go down to the gym and play basketball."

"That's my baby. I am kind of tired from cooking and cleaning the house today. You just remember that tonight is a school night. I want you back in this house by eleven."

Mrs. Hawkins's bark was worse than her bite. If JR wasn't home by eleven, she wasn't going to do a thing. She'd be fast asleep by that time anyhow.

JR was only sixteen, but he did everything that a grown man could do. He did whatever he wanted whenever he wanted since he was little, without any punishment from his grandmother. With no discipline in his life, JR was on a collision course with trouble.

He and Raynard washed the dishes and put them away. When they were done, JR ran up to his room to get his knapsack. He grabbed his .357 out of his knapsack and put it in his dip for protection, in case things got hot on the block.

Walking with a gangster swagger, JR and Raynard hit the block to pitch them *thangs*, until not one vial was left.

12

"A'ight, everybody, line up out this muthafucka. I wanna see a single-file line. Y'all know it's the same thing every damn day. You better get it together, or we ain't giving y'all shit," JR yelled at the crowd of zealous baseheads that were in front of him and Raynard. He loved talking to them greasy, because it gave him a sense of power. He was amazed at the way he could control grown folks with a crack rock.

They went through the same thing every time when they opened up shop. The crackheads couldn't wait to get one of them free testers to beam up to Scotty, swarming like a pack of roaches when Raynard handed them out.

Minutes after they were done with the testers, the baseheads ran right back to cop some more of that boomin' crack rock. Raynard cooked it up himself and made sure that he used the right blend of cocaine and baking soda so that their shit was potent. His father taught him how to take powdered cocaine and make it into a crack rock. He'd paid close attention to his lessons and became one of the best ghetto chemists around.

Raynard and JR chose the corner of Park Heights and Woodland to make their strip, the same neighborhood that JR spent his early years growing up with parents. At first, it bothered him to be in the area. Seeing his old home brought back memories of all of the constant fights between his parents. It reminded him of the fact that they had both abandoned him.

When they first set up shop, some of the neighborhood regulars recognized him from when he was younger. When they asked him about his parents and their whereabouts, he gave them a "leave-me-the-fuck-alone" look that quickly put an end to their questions. Most of those old neighbors became some of his best customers. The area was riddled with drug addicts eager to get high on whatever was being sold out on the strip. The moneymaking potential of the area was enough to make JR forget about his hang-ups of being in his old neighborhood.

JR and Raynard had to run a couple of local hardheads outta the area before they seized control. A local crew run by a guy named Mark held down the drug market before them. A bunch of pussies who were scared of competition, Mark and his crew were in it for the money but didn't have the balls or stomach to go to war for their strip. Once Raynard and JR came through with their pistols blazing, them muthafuckas broke the hell outta dodge. The locals saw how the two young gunslingers got down and didn't dare question their authority. That was how Park Heights and Woodland became their territory. They'd been holding it down for the past year without an ounce of confrontation from any potential rivals. If anybody tried to come up on their block and sell work without their permission, they would've received a lead shower for their troubles.

They usually stashed their work at Maxine's house, a local basehead. Maxine was a washed-up, broke-down rock star. JR remembered seeing her at his house as a child with his mother. When he looked at her, it made him think of his mother. Maxine used to be a pretty woman but had lost it all to the crack pipe, just like his mother.

Watching her ways and behavior when she was high reminded him of the same things his mother used to do around the house. He had a hard time dealing with the fact that he was the child of two crackhead parents. It gave him a negative complex about himself. He thought that he was inferior to the other kids in school. He always felt like an outcast and just another ghetto bastard, because neither of his parents was around.

JR used his material possessions to mask his low self-esteem. Being a drug dealer gave him a sense of self-worth that enabled him to be able to hide his self-identity issues from the rest of the world. He got more attention than he could have ever imagined due to his street credentials. It made him feel important that girls would flock to him because his pockets were swole. His need to feel like the man further fueled his young capitalist ambitions to become a drug kingpin. He craved the spotlight and the street life gave him more than enough of it to quench his desire.

JR and Raynard paid Maxine in drugs to use her house to conduct business. It was a small price to pay for the amount of revenue they generated. They never had to worry about Maxine stealing because as long as they kept her high, she wouldn't be a problem. They were given a free run of her home to do whatever they pleased. They also didn't have to worry about her snitching to the police because Maxine saw them in action more than enough times bustin' them guns to know that it was best to keep her mouth shut if she wanted to live. JR and Raynard held down their block like two guerilla warriors ready for war.

"Let me get two, JR," the hype said as he pulled out a ten-dollar bill and a handful of wrinkled one-dollar bills.

JR took the money and gave the man two jumbo-sized vials of crack.

The man stood there for a minute and looked JR up and down in strange manner.

"What the fuck is wrong with you? Why in the fuck are you looking at me like that?" JR asked, leery of the customer. He knew whenever a hype hung around after he got served, normally that meant he was up to some slick shit.

"You don't recognize me do you, JR? I've known you since you were a baby. It's me Uncle Fats. I know it's been a long time. You don't remember me?" Fats extended his arms to hug JR.

JR stepped back out of his reach. "I don't know nobody named Fats, asshole. You got what you came here to get, now get ya crusty ass outta here. Next time, don't be giving me all of these singles," JR barked. He lied because he just didn't want to acknowledge him or anybody connected with his father. He lunged forward and pushed Fats with enough force to knock his paper-thin frame to the ground. He felt good about knocking him off of his feet. It gave him a chance to take some of his pent-up anger he held against his father out on one of his acquaintances.

"You ain't gotta treat me like that, JR. Ya father and I used to be some major figures in these streets. Just because I'm doing bad you ain't gotta play me like a sucka. You could show me a little respect on the strength of your father," Fats said as he tried to flex. Nigel wasn't impressed with his attempt to stand his ground.

"Nigga, I'ma say this one last time. You better get ghost and don't come back around here unless you spending money. Fuck you and my father," JR yelled and raised his fists. He was about to give Fats an ass whipping he would remember for days.

Fats got the message clearly and jumped to his feet. He jetted away from the corner to escape the beat-down. In his prime, he would've pistol-whipped a young dude like JR for disrespecting him. Today he was in no position to win a battle with JR. He knew that if he stayed around any longer there was a chance that JR might bust a cap in him for irking his nerves.

"Yo, you a'ight? Was that nigga really a friend of ya pops?" Raynard asked.

"Yeah, he was, but fuck that nigga. As far as I'm concerned, my pops is a dead man walking. If I see that nigga around here again, I'ma do his ass just for GP." JR said. He hog-spat on the concrete. He lit up a cigarette to calm his nerves.

"Don't let that muthafucka get to you, dog. You know I got ya back. We're family. Besides, we got too much money to make to let some junkie distract us. Fuck them has-been muthafuckas. This is our time, dog." Raynard gave JR a pound.

"Exactly. Now you talking some good shit right there."

"Yo, whoever invented this crack shit was the smartest muthafucka alive. This shit is like a bird in the hand. A dumb muthafucka could make money selling this shit. I don't know what that coke does to these fiends' brains, but they will do anything to get a hit," Raynard said as he conducted a hand-to-hand sale to a customer.

"Yeah, this shit is like truth serum. It shows you the ugliest side of a muthafucka. A bitch will sell her baby just to get down. I done had my dick sucked more than enough times by some hype tryin' to get on. I don't even wanna tell you how much pussy I get. Crack done drove the price of pussy down to almost nothing."

As the two talked, they had a group of rock stars surrounding them, eager to spend the money they'd swindled somebody out of to get a blast. JR didn't give a damn where the money came from, as long as they didn't come with shorts.

"Nigga, is you crazy? You can't let any of these hoes suck

your dick. AIDS is killing muthafuckas left and right out here. I ain't fucking any of these hypes. I got too much class for that," Raynard said.

"Whatever, dog. Don't think I don't know about you taking that strawberry Juanita behind the house across the street last week and letting her give you a blowjob," JR grinned.

Raynard just put his head down. "Fuck you, man. Juanita was different. She ain't been out here like these other hoes. She's new to the game. She ain't all used up."

"A hype is a hype is a hype, nigga. It don't matter how long she's been out in these streets. You ain't no different. If I can get that shit from one of these hoes then so can you. You better hope you don't give anything to Latrice. Then your ass is gonna really be in trouble," JR said.

"Yeah, that's for real, but if I get jammed up, then so do you. She ain't gonna do nothing but go and tell Rochelle. Then ya ass is gonna be on the hot seat too, nigga, right along with me."

"That is true. She'll be on some 'birds-of-a-feather-freak-hoes-together' shit. Rochelle will be trying to smell a nigga drawers to see if I've been out here fucking around."

The next few hours they went back and forth to Maxine's house to get more work when they ran out. All in all, they'd made a little over four grand so far. The package was almost gone. They would get to keep forty percent of the profits, which added up to over a thousand dollars apiece for both of them after they paid Raynard's father his cut. That was damn good for only a few hours of work. No job in America could pay a young Black teenager that much money in a month, let alone a few hours.

JR was smart and saved his money and had close to twenty grand saved up for emergencies. He kept it stashed in a safe at Rochelle's house.

JR and Raynard were their own bosses and set their own

hours of operation. As far as they were concerned, life couldn't get any better.

JR went back to the house to get the last of their package so they could knock it off and close up shop. The way things were going, he might just make it home before eleven. As he approached the strip, he noticed a white BMW with DC plates parked in front of Raynard. A scraggly-looking White dude stood in front of Raynard. As he got closer, he saw Raynard with a big smile on his face.

"Yo, what's up?" JR asked. "What's the deal?"

"My man Pete here just made my night. He ain't from around here. He said that he has seven hundred big ones and he wants to know how much rock he can get for that from us. What you think about that?"

"Is ya money right, homeboy?" JR asked.

"Yeah, man, you can count it yaself. It's all there," Pete replied. The hair on his head looked unkempt, and he was in desperate need of a shave. His clothes reeked of alcohol and stale cigarette smoke. He gave his money to Raynard to count.

"What's a White boy like yaself doin' down here in the hood?" JR asked suspiciously. When a White boy came to cop, a brother needed to be on alert. They were usually undercover cops sent to do buy and busts.

Pete appeared to be fidgeting, and his buggy eyes raced back and forth between Raynard and JR. He couldn't stand still.

His nervousness made JR feel a little uneasy. JR put his hand in his dip as though he were about to reach for his gun. His gun wasn't in his dip, though, but was stashed on in the bushes behind him. It was close enough for him to be able to get to it if he needed to.

"Easy, partner. I don't want any trouble, bro. I just came to get what I need and be outta here. You know like I do that us

White boys gotta come down here in the hood to get that good ready rock."

His response made JR relax a little, and he removed his hand from his dip.

"Hell, yeah, nigga, his money is good. It's all there!" Raynard said excitedly after he finished counting the money.

"Then let's do this," JR said. They did the exchange of money for drugs. This was a good way to end the night. All of their work was about gone, with the exception of a few vials.

Another customer came right behind Pete and copped the remaining vials. They were both pumped up. Now they could get with Raynard's father tomorrow and talk about increasing their supply.

About five minutes after they closed up shop, several unmarked cars swarmed around JR and Raynard as they were about to hail down a cab.

"Police, assholes, get ya ass down on the ground!" one of the officers barked, and several other officers emerged from the two squad cars, their pistols drawn.

"We ain't did shit! Why are you harassing two young Black men minding their own business?" Raynard asked angrily. He got down on the ground and assumed the position, his hands behind his head. JR complied as well.

They looked at each other and shook their heads.

"Yeah, y'all ain't got nothing else to do but harass us?" JR chimed in. "You can search us all you want. Neither one of us is dirty,"

"That's real cute, you lil' scumbag, but you're under arrest. You two stupid fucks just served an undercover cop," one of the officers responded.

"When JR looked up, he saw Pete out of the corner of his eye with a police badge in his hand. "Fuck!" he said as he gritted his teeth. He looked at Raynard, who was equally

pissed off as he was being handcuffed and placed into the police vehicle.

"Yeah, that's right. You are fucked. We've been watching
you all night. Y'all need to be a little tighter with your shit.
You had everything right out here in the open for us to see.
We didn't have to break a sweat to bust up your little ring," a
Black cop said as he laughed.

"Oh, and what do we have here?" one of the other cops
asked with a devilish grin as he took a wad of money out of
Raynard's pocket. Another cop searched through JR's pockets
and took his stash as well.

The two officers looked at each other and gave each other
a familiar look. The money they'd just retrieved wasn't gonna
be logged into evidence at the precinct, with the exception
of the money that Pete used to cop.

"Man, that's our money," Raynard yelled. "You pigs can't
take our shit!"

"We're the goddamn police. We can do whatever the hell
we want and ain't a damn thing that you can do about it,
chump!" one of the officers shouted.

"Yeah, you little girls are on ya way down to the police station. You better hope ya mommies come and bail ya out," another one of the officers said as they put them into the squad
car.

JR's mind began to race with thoughts of all of the jail-
house stories that his father had told him when he was
younger. Now he was gonna get a firsthand view of what life
was like behind bars. He was mad that he got knocked off
and upset that the police seized all of the money that they
had just made. Now they would be indebted to Raynard's father for the money lost, and he would have to dig into his
savings to pay his share of the debt.

As far as the felony possession and distribution charges he
would face, he knew that he had a chance of beating it or get-

ting probation because of the small quantity of work they'd sold to Pete and the connections that Raynard's father had in the legal system. He was relieved that he didn't have his gun on him when he got knocked off because that would have guaranteed him jail time.

The arrest did nothing to deter him from staying in the game. Once he was released, he planned to be right back on the block doing what he did best—slinging pies.

13

Once they were taken back to the police station, JR and Raynard were fingerprinted and placed in separate interrogation rooms. JR used his one phone call to call Rochelle to let her know that he was locked up, and Raynard called his father so that his lawyers would use their influence to expedite the process of them getting released.

The arresting officers tried to get JR and Raynard to rat on each other or tell them who their supplier was. The old tactic of divide and conquer didn't work with these two, who were schooled well on the ploys used by police officers to get information out of a suspect, and neither one of them budged under the intense questioning. The police officers exhausted every avenue before they realized that they were up against a brick wall and placed them in separate cells, where they had to wait until the morning to see the court commissioner to find out how much their bail would be.

When they went before the commissioner the next day, bail was set at ten grand for each of them. Raynard's father had his lawyer post their bond, and they had to wait to receive a court date in the mail.

They slapped each other high-fives as they walked outta the jail and gave the finger to the officers that escorted them to the courthouse. The two of them waited on the courthouse steps for Rochelle and Latrice to pick them up.

"Yo, that shit was crazy, man," JR said proudly to Raynard. "The pigs tried everything under the sun to get me to talk, but I wouldn't budge. I told them muthafuckas I wasn't saying shit until I talked to my attorney."

"I know they did the same thing to me. They wanted to know who we were working for and said that they would drop the charges against me if I told them. Then two officers came at me with the good cop-bad cop routine. I just laughed at them making a fool of themselves. They backed up off of me when I told them who my pops was. That cell they had me in was filthy as hell, dog, piss stains on the wall and the sink up in there was filled with mold." Raynard shook his head.

"Yeah, my cell was nasty-looking too. I'm glad that we're up outta there now. I'm too pretty to be up in that filthy-ass hellhole," JR joked.

"Those pigs shoulda known that they couldn't break soldiers like us. We're true to this shit."

"No doubt, my nigga. We're gangstas for life." JR inhaled the smoke from his cigarette. When he looked to his left, he saw Rochelle pull up in the Cadillac he'd bought her. He flicked his cigarette onto the ground and they walked over to the car.

"Damn, nigga! Is you all right?" Rochelle asked, rapper Jay Z blasting from the cars speakers. "Ain't nobody try to take y'all booty while y'all was up in there, did they?"

Rochelle got out and hugged JR. He grabbed her around

her trim waist and wrapped her up in his arms. Rochelle was dressed in a pair of red capris, a matching red wife-beater and a pair of Steve Madden sandals. Her hair was in a ponytail because it needed to be done. .

"Girl, you better stop playing with me. You know if a nigga woulda tried me, I would be up in that joint for life for shanking his ass. Trice, hop ya ass in the back with ya man." JR walked around the front of the car and opened the passenger's side door so she could get out of the car.

"Raynard, why is ya boy so rude?" Latrice rolled her eyes at JR. "You need to check his ass," she added, and playfully pushed JR from behind.

"Girl, that's my dog. The only one that's getting checked out here is you. Now get ya phat ass in this car." Raynard hopped in the back seat on the driver's side.

"Okay, daddy. I like it when you get all rough and shit." Latrice smacked her lips and stuck out her tongue at Raynard and hopped in the car.

Raynard slid his hand on the seat so that he could cup her firm ass when she tried to sit down. She placed her legs across his lap. He massaged her luscious thighs with his hands and his erect penis poked her in the leg. She put her hand on his groin area to feel his manhood.

Rochelle glanced in the rearview mirror and caught them fondling each other. "Don't be back there messing up my seats, being all nasty. Y'all need to get a hotel room."

Raynard cracked a smile and burst out laughing.

"Oh, yeah, your father said that he wants to see y'all right away. He told us to bring y'all by the club as soon as we scooped y'all up." Latrice pushed Raynard's hand away when he tried to undo the top button on her shirt.

"He can wait. I'm tryin' to get my groove on with my shorty." Raynard took his hand and placed it on Latrice's crotch.

"Nah, nigga, we can do the damn thing later. He said he wanted to see you right away," Rochelle told him.

"Yeah, Ray, we gotta go see what's up. It's business first."

"Aaah, nigga, you just saying that because Rochelle ain't gonna give you none, with her stingy ass."

"It ain't even like that, homey. My baby takes good care of me in that area." JR rubbed his forehead. "I'm just staying focused on our money situation. Rochelle, I know y'all got some weed up in here for a nigga. I need to spark up a blunt to relax my mind."

"I got you, boo. You know ya queen is always on her job." Rochelle handed JR a phat sack of bud and a fresh Philly to roll it up in.

JR said with a smile, "I knew there was reason why I made you my wifey."

"Aaah, nigga, stop being mushy and spark that shit up."

"I know that's right!" Latrice added.

Like a surgeon, JR sliced the blunt down the middle with precision and emptied out the tobacco into a plastic cup in the cup holder. Next, he took the weed and gently spread it out evenly across the blunt paper. He rolled it up carefully, making sure not to spill any of the weed, licking the edges of the paper to seal the blunt. Before lighting the blunt, he put it up to his nose to inhale the sweet aroma of the cannabis sativa.

He took two strong pulls into his lungs and relaxed his head up against the headrest. Then he passed the blunt to Raynard, who did the same:

Latrice got her turn to puff and took in a monster-size gust of smoke into her lungs. She handled it like a trooper. Then she passed the blunt to Rochelle, but she didn't want a hit. She hadn't smoked weed with her for the last couple of weeks, and Latrice figured something must be up. "Damn, bitch! Why you ain't trying ta smoke?" Latrice asked as she coughed.

"I ain't in the mood to puff today, that's all," Rochelle lied.

"Suit yaself. I'll just take your hit." Latrice put the blunt to her mouth and inhaled.

By the time they reached Raynard's father's lounge, The Gentlemen of Quality Social Club, the three smokers were giggling nonstop and had a bad case of the munchies. The smoke they had was of a good quality.

The girls dropped JR and Raynard off so that they could handle some business while they hit the mall.

Raynard Sr. gave both of his young soldiers a big hug when he greeted them. The lounge served as a front for his drug organization, and was where he conducted most of his business. "Gentlemen, I'm glad to see that you're all right," he said, walking into the lounge. "My favorite two young G's, come on in and have a drink with an old man."

They all took a seat at his reserved table in the back of the lounge.

Raynard Sr. was dressed in a cream linen set, with a pair of Stacy Adams sandals on his feet. He had a baldhead and a beard full of gray hair. A slim man with distinct facial features, he and his son looked nothing alike. Raynard got most of his physical features from his deceased mother's side of the family.

Raynard Sr. was in the game for a long time and had a lot of wisdom to impart to his young understudies. He sat back in his chair, crossed his legs, and began to speak, his two students attentively waiting to hear what he had to say.

"What would you two like to drink? I know you're both underage, but I ain't the police so it's cool."

"Let me get a Heineken, Pops."

"I'll have a Hennessy and Coke, Mr. Polo."

Polo was the nickname that Raynard's father went by in

the streets. The only one that was allowed to call him by his first name was his mother.

"Maria, come get my boys some drinks, you sexy lil' thing you," Polo yelled to the young Hispanic waitress. When Maria came over to get their drink orders, he slapped her on her butt when she stood next to him.

Maria blushed and placed her free hand on his shoulder, playfully massaging his bald head. Raynard and JR's eyes were glued to her rump as she put an extra lil' something in her strut on her stroll back over to the bar.

"Dag, Mr. Polo, is it like that?"

"JR, how many times do I have to tell you that you can call me Polo and drop all of that calling me *Mister*, like I'm your grandfather or something? But yes, son, women like Maria come a dime-a-dozen when ya paper is right. I can have any woman that I want. It doesn't matter if the bitch is one of them high-society broads or if she's from the bricks. It don't matter if she's twenty-one or forty-one. It don't even matter if she's got a man. When Polo wants a bitch, you can bet the whole bank that I'ma get that ho," he replied referring to himself in third person. His swagger and confidence only increased his standing with his two young cohorts. They wanted to be just like him—rich, respected, and to have any woman in the world.

"Yeah, my father is a mack from way back," Raynard joked.

While they all shared a laugh, Maria returned with their drinks. She winked her eye at Raynard, and he blushed.

"I wanna toast to us having much success in the future," Polo stated.

They all tipped their glasses back and took a drink.

"So, why did you wanna see us, Pops?"

"I just wanted to thank you boys for keeping ya mouths shut and not mentioning my name to them pigs when they ran down on you. Those muthafuckas have been on my ass for years. I've always managed to stay two steps ahead of them in the game," Polo replied.

In fact, the reason the police were never able to build a case against him was because he had the chief of police and all of his top lieutenants on his payroll for years, tipping him off if he was under investigation.

"You ain't gotta thank us for that, Pops," Raynard said boldly. "Those pigs ain't got enough time to give us that would make us turn on you. We ain't no rats. We exterminate them type of niggas."

JR nodded his head in agreement as he finished his drink.

"That's what I like to hear. I also wanted to tell you not to worry about the money that you lost last night. I'll take that hit. That money is small potatoes. What I have in store for you fellas is much bigger than that. I fronted you the work you've been getting from me for the past year just to see how you could handle yaselves out in the streets. I must say that you passed the test with flying colors. I'm thinking about giving you a bigger role in my organization. I know you're both young, but you're smart and hungry, unlike some of these lames that I got working for me now. My top men are getting old and not as sharp as they used to be. I need some young eyes and ears to keep business running smoothly with all of this new technology that these pigs are coming up with to jam a brother up." Polo's business offer piqued JR's interest.

"So, Polo, what did you have in mind for us?" JR asked.

"Well, first we have to get you both through this legal thing. My lawyers will see to it that you both just get probation when you go to court, so that's nothing for you to sweat about. Once that's taken care of, I plan on making you both my new lieutenants. You'll work directly under me and only take orders from me. I'm gonna give you both your own crews to run because I think both of you have leadership potential. The game is about to change, and things are gonna be on a whole new level. I think that you both can handle it, though. Along with a new job comes more responsibility. Oh, yeah, it also means a whole lot more money will be coming your way. Are you boys ready to get paid or what?"

"Hell yeah. I'm trying to get rich and live like you be living!"

Polo smiled at JR's enthusiasm. He used to be just like JR when he was younger.

"Daddy, you've just made us two happy young dudes. You just don't know what you've started. All I see is more money, more money, and more money!"

"So be it. I have a meeting with all of my top lieutenants next week, and I want you both to be there. I'll inform them all of your new positions in my organization at that time. It's good to see my two sons standing next to me and joining the family business. Raynard, why don't you take Maria in the back and let her entertain you for a few while I talk to JR in private for a minute. I think she has a little crush on you."

"A'ight, Pops."

Raynard tried to act nonchalant, but hearing his father refer to JR as his son made him feel a little jealous. He was an only child and even though he and JR were best friends, he didn't like sharing that space in his father's life with anyone. Nonetheless, he kept his thoughts to himself.

He motioned for Maria to join him in the back in his father's office. As horny as he was at the moment, getting some pussy was more important than dealing with his jealousy issues.

Polo had a private bedroom area built into his office space to entertain female acquaintances and allowed Raynard to bring females there on occasion. They were more like brothers than father and son.

"JR, I know you're wondering why I wanna talk to you in private, don't you?" Polo sipped on his second drink.

"Yeah, I ain't gonna lie, you did catch me off guard with that one," JR told him.

"Relax, lil' buddy, you ain't do nothing wrong. I meant what I said when I said that I thought of you both as my sons. Since you and Raynard have been friends I've come to see you that way, and I hope that you look at me as someone you can come to if you need advice about anything. I know your father's not around to teach all the things you need to know about being a man, but I'm here for you, young blood."

"Thanks, Polo. You all right, man. I ain't never had nobody say no shit like that to me. That means a lot to me. My pops ain't shit, and I don't want nothing to do with him. He's a loser." JR got up and gave Polo a hug. A tear formed in the corner of his eye, and he wiped it away quickly.

"A'ight now, soldier. Don't go gettin' all emotional on me and shit. I can't have one of my top gunners showing any signs of weakness. This conversation stays between me and you. Don't say anything to Raynard about this because I know my son. He will definitely be jealous," Polo stated seriously.

"You got that, Polo. This little conversation never happened," JR replied.

"Now, let's move on to a lighter subject. What's up with you and that crazy girlfriend of yours?" Polo asked. He had developed a strong bond with JR and Raynard and their girlfriends. He looked at them all as his kids. He had them over to his house all of the time for dinner or just to chill by his Olympic-sized pool.

"Ahh, man, Rochelle is good peoples. In fact, I'm glad that you mentioned her. I have something I need to bend your ear about. It's been on my mind real heavy. Last week she told me she was pregnant. I haven't even told Raynard about it yet. I don't know what I'm gonna do." JR looked down toward the ground.

"What do you mean you don't know what you're gonna do? You were grown enough to put ya dick in her and get her pregnant, weren't you? You're gonna be a man and step up to the plate, son." Polo's powerful voice commanded JR's undivided attention.

JR sat upright in his chair. "I don't know if I'm ready for that kind of responsibility in my life right now."

"Well, son, you better get ready. I can't have no son of my having his woman going to no abortion clinic, getting her body all jacked up by some doctor trying to make a fast buck. Tell that girl that you're gonna help her raise that child," Polo said, reaffirming his original position.

"Yeah, I know what you're saying is right. It's just that I don't know if I'm cut out to be a father. My father ain't do nothing to show me how to be a man," JR said.

"Son, you know what . . . I never said anything about it, but when Raynard first brought you around and he told me your name, it threw me for a loop. You see, I know your father very well. We grew up together. I turned him on to the drug game. Eventually, he turned on me. He burned me for a lot of money. He also stole your mother away from me. She was my girl before they got together. If it wasn't for him, I could have been your father."

Just the thought of the betrayal made Polo angry, but he didn't let it show. He didn't want to let JR see that side of him just yet.

JR was shocked to learn how their lives were so interwoven by the history that Polo shared with his parents. "I hate her too. She abandoned me just like him. I haven't seen or heard from her in years. I hope she's dead." He pounded his hand on the table.

"It's all right, son. These things happen in life. You can't let them fester inside of you. You have to move on. They would both have been dead, and you would have never been born if I let my anger get the best of me. I spared their lives on the strength of the love that I had for both of them. I let karma take care of them, and you see how their lives turned out, as opposed to mine. So when you say that your father ain't shit, I have to agree with you. But, as I just told you, I'm here for you to help guide you and Rochelle through this child-rearing thing. That's what family's for." Polo patted JR on his back to let him know that he was not alone in this dilemma.

"Polo, I wish that you could have been my father instead of that piece of shit Nigel Hawkins. Maybe I wouldn't have some of the fucked-up thoughts that I have now," JR said angrily. It made him feel good to know that somebody shared his hatred for the sperm donor that helped bring him into existence.

"Well, we can't control genetics, but we can control who we allow into our personal circle. Your family is whoever you want them to be and not necessarily somebody that shares your same bloodline. Remember that, young blood."

"Polo, you're a wise dude. I wanna learn all I can from you." JR's mind was like an empty glass eager to be filled to capacity. He yearned to hear a grown man give him direction in his life, but didn't know how to ask for guidance. Now it was being given to him, and he was eager to receive every ounce of wisdom imparted onto him by Polo.

"Stick around, young blood, and you'll be sharper than me," Polo said with big smile on his face.

Polo could tell that he had JR under his thumb and eager to do whatever he commanded. His trap worked like a charm. He saw a weakness in JR and jumped at the opportunity to exploit it. He could tell that the young JR wanted a father figure and planned to be just that to him. By gaining JR's trust and loyalty, he knew that he would one day become a useful tool for him.

Polo reclined back in his chair and sipped on his drink as they continued their conversation. His mind was partially elsewhere, thinking about how he could best utilize JR to carry out his plan of revenge against his father.

Many years might have passed since he had run across Nigel Hawkins, but time didn't dim his feeling of hatred for the man. It was a shame JR would have to be caught up in the middle of his secret game of revenge.

14

JR made his way home to face the music. He knew that his grandmother would want to know where he had been. This wasn't the first time that he had stayed out all night, but he usually called her to let her know he where he was. He usually lied and told her that he was spending the night at Raynard's house when he was really over at Rochelle's place. She would definitely be steamed at him for not calling her.

When he put his key in the door, he expected for her to be seated in the living room waiting on him, but she was nowhere to be found. Instead, he was greeted by his uncles, Albert and Franklin.

"It's nice of you to finally come home, JR. Do you mind telling us where you've been? You're not grown. I'm not gonna let you have my mother worrying herself sick about you." Franklin rose up off the couch and stood in front of JR.

"JR, what is wrong with you, boy? I think that it's about time that we all sat down and had a talk. We need to lay down some ground rules around this house. You can't just come and go as you please. This is our mother's house." Albert got up and stood next to his brother.

"We don't need to talk about anything. Neither one of you are my father. I ain't in the mood for this. I don't need to explain anything to either one of you. Where I've been is none of ya business." JR boldly attempted to walk through the wall they had erected in front of him.

"The hell if it ain't. You better sit your ass down and listen to what we've got to say!" Franklin grabbed JR's right arm and Albert grabbed a hold of his left arm in an effort to stop him from leaving the room.

"I ain't doing a damn thing. You've got three seconds to get ya hands off of me or I'ma forget that you're Grandma's sons and beat you both down like you stole something from me," JR said sternly.

In an instant, they let his arms go. Physically, neither one of them was a match for JR's muscular and youthful frame. He could whip both of them at the same time.

"You ain't even worth me going to jail for, JR. I'ma let Momma handle you," Albert said.

JR laughed in their faces. "Yeah, that's what I thought. I ain't got time to be wasting with you fools. Grandma, where are you at?" He brushed past both of them and went upstairs to his grandmother's bedroom. When he entered the room, he saw her seated on the edge of the bed with tears in her eyes.

"Come on in here, boy. I just don't know what to say anymore. I am so disappointed in you. I did everything in my power to try and keep you away from being just like ya father, but it just didn't work," she said sadly.

"What are you talking about, Grandma? I am nothing like that bum. I'm my own man. I ain't strung out on drugs like him." JR sat down on the bed next to her and wrapped his arm around her shoulder.

"JR, where have you been all night?"

"I was at Raynard's house. It was late when we left the gym, so I decided to spend the night. I know that I should have called. I'm sorry, Grandma." JR had an innocent look on his face.

"I ain't no fool, boy. You probably were with Raynard, but you two weren't playing basketball. I've let you pull the wool over my eyes for long enough. I was cleaning up your room and look what I stumbled across." Mrs. Hawkins extended her arm and opened up her hand so he could see the three crack vials. She pointed at the scale on her dresser. She'd found it under his bed.

JR was caught off guard and had to come up with a lie fast. "That's not mine, Grandma. I don't know how any of that got in my room!" JR swore.

His lie did nothing to convince her of his innocence. She was so upset that she hauled off and slapped him across the face.

JR was stunned and couldn't believe what just happened. He was hurt that she struck him because she had never done it before.

"You ungrateful fool. How are you gonna stand up here and lie to me in my face? I didn't bring it in this house, so I know that it was you. I went through this same stuff with ya father, so don't play me like I'm some airhead."

"Grandma, I'm not lying. That stuff is not mine! I don't use drugs. It might be Raynard's. I swear, it's not mine!"

"Well, you know what, JR? You don't have to admit that it was yours, but I am gonna tell you something. Since you are old enough to stay out all night and do whatever it is that you wanna do, I think that it's time that you leave my house. I am not gonna have the police running up in here, tearing up my house behind you." It hurt Mrs. Hawkins deeply to come to the decision to put him out, but she had to consider herself first.

"You're puttin' me out, Grandma, over something like this?

I didn't do anything. I can't believe that you are treating me like this. You don't love me anymore?" he asked, trying to gain sympathy.

This time his grandmother didn't budge.

Dealing with rejection was always a hard thing for him. It was even harder this time because he thought that she'd never turn her back on him.

"I do love you, JR. That's why I always made sure that you always had the best of everything. I sacrificed so much to give you whatever you wanted because your mother and father weren't around. I looked the other way when you used to get in trouble in school even though I knew that you were guilty. I did all of that, and it still didn't matter. You would think that seeing what drugs did to your mother and father would have made you leave that life alone, but it didn't. I see now that you have to learn the hard way. Right now, I need you to leave my house, JR. Pack your stuff and just go. I don't care where you go, just as long as it is out of here!" she yelled as she pushed toward her bedroom door.

"Fine, if that's you want, then I will leave. You don't love me. You never did. You're just like everybody else. I don't need you. I was just lying to you to spare your feelings, but now I don't care. Let's get it all out in the open. Yeah, I sell drugs. I make more money in a day than most people make in a month. If you want me out of your house, then I'm gone. Don't ever call on me when you need something. I'ma be so rich that one day you will need me and I'ma turn my back on you just like you are doing to me now. You lied when you said that you would always be there for me. I don't need love from nobody. As long as I got money, I can have anything that I want outta life. I'm outta here. As far as I'm concerned, I don't have a family anymore!"

JR picked up the scale and the vials of crack. He ran out of her room to pack his stuff.

Mrs. Hawkins wanted to run behind him, but she re-strained herself. She loved JR with all of her heart and prayed that he would come to his senses before the streets took his life away.

Lord, please watch over that boy. Please protect him from harm. He doesn't know what he's doing. Keep him safe, Lord. I've done all that I could with him and now he's in Your hands. I know that you will guide him through this storm. I trust in You, Lord. Take care of my baby. She watched JR walk out of her front door with his belongings in tow. He was so enraged that she put him out of the house that he didn't even speak or look in her direction when he walked past her. Mrs. Hawkins wished there was an-other way for her to handle this situation, but there wasn't. Nothing positive awaited JR in the journey that he was about to embark on. He was a lost child in a grown man's body and would need every one of her prayers, as well as God's mercy, to help him survive in the urban jungle.

15

"Girl, what you gotta do today when we get outta school?" Rochelle asked Latrice.

"I ain't doing shit."

"I was thinking that we could go over to Mondawmin Mall and get some shoes. I got some money from JR that I'm trying to spend. Are you trying to go or what?" Rochelle asked.

"Yeah, that's cool. We can do that. I wanna get me some new sneakers anyway," Latrice stated.

"Girl, I can't wait until my baby save up enough money so that we can move together one day into our own house." Rochelle often visualized her and JR living happily ever after with kids and a big house.

"Shit, the way them niggas is getting that paper that's gonna happen real soon for all of us." Latrice too shared the same fantasies about her and Raynard and wanted their kids to grow up and become best friends like the four of them.

"I know that's right, because my baby is fixin' to be the next Peanut King in this city. Shit, he's gonna be larger than him!" Rochelle said, referencing the fallen Baltimore drug kingpin from the eighties.

"And my man is gonna be right there with him, clockin' that dough."

"That's without a doubt. I've got something to tell you, Trice. I'm pregnant. I told the news to JR the other day." Rochelle awaited Latrice's response to the bombshell she just dropped.

"Are you for real? I'm just jealous that you ain't tell me first. How did he take the news?"

"At first, he was on some I-ain't-ready-to-be-a-father bullshit, but then he started talking about he wanted me to have the baby."

"So, what are you gonna do?"

"Girl, I'm having this baby. This will guarantee that I got JR's ass for life."

"I feel you, girl. Shit, I wish that Raynard's trifling ass would get me knocked up. You know them niggas be out here chasing all the bitches they can when we're not around." Latrice thought about the numerous occasions she'd caught Raynard creeping.

"Yeah, I know JR's got other bitches, but I don't care. He don't trust none of them hoes to hold his money for him. As long as I'm wifey and he don't bring no shit home to me, he can do him. What I don't know won't hurt me."

Latrice spoke in agreement.

The two of them spent hours on the phone daily talking about their future plans and mapping out their shopping expeditions. As they continued to go on and on about their big dreams, Rochelle lay across her bed wearing an oversized T-shirt with a pink thong on underneath it that hugged her tender, juicy ass. Her Coke bottle-shaped figure fit snugly on top of her queen-sized bed. She wore micro braids in her hair, and the extensions made her hair come down to the middle of her back. Her olive complexion was flawless. She didn't have as much as a scratch anywhere on her body and stood a solid five feet, five inches tall, and her long legs made her look taller when she wore shoes with high heels. Her stomach was as flat as an ironing board. That would soon change.

Even though she was only seventeen years old, she made grown men stop and stare whenever she walked down the street. She had the attitude to match her good looks. As fine as she was, she wasn't too cute to roll up her sleeves and scrap with another bitch if the situation called for it.

Rochelle was very intelligent and had plans to go to college when she finished high school. She lived in a tiny row house with her mother and two little sisters, Keona and Lita. Her mother worked in a warehouse packaging cosmetics. Her job required her to work long hours and usually left Rochelle with the responsibility of caring for her two little sisters, getting them ready for school in the morning and picking them up after school. She also had to cook for them and help them with their homework, not to mention keep the house clean, because if her mother came home to a dirty house, then there would be hell for her to pay.

When Rochelle first met JR, she wasn't feeling him at all. She thought that he was cute, but the mean look that he always wore on his face made him look like a demon child. On their first two dates, they bumped heads constantly, but anyone could see that there was an attraction there.

After Raynard explained to her JR's family issues and how rough he had it growing up, she began to look at him differently. Raynard was the one who introduced her to JR after he and Latrice had been together for a couple of months. She sympathized with his situation because her mother used to be on drugs as well, until she got clean five years ago by going to NA meetings.

She came up with the idea of killing JR with kindness, and it worked like a charm. Slowly, he started to open up to her and within six months they were a couple. She became his lover and best friend and had gained his trust.

Rochelle had just hung the phone up from talking to Latrice when she heard something hit up against her bedroom window. She got up off of her bed to see what the heck had struck her window. When she looked outside, she saw JR standing there with several bags in his hand. He looked like he was in a daze. She was puzzled as to why he was carrying so many bags. Also, he usually called her first before he came over at night, to make sure that her mother was at work. She sensed that something wasn't right. She went downstairs to open the door to let him in, to see what was up.

She opened the door, and JR walked in. She tried to hug him, but he walked right past her and dropped his bags on the floor.

"What the hell is wrong with you tonight?" she asked.

"Nothing is wrong with me. I need a place to stay tonight. My grandmother and I got into it, and she put me out."

"What happened, baby?" she asked, sitting in his lap.

"I don't wanna talk about it."

"You don't have to be so short with me. I ain't do shit to your ass." Rochelle got up from his lap and stood up.

"Look, I ain't in the mood to answer no questions. I just wanna go to sleep so I can block this shit outta my mind."

"Well, with that attitude you ain't staying here. This is my house, and you will treat me with respect or leave. I was just trying to be there for you, Mr. Evil."

Rochelle always stood her ground when they argued and had no problem putting him in his place when he got out of line. It was one of the things that JR loved and hated about her.

"Baby, I'm sorry. My mind is just fucked-up right now. My grandmother found my scales under my bed and a couple of crack vials that must have fell outta my bag. She was heated and told me I had to leave her house. I can't believe she could turn her back on me. I just need somewhere to stay tonight. I'll figure out tomorrow where I'm gonna stay at for good."

"Yeah, that is messed up. She's just upset, JR. She still loves you. Just give her some time to calm down. Don't worry about a thing, baby. Grab ya bags and come upstairs. Let Mommy take care of you tonight. I know how to ease ya pain." Rochelle extended out her hand.

JR picked up his bags and followed her up to her room. He watched the silhouette of her ass through her T-shirt as he walked behind her up the steps and felt his manhood rise in his jeans.

When they reached her room, he dropped his bags on the floor and sat down on the bed. She stood in front of him and lifted up her shirt over head and revealed her firm young breasts. JR took one of his hands and massaged them gently. He rested his other hand on her ass and pulled her toward him.

He took his tongue and swirled it around her navel. "How does that feel, baby?"

She closed her eyes and moaned a sigh of ecstasy.

"Boy, if you gotta ask, then you must not be my man. He knows what to do to please me," Rochelle said playfully. She bent down and used her tongue to probe his right ear lobe. She licked it so sensuously that JR lay back on the bed and pulled her down on top of him. She put her hands on his chest and bit his bottom lip.

"Girl, you better stop playing with me. I wish some other nigga would be all up on you like this." JR squinted up his eyes, and a vein popped out in his neck. The thought of another touching Rochelle evoked thoughts of homicide in him.

"You are such a silly boy. Ain't nobody hittin' this ass but you, big daddy." Rochelle tongue-kissed him passionately while unzipping his pants. She released his penis from its captivity and stroked it slowly. She could feel the blood pulsating through his veins, as it grew to full size.

"Now that's more like it," he said, enjoying her hands on him.

"I know what can take all of your problems away, baby."

"And what's that?"

She responded by getting down on her knees and pleasing him orally, using her mouth to massage his member. She sucked on it for about ten minutes before he climaxed.

Seeing he was still upright after having an orgasm and not wanting to waste a healthy erection, Rochelle mounted his dick and rode it until he came again. She had three orgasms of her own throughout the ride.

They were both sexually satisfied as she lay in his arms to rest.

"So, are you still thinking about that drama from earlier?" Rochelle asked.

"Nah, baby, I'm moving past that BS. You're tight with ya shit. That was just what I needed. You know how to make a brother feel like a straight soldier." JR ran his hand along the small of her back. Getting some pussy had a way of blocking out his problems, even if only temporarily.

"I always take care of my boo," Rochelle said, her head up against his chest.

"I know, baby. That's why I wanna make this promise to you. My seed that you're carrying is gonna always have the best. I'ma be there with you through every step of this thing. I'ma show my lil' man all the love that I never got from my so-called father. I'ma be there for him to teach him how to be a man. I ain't gonna never turn my back on him, no matter what."

"That's what's up, baby. But how you so sure it's a boy? Shit, I might wanna have a lil' girl so that I can raise her to be a gangsta-ass bitch like me," Rochelle said jokingly. She kissed him gently on his lips.

"Whatever we have, it don't matter, as long as we both handle our business. Now let a brother get some rest with ya freaky behind. I gotta a lot of shit to do tomorrow. I think that I'ma ask Raynard if I can crash at their crib until I'm able to get my own place."

Within minutes, the two young lovers drifted off to sleep.

JR would need the rest, with all of the decisions he was faced with making about his future once he arose in the morning. He was about to be knee-deep in the game and had to be fully prepared for his new duties as a lieutenant if he wanted to make Polo proud.

16

After eleven years in jail, Nigel's life went from bad to worse. His dual addiction to cocaine and heroin grew to monstrous proportions. In fact, he started doing more dope than coke. The physical dependence that came along with a heroin habit made him have to have it every day to not get sick. At first, he had Rodney to supply his habit. When Rodney's brother Carmine got knocked off by the Feds six months earlier and was sentenced to fifteen years for conspiracy to distribute cocaine, their pipeline to free drugs dried up.

New suppliers moved into the market that Carmine once controlled. With Carmine locked up, Rodney didn't have anybody to put money on his books so they were forced to work for rival drug crews to support their habit. They had to do whatever was necessary to keep the monkey off of their backs. The last year and a half was pure hell for them. They argued constantly over the limited supply of drugs they had.

Years of drug abuse wore Nigel's body down. He had a

head full of gray hair that made him look ten years older than he really was. When he used heroin, it made his skin feel like there were ticks crawling on him. This led him to scratch himself constantly and left his arms and legs filled with scars. His teeth were yellow from the residue left on them when he smoked coke. He weighed approximately one hundred and forty pounds, and that was a generous estimate. The doctor in the prison infirmary informed him that he had developed an irregular heartbeat, from smoking cocaine. He told Nigel that if he didn't stop using drugs, he might have a heart attack and die. Not a warning from the doctor was enough to deter him from using. In fact, he used even more.

Everything hit the fan for him recently when Rodney got a hold of some bad dope and OD'd in their cell. Luckily, it happened before Nigel got a chance to sniff some of the same package of dope, or he would have been dead as well. Nine other inmates died from the same batch of heroin. It was discovered that the heroin was laced with the powerful narcotic fetanyl, which made it far more potent and deadly. The series of deaths led to an investigation of the entire prison by the prison administration. They ransacked all of the cells in search of drugs and gave urine tests to all of the inmates. Their search never uncovered who was responsible for the distribution of the heroin.

Nigel's urine test came back dirty for coke and dope. He was sent to isolation for a week and then required to attend a recovery support group, once he was returned to general population. Even though he got busted and his road dog died as a result of drugs, he still didn't stop getting high. In fact, he started using even more. He would rather be in his cell getting beamed up to Scotty than sitting in a meeting with a bunch of niggas talking about recovery like he was right now.

What in the hell am I doing here with all of these lames? I ain't got no muthafuckin' drug problem. These niggas have a fuckin' drug problem. I love getting high, and I don't wanna stop. Coke and dope are my best friends. Shit, they're helping me pass the time away through this bit. I need that shit to deal with all of these crazy muthafuckas up in here. Nigel sat up in the meeting as defiant as ever and with a stony look on his face. He had just done a few lines of heroin before he entered the meeting. The drugs did the thinking and acting for him. He was a living example of denial because a blind man could see how much damage drugs had done to his life. His conscious mind wanted to stop using drugs, but it was powerless against his lower self. He didn't know how to ask for help. He did what most addicts did—continue to use drugs to escape the responsibility and hard work required for them to obtain sobriety.

Nigel had attended the support group for the past few weeks and always sat in the back of the meeting, out of the clear eyesight of the meeting chairperson, Reverend Johnnie Mitchell. He figured that if he stayed in the back, he could go unnoticed without having to speak and be able to skate through the program to fulfill his requirements.

"Good evening, my brothers. How is everyone doing this evening? It's time to start the meeting," Reverend Johnnie Mitchell said loudly. He was greeted with a loud applause by the thirty-plus inmates seated in the prison classroom.

Reverend Mitchell was the charismatic leader of Redeemed Souls Outreach Ministry. He was an ex-dope fiend-turned-minister who had served over half of his life in jail for almost every crime under the sun. He claimed to have had a revelation from God while incarcerated that made him turn his life around. He was dressed in a tailor-made black suit and wore diamond rings on every finger. He said that his jewelry and expensive clothes were gifts from God that were bestowed upon him for living a righteous life. His message was that all of the inmates could be just as fortunate if they would free themselves from the bondage of drug addiction and a life of crime.

His prison outreach ministry was his way of giving back to the community for his own salvation, and he ran a string of recovery houses across the city as well as a host of other local businesses. He offered employment to many of the brothers who completed his six-month program in the jail, once they were released from prison.

"What's the good word for today, Reverend Johnnie?" one of the inmates in the crowd asked.

"The good word for today my brother is that God wants us all to come clean and purify our souls of the demons that have been holding us back. He wants us all to get ourselves together and stop wasting time giving Satan power in His kingdom. You can't go to Heaven my brothers until you leave behind all of the deathtraps that Satan has laid for you in your path."

Rev. Mitchell's words were greeted with nods of agreement from those in attendance.

"Preach, brother!" one inmate shouted out of the crowd.

"I too was just like all of you brothers. I know the walls of these penitentiaries oh so well. I know all of the insane things that drug addiction can lead a man to do. I started using heroin when I was only twelve years old. I got turned on to it by my older brother David. He was five years older than me. I looked up to him because my father wasn't around. He had died in the Vietnam War. My mother did her best to raise us, but without a man around, we ran all over her. She couldn't control us. I used to see David and his friends in a dope nod, and I thought that it was cool. David sold drugs and always had money. He gave me anything that I wanted. He drove fancy cars and always had a different beautiful woman by his side every time that I saw him. I wanted to be just like him and his friends.

"When I walked in on him and his crew getting high one day, I begged him to let me try it. He agreed to let me do it, but made me promise to only get high around him. Once he put that needle into my arm, I was in a paradise. Heroin gave me the best feeling that a teenage boy could experience. It warmed my soul. I didn't know that I had set myself on a course for self-destruction." Rev. Mitchell spoke with emotion. You could tell that his story was sincere and came from the heart.

"Keep going, brother! We need to hear the good word!" another inmate shouted.

"My addiction to heroin grew day by day as did my brother's. I started selling drugs with him and his crew. The money was good to me, and I started getting some of the same things he got from the lifestyle—the women, the fancy cars, and what have you. When David got killed in a drug deal, I was on my own out in the streets to find drugs to support my habit and to provide for myself financially. I did what I knew how to do best. Being the hustler that I was, anybody was fair game. I stole from my mother. I stole from stores. I stuck people up with guns. I sold drugs. I pimped women. You name it, I did it just to get high. If you asked me while I was actively using, I would have told you that drugs weren't my problem. I would have said that they were just another part of my fast lifestyle. I thought that I was in control of my life. In reality, that narcotic controlled me." Sweat streaming from his brow, Rev. Mitchell banged his hand on the podium to further bring home his point.

His charged speech captivated all of the audience except for Nigel.

"Man, all you're spitting out is a bunch of hot air!" Nigel

yelled from the back of the room. He couldn't wait for the meeting to be over. He wanted to be back in his cell zoning out on the last bit of dope he had left.

"Who said that?" Reverend Mitchell's eyes scanned across the room for the naysayer. All of the other inmates turned around as well.

"I did. You come up here preaching that nonsense to us brothers up in the joint about how you don't get high no more and you changed your life around. Man, you ain't no damn Malcolm X."

"I'm sorry you feel that way, brother. You're right I'm not Malcolm X, but I am a brother that has changed his life for the better. I've noticed you in the back of the meetings the last couple of weeks sitting quietly with ya mug broke down. Why don't you come up here to the front so I can see you while I'm rapping with the group?"

The other inmates watched as Rev. Mitchell confronted Nigel about his disbelief. They all knew from seeing Nigel around the yard that he was still a heavy user and a knucklehead, but they had also seen Rev. Mitchell first-hand break down brothers like him before. He was a master craftsman in the trade of reforming addicts.

"I can hear you just fine back here. I don't need to be up close to peep out somebody who's just popping off a crock of shit. Shit smells the same whether you're standing in it or smelling it from a distance," Nigel replied sarcastically.

Rev. Mitchell grinned to himself. He had been in this situation many times throughout his ministry. He could recognize a soul in need of saving that was too caught up in the perils of drug abuse to get the help he needed. He was time enough for Nigel's antics.

"I'll tell you what, brother . . . if you think that I'm full of crap, then why don't you come up here and prove it. If nothing that I say holds any weight, then nobody in this room can come out of the dark hole that their addiction has placed them in. If my words can produce a change in ya life, then give God the credit. Don't give it to me. I'm just a man like you. God shined His light on me and made me come out of my cave of shame to become a respectable man. He can do the same thing for you, brother. Do you wanna spend the rest of your life chasing that dragon?" Rev. Mitchell noticed that his words had struck a chord with Nigel, who was silent and listening to him attentively.

"Man, don't nobody get clean from drugs altogether. A nigga might stop using for a minute to please his mother or his children, but once that jones kicked in, he's off to the races. I know I'm a junkie and I have no problem admitting it. I love to get high, and so does everybody else in this room." Nigel looked around for the other brothers in the room to co-sign his statement, but found no supporters.

"Well, brother, it's good that you know that you're an addict, but let me pull ya coat to a few things. First of all, just because drugs have controlled ya life all of these years, it doesn't mean that you have to die using them. A man can accomplish whatever his will and desire leads him to want to achieve. Just as vigilant as you have been out there chasing that narcotic, you can be just as determined to stay away from it if you put in the right amount of hard work. I'm a living testimony to that fact. Drugs have no power in my life today. I gave the streets fifteen of the best years of my life, but then I told the Devil that I wanted my life back. Once I submitted my will to God, He carried me until I was strong enough to stand on my own two feet. Now I stand before you a man that has been clean and sober for ten years and six months," Rev. Mitchell stated proudly.

The other group members clapped loudly in approval of his testimony. His message produced the desired effect. He'd put Nigel on the spot.

"So, you mean to tell me that you haven't used any drugs in over ten years? You haven't slipped up not once to get you a 'one on one'?" Nigel asked.

"I most certainly have not, brother, because when I came to the thorough understanding that I was destroying my life with drugs, I wanted something better for myself. The fun and euphoria that I felt when I first started using had turned to pain, degradation, and nothing but suffering for me. My life was a wreck. I don't want that kinda life anymore. I want to be alive to raise my son and see him go off to college. I want to live a long life with my beautiful wife. It makes me feel good today to know that my mother doesn't have to worry about me anymore. It brings a smile to her face for her to see me doing so well when I used to fill her eyes with tears of worry. I know today if I used even once, I'm back off to the races and I will lose everything that I've been able to build."

"I find that hard to believe. I know none of y'all fellas up in here believe him either, do you?" Nigel looked around the room to see if any of the other brothers shared his skepticism.

Once again, nobody said a word to back him up. All of the other men were in the group for much longer than Nigel and were serious about their recovery, leaving Nigel all alone in his efforts to discredit the minister.

"This is the real deal, my brother. God raised me up to speak to brothers like you. He wants me to share my blessing with the world. He resurrected me from a spiritual death for me to be a witness to His majesty and beneficence. You were sent to this group for a reason, whether you realize it or not. God wanted you to be here to hear my words and for them to touch ya spirit. Come take this walk with me down the road of sobriety, brother, so you can see for yourself how good life can be." Rev. Mitchell extended his hand out to Nigel.

Nigel was in uncharted territory. In all of his life, nobody ever questioned him about anything. He always did what he wanted, when he wanted, to whom he wanted without regard for the consequences. If he got what wanted, then that was all that mattered. Now, here he stood with his foundation shaken by a man that he didn't even know. Reverend Mitchell struck a nerve with him like no one else was able to do.

He began to think about JR and his mother. He thought about the pain that he had caused them due to his drug use. Every word that the minister spoke hit home with him and was similar to something that he had experienced in his own travels down the road of addiction. He was filled with feelings of guilt and shame. His defiant stance was undermined by the minister's cold, hard truth. His conscious mind, asleep for so many years, was awakened by the sermon.

Unconsciously, he started walking toward the front of the room.

Rev. Mitchell stepped away from the podium and walked toward Nigel. He embraced him like a father would do his son.

Momentarily, Nigel forgot that he was in jail in a room filled with hardened criminals where it was not smart to show a sign of weakness. Tears began to pour from his eyes. His defenses were down. Once he realized where he was, he took his hand and wiped his tears away before he spoke.

"Well, tell me how you did it then, brother." Nigel was open to the possibility that he too could change. His spiritual self was relieved to finally be unbound from the stranglehold that his addiction had placed it under.

"It's okay to cry, brother, because that's a part of recovery. All of the crazy things we all have done in our addiction is enough to bring a man to tears once those feelings of shame and regret kick in. You wouldn't be human if you didn't cry. Ain't that right, brothers?" Reverend Mitchell asked the other members of the group.

Chants of "Hell yeah!" and "True indeed!" echoed throughout the room.

"So, what's the secret to me getting clean from drugs?" Nigel asked humbly, which was totally out of character because Nigel Hawkins never asked for help or advice. For most of his life, he was the one who gave orders out in the streets to his crew.

"It's no secret, brother. You've already taken the first step, and that's to surrender to the power of your addiction. You also have to be sincere in coming up with a plan for yourself. You have to decide what you want out of life. Not only do you have to come up with a plan, you have to stick to your plan to the letter. Any deviation from your plan will lead you right back to where you started. Keep coming to the meetings and more will be revealed. You don't have to say much. Just listen. You're early in the process, so it's good for you to get as much insight as possible. Take what you get from these meetings and apply it to your life. Just because you're in jail is no excuse to continue to self-destruct. You will eventually return to society. I want you to use this time behind bars to become the best man you can become so that when you are released, you can be an asset to your family. Also, know that you're not alone in this journey. Every brother in this room is a part of your support system. If you feel the urge to wanna use, then get with one of these cats before you go use. Go to the NA meetings offered here at the jail. You're gonna have to put in some work, but I know you can make it, brother. Our time is up, but we will pick this up next week. Give recovery a try. It works," Reverend Mitchell reassured Nigel as he concluded his speech.

Reverend Mitchell felt proud to know that he had converted another soul. As he exited the room, he heard a loud applause of approval. The group had just witnessed a miracle.

A seed had been planted in Nigel. Only time would tell if it would come into full bloom.

For now, the minister had left Nigel with some serious things to think about. The God that Nigel's mother had talked about for so many years spoke to him through Reverend Mitchell. Now it was up to Nigel to answer the call to redeem his lost soul.

17

Becoming a father changed JR in a good way, to some degree. From the moment he and Rochelle brought Quentin Maurice Hawkins home from the hospital, JR accepted his responsibilities as a parent. He loved spending time with him. When he wasn't out in the streets conducting business, he was at home with Quentin, helping Rochelle out in every way possible. He changed his son's diapers, fed him, and played with him until he got tired and fell asleep. Quentin was his pride and joy. Seeing a smaller version of himself made him appreciate life a little more. He wanted to be around to see his son grow up to become a responsible man. He didn't want him involved in the street life. That life was for men like him and Raynard. He planned to send him to the best schools and shield him from the thug life as much as possible. In his mind, JR believed that he was bred to be a part of the drug culture by his father and not given a choice. If it were up to him, Quentin would have a choice as to what road he traveled in his life.

Since he was made a lieutenant in Polo's organization, JR came up big time, his crew up on Harford Road pumping out close to fifteen grand a day. He was getting money like he had never seen before in his life. Raynard did okay with his crew, but nowhere near as good as JR.

Polo was so proud of how much money JR made for him that he bragged about him all of the time in front of his other workers and would taunt them, telling them they should step their game up so they could become a top earner like JR. Some of them were jealous of JR, but never let it be known outright. If they did, Polo would've dealt with them personally.

JR was the golden boy and could do no wrong in Polo's eyes. His ego soared through the roof being talked about in such a high regard by an OG like Polo, and he thought he was untouchable.

In accord with his new status in the drug game, JR had to play his part to the hilt. He spared no expense in adorning himself with the most expensive jewels and clothing. He and Raynard would go on shopping sprees to Tyson's Corner in Virginia and drop anywhere from ten to twenty grand in a day. If he saw something that he wanted for himself, Rochelle, or Quentin, then he bought it without a second thought. He drove around town in his black Mercedes CL600, tricking it out with chrome rims and a booming custom stereo system. He bought Rochelle a luxury-equipped Chevy Tahoe to transport his son around in style. Even though he didn't want his son to be part of the game, there was no way in hell he could give it up for himself. The streets had been too good to him.

With all of the money and power he now possessed, the one dark cloud that lingered over his head was his relationship with his grandmother. Ever since she put him out of her house, he had been true to his word of not speaking to her. It killed him inside to not have her as a part of his life, but he was too stubborn to break down and call her. On several occasions, he drove past her house and just looked on at the house that he once called home. He wanted to walk up to the front door, put his key in the lock, and be greeted by the smell of one of his grandmother's home-cooked meals, but he just couldn't bring himself to get out of his car and ring her doorbell. He loved his Grandma Hawkins, but his bitterness and inability to swallow his pride kept him from bringing her back into his life.

Rochelle had tried to get him to call her several times to make amends, but that conversation usually wound up in a bitter argument. She even went as far as to invite Mrs. Hawkins over to their place when JR wasn't home so that she could see Quentin. When she broke down and told JR what she had done, he was so irate that she went against his wishes that he hauled off and slapped her. That was the first time throughout their relationship that their argument ever got physical. Eventually, Rochelle gave up on her efforts and just hoped that time would heal their wounds.

All JR did was block the thoughts of his grandmother out of his mind in a haze of weed smoke. Smoking marijuana was usually how he dealt with his emotional issues.

"Come here, boy," JR yelled playfully at three-year-old Quentin. "I'ma get ya lil' bad behind!" JR chased him around the living room of the two-bedroom condominium that he shared with Rochelle.

Quentin ran to escape from getting a beating from JR after he accidentally punched him in the jaw while they were play-fighting. Quentin smiled as he maneuvered out of his father's grasp and ran into the bathroom so Rochelle, who was fixing her hair, could rescue him. He grabbed on to Rochelle's leg. "Daddy's gonna get me! Mommy, help me!" Quentin was giggling the whole time.

Rochelle picked him up. "What's wrong with Mommy's baby? Is Daddy bothering you?"

Quentin nodded and laid his head on her bosom.

"I ain't did nothing to that lil' chump. He just hit me in my jaw. It hurts like hell. My lil' man is gonna be a beast. He punches like his Daddy. Ain't none of them little boys gonna give him any problems when he starts school." JR grabbed Quentin out of Rochelle's arms and threw him over his shoulder. He walked back into the living room and spun him around in circles until he was dizzy, Quentin laughing loudly the whole time.

"You are a nut. I am so tired, man. I need some rest." Rochelle rubbed her protruding stomach. She was three months pregnant with their second child and hoped that this one was a girl.

"Where are you going, baby?" JR asked, walking back into the room, Quentin on his heels crawling right behind him.

"I'm going to school," Rochelle told him. "That's where you need to take your butt as well."

Since he'd dropped out of high school, she'd been on him to go back and get his GED, but the only education JR wanted was his Ph.D. in street pharmacy and masters in urban combat.

"Nah, baby, you got it twisted. You're the brains in this operation. I'm the one that goes out and makes the money."

"Okay, Bill Gates, make that money then. Nah, on the real, I told you that I have to go to class on Monday, Wednesday, and Thursday nights. You don't pay attention to anything that I say."

Rochelle was in her second year at Catonsville Community College, working toward an AA degree in business management, and she planned to pursue her bachelor's degree in the same field after graduation. JR had suggested that she study business in school because he could make good use of her to help him transfer his illegal money into legitimate businesses.

"Oh, I forgot. My memory is bad. It's probably that way because of all the weed I smoke," JR joked.

It was only noon, and he had already blazed up two *L*'s to jumpstart his day. He puffed over an ounce of bud a day, starting from the time he woke up in the morning until he shut his eyes to rest at night. The tips of his fingers and his lips were pitch-black from the residue of the smoke, and he had developed a nasty hacking cough from all of the damage the weed smoke did to his lungs. He had to have his weed shot on a regular because, if he didn't, he was one irritable muthafucka. Whenever he went without some weed due to a drought out on the streets, his mood would change drastically. He was addicted to marijuana like a crackhead was addicted to the rock, but, of course, he didn't see it that way.

"Well, just don't forget to feed our son. I'll be home around nine." Rochelle grabbed the keys to her Chevy Tahoe truck, kissed JR and Quentin, and was out the door.

JR was seated on the living room sofa, with Quentin right by his side, in his favorite position, in front of the 50-inch television playing NBA Live on the PlayStation 2. His favorite team was the Philadelphia 76ers, and he was whipping the crap outta the game 96-50 when his phone rang.

"Yo, what's good, kid?" Raynard asked.

"Nothing much, dog. I'm just up in here with my lil' man, playing some NBA Live. Are you trying to slide through so I can whip up on you?" JR asked. The two of them would play video games for hours and hours, often gambling for money to see who was better at basketball or football. JR usually won, but that never stopped Raynard from betting.

"Nah, homes, I got some serious shit on my mind right now. I'ma need ya help with something," Raynard said, a sense of urgency in his voice.

JR picked up on the vibe and paused his game of NBA

Live to give Raynard his undivided attention. "What's the deal, homes?" he asked.

"Man, this shit is too serious to talk about over the phone. I'ma be over ya crib in a few to tell you in person."

"A'ight, hit me when you're downstairs so I can buzz you up."

JR noticed that Quentin had fallen asleep on the couch. He picked him up and took him into him his room to lie down in his bed. Once he did that, he walked out onto his balcony and lit up a blunt to pass the time while he waited for Raynard to arrive. He never smoked in the house around his son because he didn't want the smoke to get into his lungs.

JR sensed that Raynard wanted to talk about something heavy, since they had to have a face-to-face to discuss it.

After waiting about fifteen minutes, he heard the intercom system in the living room chirp. He pushed the button on the front to buzz Raynard into the building. Shortly, thereafter, he heard a knock at the door and let him in. They embraced in a brotherly hug and walked into the living room to talk.

"So, what's the business, Ray? You got beef with somebody? Do I need to lay a nigga down for you?"

Even though they both had come a long way, from pitching on the block to running their own crews, nothing had changed as far as the camaraderie between them. They were still as tight as ever.

"Yeah, actually it is something like that, man. You remember that dude Mark that we bum-rushed a long time and took over his spot on Park Heights? Well, the nigga got some New York dudes backing him up now with serious firepower. He came through the block two days ago and threatened my workers, telling them that his team was coming through to take over my territory. They shot one of my young niggas to send a message to me. Shorty ain't die, but I still gotta answer for that shit. That's where you come in. I want you to do me this solid and help me take care of this nigga."

"Why don't we just go to your pops and let him send some of his heavy hitters at them crab-ass faggots?" JR asked, knowing Polo had a team of cold-hearted killers on call, ready to put in work for these kinds of situations.

"Because I don't want my pops to know nothing about this until I've handled the situation. You know how fast word spreads on the street, so I gotta take care of this quick, fast, and in a hurry. For one, them New York boys need to know that us B'more niggas are not to be fucked with and that we can hold our own. Another thing is that I don't want Polo to think that I can't pull my own weight and have to run to him for help when the block gets hot. I gotta handle this on my own." Raynard knew that even though he was Polo's son, if he showed any signs of weakness, his father wouldn't hesitate to replace him within the organization. That was how serious he was about his money and reputation in the streets.

"I feel you, man. You know I'm in. If a nigga fucking with you, then he's fucking with me, and I ain't the one to be fucking with. Just let me know when and where, and it's a done deal."

"Well, we gotta set this thing off tomorrow night. I've been scoping the nigga out since yesterday. The lame fuck didn't even know that he was being followed. His crew be pumpin' up on Biddle Street. They got that shit on lockdown over there, so it wouldn't be smart to hit him up in his territory. He fucks with this bitch named Catrina that lives in Cherry Hill. I hollered at some of the niggas that I know out that way who be slinging, and they say he's over her crib every night. Them niggas don't like his ass because they say he be flossing heavy like he's a boss playa. They know he's really a cupcake, and the only reason they ain't get at him was because the niggas he be rolling with are quick to let them guns go off. I think one of them New York boys is his cousin or something. It don't really matter to me, because they all can get it, as far as

I'm concerned. I say we catch Mark at her crib and rock his cradle. I got the guns and a car ready, so we can do the damn thing." Raynard knew that JR loved to put the murder game down and knew he would have his back in his time of need.

"I'm ready to ride, my nigga," JR said, short, sweet, and to the point. Other than money and pussy, nothing got his dick hard more than some gunplay. He got a rush when he wrapped his hand around a piece of cold steel and squeezed the trigger. He had pushed several niggas' wigs back in his years on the streets.

"That's what's up, my nigga," Raynard told him. "Now break out them controllers so that I can spank that ass in some Madden. You got me in NBA Live, but on the gridiron, I'm that nigga!"

"Put ya money where ya mouth is. I got a stack I'm putting up that says you won't score one touchdown!" JR pulled out a rubber band full of cash out of his pocket and threw it on the living room floor.

Raynard reached in his pocket and counted out enough money to cover the bet. "Let's get it on, fool," he said as they started the game.

The two thugs went from plotting a murder to playing a video game in just a matter of minutes. It might seem crazy to some how they could switch modes so quickly, but in the streets that quality was a necessity. One had to be prepared to respond to any situation at any given time. That was especially true if you were a boss type of playa. All Raynard needed was for any member of his crew to question his leadership, and it would only be a matter of time before they came for his spot as the boss. If a nigga wasn't able to improvise on his feet, then he would be swallowed up by the dangerous elements in the streets that lie in wait to knock him off his throne.

Raynard and JR planned to be on top of the game for a

long time and had it etched in their brains that they would do whatever it took to stay there. By this time tomorrow, their playful mood today would be one of naked brutality. Mark was about to be introduced to a dark side of the game that he never saw before.

18

"You better recognize a pimp when you see one, girl. I'm that nigga in Baltimore City that all of these other hustlers wanna be like," Mark bragged to Catrina as they cruised down I-95 South en route to her apartment in Cherry Hill. The song "Let Me Ride" by Young Buck was playing on the stereo of his black Hummer. He boosted up the volume and nodded his head to the beat:

Nigga, please stop sweatin' yaself. You ain't no balla. Your tired ass is just another dumb trick that I've been workin' for his money. I'm the real pimp because once I gave you some of this good stuff between my legs, I made you run them pockets like you was my ho!

Catrina just smiled at Mark's comment. Catrina had one of those bodies that would make any man turn over his fortune just to hit it one time. She had smooth dark skin like Naomi Campbell, tall and thick model legs like Tyra Banks, with Vida Guerra's ass and titties. She was twenty years old, with a ninth-grade education and no job, but God blessed her with a body so fierce that she could get anything she wanted from a man. She knew how to wrap a man's mind up in her spell so good that it was a shame. No man stood a chance, once he got a glimpse of her in her birthday suit.

Mark had come up big since he got ran off of his drug strip by JR and Raynard. After word spread across B'more about him being run off of his block, his name was mud in the streets. But since he hooked up with his cousin Shakim from Far Rockaway in Queens, New York, he re-established himself in West Baltimore as a major figure. Shakim had a crew of rowdy New York niggas that he relocated to Baltimore and served as muscle for Mark. As a result, Mark was able to set up shop again.

Mark ran one of the few successful drug crews in the city that Polo didn't supply with cocaine and was too afraid to get his revenge on Raynard and JR, until Shakim vowed to have his back if they went to war. With some trigger-happy New Yorkers behind him, he figured that the time was right for him to get some payback. The move that he'd brought to Raynard the other day was only the beginning of what he had in store for his old rivals.

When they pulled up in front of her complex, Catrina climbed out of her truck and walked toward her apartment. A couple of local teenage boys were playing a pickup game on the basketball court across from her building. All of their heads turned at the same time to get a peek at Catrina's ass as it jiggled in her tight Baby Phat shorts when she walked by.

"Damn, girl! You phatter than a Philly cheesesteak with extra meat!" one of the boys yelled.

"Catrina, you need to cut that nigga loose and let me get up in them guts!" another one of the boys yelled.

Catrina just grinned at their comments about how phat she was because she knew she was a beast, but Mark wasn't amused by their antics. "Y'all niggas better keep ya young-ass game on the court where it belongs. If I hear another one of y'all niggas say something to my girl, I'ma give every one of y'all something to scream and holler about!" Mark stuck his hand in his dip to make it appear as though he was reaching for his strap. In reality, he was unarmed, but the front worked well enough. The young boys shut their mouths and went back to shooting hoops, and he and Catrina continued walking toward her building.

"I don't know why you even pay them lil' boys any mind. They don't know any better. Baby, can you give me a hot oil massage tonight?" she asked as they entered her building. She took his hand into hers and led him to the stairs, and they walked down the stairs to her basement-level apartment.

"Anything you want, you pretty thang, you can get it. Just as long as I can slap it up, flip it, and rub it down once I'm done. I'm trying to get deep up in them guts." Mark pressed his body up against hers while she fumbled through her purse to find her door keys.

"You can do what you want with this pussy, if you can make my toes curl when you give me a massage." Catrina knew exactly what to say to position him right where she wanted him to be.

"Trina, I'm not only gonna make ya toes curl. I'm gonna make the hair stand up on ya spine, ya thighs shake, and ya eyes roll into the back of ya head when I'm done."

"That's right, baby. Talk that nasty talk. I'm trying to feel that big juicy dick all up inside of me," Catrina said as she put her key in the door.

When they entered the apartment, Catrina flicked the light switch on the wall. Mark entered behind her and shut the door. She was startled to hear her television playing in the living room because she swore that she had turned it off before leaving the house. Catrina's eyes opened wide when she walked into the living room and saw two strange men seated on her couch, as Mark stood right by her side scared to death like the bitch-ass nigga he really was.

"It took y'all long enough to get here. We've been waiting almost two hours," Raynard said. He and JR got up from the couch, and Raynard motioned with his gun for Mark and Catrina to join them in the living room.

Mark had a petrified look on his face as he sat down on the couch.

"Who the hell are you? Why are you in my house, and how did you get in here?" Catrina asked. Most females would have been frightened in this situation, but she wasn't. She grew up with three brothers who were hustlers, and had long since gotten over her fear of having a gun pointed at her.

"Calm down, baby girl. We let ourselves in through your bedroom window. Why don't you ask ya boy Mark who we are. He knows us very well. Don't you, homey?" JR gazed up and down Catrina's body and wondered to himself what it would feel like to hit her pretty ass from the back.

"Man, we don't need to handle our business like this," Mark said. "Let's sit down and talk like businessmen. I don't want no more beef with you two cats."

"Well, nigga, you should've thought about that before you had ya niggas roll through my boy's block!" JR bitch-slapped Mark so hard that he wanted to cry. His face stung, and his light skin was red in the spot where JR struck him.

JR pushed him onto the ground and buried his face in the carpet.

"Nah, man, let's not be so cruel to Mark. He said let's be businessmen about this situation. It's not his fault that my lil' homey is in the hospital after his boys shot 'em up. Mark, let me help you to ya feet," Raynard offered.

When Mark attempted to get up off of the ground, Raynard kicked him in the groin, and JR came from behind and kicked him in the back of his head, and he fell flat on his face once again.

"I'm sorry, man. I didn't want that shit to happen! My

New York peoples forced me to come through ya block. They saw how much money y'all was making and wanted to take over ya strip. They told me if I didn't do it, I was a dead man. I'm sorry! I'm sorry! I don't wanna die!"

"Mark, stop crying like a bitch. Be a man for once in ya life. That's fucked up that you ain't man enough to take ya own weight out in the streets. Kick his ass a few more times for me." Catrina knew that they planned to kill Mark and wanted to get on JR's and Raynard's good side so they wouldn't kill her along with him. She crossed her legs in a sexy manner as she sat on the couch.

"Yo, I think I like this bitch, homes. She's got some gangsta shit up in her."

JR nodded in agreement and stopped pounding on Mark to get a better view of Catrina's body.

. "Trina, what are you doing, baby?" Mark asked. "Why you acting like this?"

"Mark, stop being a bitch all ya life. I was just using ya faggot ass to get what I wanted outta you. Once I got me a Benz at ya expense, I planned on dumping you. Your little dick ain't do nothing for me. I just told you what you wanted to hear to get what I wanted. That's it and that's all. He has a secret stash hidden here. It should be like forty grand in there. If you give me ten thousand," Catrina told them, "I'll tell you where it's at."

"I'm liking this girl more and more," JR said in response to her offer.

Mark yelled at Catrina, "You ain't nothing but a backstabbing little whore. How the fuck you gonna play me like that!"

As soon as the words left outta his mouth, he was greeted with a right cross to the jaw by Raynard, and blood splattered from his mouth. "That ain't no way to talk to a lady, especially not one that's about to show us where ya money is at." Raynard slammed Mark's face to the ground.

JR took his gun and put it up against Mark's temple. "Yeah, nigga, I want you to apologize to this fine sista for calling her a whore."

"I'm sorry, Catrina! I didn't mean to call you a whore! Man, y'all gotta let me go. If anything happens to me, my cousin Shakim and his boys is gonna kill both of you. If you let me live, I'll make sure that he gives you a pass and promises not to make any more moves on ya territory."

"Nigga, you are a joke. A few minutes ago you told us that they forced you to bring us a move, and now you want us to think that you have enough pull to give them orders not to murk us. Them niggas can come through the block if they want to, but they're gonna get the same thing we got in store for you," JR said, pulling the trigger on his .38 three times.

All three shots went straight to Mark's face, terminating his earthly existence. The silencer on JR's gun muffled the sound, preventing the neighbors from hearing the commotion.

Catrina didn't even flinch as she watched Mark die in front of her eyes. In fact, she was turned on when JR glanced at her with a cold stare.

Raynard pointed his gun at her. "Now where's that money at, pretty thing?"

"I'ma show you where it's at, but first you have to put those big shiny guns away and promise not to kill me. I'm harmless. I wouldn't hurt a fly," she stated, sprawling herself across the couch. She lay on her stomach with her ass positioned in such a way, they had to admire its perfect shape.

JR caught himself fantasizing about taking Catrina from behind and mashing that phat ass. "How do we know that you won't run to the police and rat on us?"

"You can trust my word because I've been in the streets all my life and any nigga that I really fucked with will tell you that I'm a ride-or-die bitch when it comes to staying true to the code of the streets—No snitchin'. You probably know my brothers, Riley and Nemo. They used to be kings out here in Cherry Hill before the Feds came through and bagged them." Catrina ran her fingers through her braids and licked her lips.

"Oh, yeah, I remember them niggas. They got knocked off last year. Them niggas was moving some serious weight. They got caught with like twenty kilos, right?" Raynard lowered his gun and felt more at ease to know that she came from a family of hustlers and was familiar with the life.

"Yeah, they did, and now they're doing life in the federal pen. So, you see this little thing right here is nothing new to me. I was raised up around this my whole life. I used to hold work and money for my brothers." Catrina took her fingers and placed them in her mouth one at a time.

Watching her suck on them made Raynard's eyes open wide.

JR put his gun in his dip. "I guess we can let you live, shorty."

"Now that's a whole lot better. I feel more comfortable now. Before we get to the money, I say that we have a little fun. I'm talking about the three of us." Catrina undid the buttons on her blouse and slowly revealed her cleavage.

JR became hard instantly as he watched Catrina undress. Her breasts were a nice size and smooth without a scar on them. "Dog, what you think about that?"

"I say it ain't no fun unless the homeys share some!" Raynard replied.

"I totally agree with you on that tip," Catrina added.

"So, you ain't scared being here with us after we just killed ya boy?" JR asked.

"Scared? Shit, that nigga was a busta. I love to see a thug nigga put his thing down. Seeing you shoot that fool made my panties wet. You wanna see?" Catrina threw her shirt across the couch.

"Hell, yeah!" they both said at the exact same time.

Catrina stood up and untied the drawstring on her shorts, dropping them to the floor. Her lavender-colored thong fit snugly around her waist and hugged her ass. She could tell that the two assassins were impressed. She reclined back on the couch and spread her legs, slid her thong to the side, and parted her pussy lips. She took one finger and stuck it into her vagina. When she took it back out, she reached her arm out so that they could see for themselves. Sure enough, it was soaking wet with her juices.

"Dog, this is one wild-ass bitch right here!" JR said, grabbing his crotch.

"I think I'm in love!" Raynard yelled excitedly.

"Oh, I like to be called a bitch. Now let's take this thing in the other room so that I can see if you two boys know how to make a bitch like me scream ya name. Follow me." Her thong now on the living room floor, Catrina got up from the couch and guided them both into her bedroom.

When they made it into her bedroom, Catrina bent down on the edge of the bed and hoisted her ass up in the air. Raynard came behind her and started to grind his dick up against her butt, while JR stood to the side and watched as Raynard undid his pants and slid his dick into her pussy. His back-and-forth motion made the bed squeak loudly.

Catrina moaned sighs of approval as Raynard banged her back out. She motioned for JR to come join them.

JR got undressed and got on the bed in front of Catrina. He sucked on her breasts, making her nipples hard.

"That's right, baby, work this ass. Fuck me harder. Oooh . . . yeah . . . like that!" Then she told JR, "I wanna feel you in my mouth while he's fucking me."

JR was happy to give her just what she wanted. He closed his eyes and enjoyed her deep-throat action. She had the head game of a veteran porno star and sucked dick like he saw

Heather Hunter do so many times in the dirty movies he used to watch as a teenager. "Damn, bitch," JR yelled. "Your mouth feels so good. Suck that shit."

As she sucked and slurped and saliva dripped from her chin, JR grabbed her head and pumped his hips steadily as he made love to her mouth, every thrust bringing him closer to his climax.

"Y'all niggas can fuck. My legs are getting tired. It's time to switch up. I wanna fuck you while I suck his dick."

As Catrina lay back on the bed and spread her legs, JR got in front of her and fucked her missionary style. Catrina reached up and grabbed Raynard's stiff manhood and pulled it into her mouth slowly.

The two best friends gave each other a high-five because the sex was off da chain. Running a train on a fine broad like Catrina was worth a celebration.

"This is it right here. That's right, keep hittin' that spot! I'm about to cum! Oooh, yeah! I want you to cum all over my face while he cums in my pussy!" Catrina shouted.

They all climaxed at the same time.

"Damn, what's ya name again, shorty?" JR asked, breathing heavily. He wiped sweat from his forehead with his hand, and his back was drenched as well.

"It's Catrina. And yours?"

JR winked at Raynard. "Bishop, and this is my brother Brad."

Raynard grinned. He knew exactly what JR was up to.

"Not to be short with you," Raynard said as he got dressed, "but we got moves to make. Where's the money at, Catrina?"

"It's in my other room in the closet. Mark keeps it in a safe. I know the combination."

"Well, go take care of that for us so we can be on our way.

We've gotta get that dead body outta here while it's still dark," JR explained.

Catrina jumped up off the bed. "A'ight, let's go get to it then. I want my ten *G's* now. Don't forget about our deal."

"We got you, lil' mama," Raynard promised. "Come on now and take care of that for us. You don't have to worry about a thing."

When Catrina returned to her bedroom with a satchel containing the money, Raynard and JR were sitting on the edge of the bed with guns drawn.

"Here's the money. Why y'all got them guns out?"

"The plan has changed. We don't wanna split the money with you. We're taking it all for ourselves." JR had a steely look on his face that let Catrina know she was in serious danger.

"Come on, fellas, didn't we just have a lotta fun together? Y'all don't have to kill me. I promise I won't tell!"

The two friends looked at each other and bust out laughing.

"We know that you won't tell because a dead person can't tell nobody a damn thing!" Raynard pointed his gun at Catrina and squeezed the trigger twice.

Both shots lunged into her midsection, and she fell to the ground. They watched her squirm and squeal for about three minutes as she bled to death.

JR said as he took one last look at her. "That bitch had a nice ass, dog."

"True indeed, she did. I wish we didn't have to kill her, but shit happens." Raynard reached down and grabbed the satchel. He opened it and saw that it was filled with brand-new hundred-dollar bills.

"Let's see how this plays out for us. We got rid of the fool Mark, fucked his girl, and we're leaving outta here with forty grand of his money. Not bad for a night's work, wouldn't you say?" JR asked gleefully.

"Not bad at all. Let's get outta here."

The two friends exited the apartment from her bedroom window so that no one would see them leave, leaving behind two dead bodies for the Baltimore City Police Department's Homicide Division to clean up.

19

Dear Ma,

I know that it's been quite sometime since we've corresponded with one another. I've read every letter that you've sent to me numerous times. I never responded to any of them because my drug addiction had me sidetracked and living like a savage. I was too busy killing myself with drugs to appreciate the love and compassion that you have shown me in the midst of my craziness. You are truly the best mother that a man could ever have. I've wasted away most of my adult years doing absolutely nothing constructive with my life. In the past, I always wanted to blame someone else for me going back and forth to prison, be it the White man or the police. I have no one to blame for putting me in prison but myself. I can see that clearly today. I have grown over the past few years to accept responsibility for my actions.

I'm writing you this letter because I have a lot of things on my mind that I wanted to share with you. First of all, I want to apologize for all of the heartache that I've caused you throughout the years due to my drug addiction. I want to apologize to JR for not being there for him while he was growing up. It's my fault that he is the way that he is today. I want to thank you for doing the best you could for him. When I read your letters and you talked about how he was caught up in the same mess in the streets that I was at his age, I wanted to bust out of this prison and save him from taking that road, but I couldn't. I promise you that I will do whatever it takes to get him to leave the streets alone. I want to apologize to Albert and Franklin for not being a better brother to them as well. All of the petty fighting and jealousy that has existed between us over the years is silly and has done nothing but drive a wedge between us when we should be sharing a brotherly bond with one another. I can see now that family is the most important thing that a man could have in his life. I no longer take any of you for granted. In fact, I need you all more now that I ever have in my life.

I just wanted to let you know that I have made some significant changes in my life. I'm no longer the man that I used to be. I'm reformed now. I've been drug free for over two years now and have no plans on going back to being my former self. I know you might not believe me, but my transformation is sincere. While I've been incarcerated, I met a man named Reverend Johnnie Mitchell who has helped me to see that I can have a better life without drugs. Reverend Mitchell runs a drug program here in the jail that I was forced to attend due to my drug use. While in the program, he challenged me to do some serious soul searching to find the man that I truly am and to bury the heartless thug that I used to be. I have to thank him for saving my life. God put him in my life at the right time to give me just what I needed to deal with my personal issues.

I know it sounds crazy to hear me talking about God, seeing how I used to fight you as a child not to have to go to church. Reverend Mitchell has shown me that God is at the center of everything that we as humans do and that we can do nothing in life without his permission. When I was using drugs, cocaine was my God. It was my Higher Power. I had to have it to survive. It led me into many dark and desolate places and to do many regrettable things. Now I see that there is only God and that my Lord and Savior is Jesus Christ. With the two of them in my life, I know that I can prosper in spite of my past criminal background. I'm no longer a soldier for Satan, but I'm a soldier walking a righteous path for God. I attend church services here at the jail every Sunday and I go to NA meetings daily to stay focused on my recovery. When I return to society, I will return a redeemed man, a renewed spirit eager to do many righteous things!

I'm saying all of these things to you because I will be going up for parole very soon. There is a good chance that I will be granted parole and would like to stay with you once I am released. Reverend Mitchell has promised to put in a good word for me with the parole board as a testament to my transformation and my ability to become a productive member of society. He also has a job for me when I get out. Yes, Mama, your baby boy is gonna get a job! (Smile) I no longer want the fast money and am willing to put in hard work to get the things I want outta life. I'm not trying to run game on you for a place to stay. That Nigel Hawkins is long gone. I want you to have a chance to see me in this lifetime doing something positive with myself. I want to make you proud of me.

Once I get out of here, the first thing that I have to do is to find JR and try to build a relationship with him. I wanna save him from continuing down the same path that I did. It's not too late for me to reach him. I know that it's gonna take a whole lot of work for him to forgive me, but I'm willing to do whatever is necessary to undo all of my faulty lessons that I gave him about being a criminal. All of the stories that Daddy fed me when I was a kid about the honor that came along with being a thug were a bunch of crap. The streets have done nothing but destroy hundred of thousands of Black men like myself. Reverend Mitchell has shown me that a man is somebody that is responsible and takes care of his family. These are two things that I have never done, but I plan to once I am free. If it is God's will, JR will not be another statistic in the jails or funeral parlors of Baltimore City. I'm prepared to give my life to save his from suffering such a dreadful fate.

It's time for me to wrap this letter up, but I just wanted to get these things off of my chest. I feel much better now. Reverend Mitchell has taught me that making amends to the persons that we as addicts have harmed is crucial to us relieving ourselves from the feeling of shame and guilt. I'm now ready to confront my addiction head on but I need your help. Please find it in your heart to see that I am ready to do the right thing. I hope to get a response from you soon. Oh yeah one last thing. Happy Mother's Day!

Your Loving Son in Christ,
Nigel Hawkins

Mrs. Hawkins wept as she read Nigel's letter. His words touched her in the most profound way. She couldn't believe that this was her son talking this way. She wondered if this was just another game that he was running, only to disappoint her once again. Her heart wanted to believe that he was sincere about his change, but her mind remained a tad bit skeptical. Nigel had told her too many times that he would stop using drugs, but never did. It was something about the tone in his speech throughout the letter that made her lean toward believing that her son had finally seen the light of salvation that God had in store for him.

"Mama, what are you up here doing?" Albert asked as he walked into her room and saw her reading the letter.

"Nothing. I was just reading this letter from Nigel. It looks like he'll be coming home soon."

"Well, I hope he has a place to stay. I don't want him coming here to drive you crazy," Albert stated firmly.

"Hush ya mouth, boy. This is my house. You don't tell me who can and can't stay in my home."

"I'm sorry, Ma. I just don't want him having you up all hours of the night worrying about him like you did before he went to jail. So, what did he say? He ask you for money?"

"No, actually he wanted to let me know that he done left that stuff alone and turned his life over to God."

"Say what? Nigel and God don't belong in the same sentence. People like him never change, Ma."

"With God, anything's possible. He's capable of taking any man, no matter how low he's gone in life, and making him whole again."

"I hear you, Ma. I can't say that I believe in him though." Even though it had been over ten years since Albert last saw Nigel, his hatred for him was just as passionate.

"He even wanted me to tell you and Franklin that he was sorry for the way that he acted toward you all of his life. He wants to build a brotherly relationship with you two when he comes home. I don't know if he's sincere or not, but I hope that he is. All of you are my sons and I love you all equally. If your brother has made a change, then you are obligated to give him a fair chance. If you refuse to accept his offer to reconcile ya differences, then you will block your own blessings from God."

"You're right, Ma. I'm just thinking about you is all. Nigel and JR have brought you nothing but grief. I just want you to be happy," Albert stated.

"Well, son, I'm not happy until I know that all of my babies are okay. I carried all three of you boys in my womb. I worry about all of my children because that's what a mother does. I worry about JR every day because I know that he is blind and doesn't know what he is doing with his life. I worry about his children, but I'm glad that he has that young girl Rochelle by his side. She seems to have a good heart and a somewhat level head on her shoulders. Right or wrong, Nigel is my son and JR is my grandbaby, I have no choice but to worry about them. Love makes things that way."

"I know it does, Ma, but today is your day. I want you to put them aside just for tonight. We have a reservation for dinner at eight. It's seven o'clock now. We have to get ready to leave. Franklin and his family are already on their way to the restaurant."

"Okay, let me grab my coat."

Mrs. Hawkins grabbed her coat, and they were on the way. The whole ride to the restaurant, her mind was on Nigel's letter. She couldn't wait for him to come home from jail. If he had truly turned his life over to God, then she would do whatever she could to help him get back on his feet. She didn't know how, but she would also have to find a way to reunite him with JR. She wanted all of her family to grow to share a closer bond with each other.

For now, all she could do was play the waiting game until Nigel's release.

20

JR and Rochelle were getting ready to go over to Polo's mansion for his annual Memorial Day cookout to which he'd invite only his closest associates for the grand event. It was always a festive occasion for all of those privileged to attend, and JR looked forward to attending every year.

Polo was nice in the kitchen, and the food spread was immaculate. He specially prepared and seasoned his meats so that they were all nice and tender. He blended up a homemade barbecue sauce with his own secret ingredients, and it was absolutely delicious. Everybody at the party was free to eat as much as they wanted, drink all of the alcohol they could consume, and dance the night away to the sounds provided by the DJ hired for the event.

Rochelle searched through her closet. "JR, have you seen my green sandals?"

"Nah, girl, I can't keep up with ya shit," he shot back. "That's why you need to clean out that junky closet of yours." JR was out on their balcony smoking his midday blunt. Blazing up trees had started to become more and more a part of his daily routine, and he'd moved up from smoking regular weed to the more expensive and more potent brand of cannabis called purple haze.

"Whatever. You need to stop smoking that weed and come in here to get ya sons ready so we can be outta here." In addition to Quentin, they now had their second son, Savion.

Rochelle had grown to know JR better than he knew himself. Even though he wasn't within her eyesight, she knew that he was in his favorite place in the house, the balcony, doing his favorite thing, smoking weed. She'd stopped getting high after she had Quentin and started school.

"Don't you worry about my lil' niggas because I've got them. They're already dressed. You just take care of you."

Before JR went out to get his smoke on, he made sure he had his sons dressed in their fly little Enyce outfits. They were in their room playing quietly with their toys.

JR finished off his blunt and walked back into the living room. Just as he was about to sit down on the couch, he heard the buzzer go off, signaling that they had a visitor.

Rochelle yelled from the bedroom. "JR, see who that is."

"I got this out here. You just finish getting ready. Yeah, who is it?"

"JR, it's ya grandmother. I need to talk to you right now!" she shouted.

Rochelle heard her voice from the bedroom and came into the living room. She saw an angry look on JR's face. She threw her hands in the air and shrugged her shoulders, as if to say she didn't invite her over and had nothing to do with her showing up unexpectedly.

"Well, I'm busy right now. You'll have to come back some other time."

"JR, you better stop playing with me. I am not leaving until we talk. I will sit down here in this lobby and raise high hell if you don't buzz me up there. This nonsense between us has gone on long enough."

"Baby, you might as well let her up and see what she has to say."

JR darted his eyes in Rochelle's direction. "I better not find out that you had anything to do with this," he said as he buzzed his grandmother in the building and told her to come up to the fifth floor.

She arrived at their front door in no time.

"Hello, Mrs. Hawkins." Rochelle let her into the condo. "How are you doing today?"

"I'm fine, Rochelle. How are my lil' babies?"

"They're fine. Savion is getting big. I know I'ma have my hands full with these two boys."

"That's good. You are such a pretty girl."

"Thank you. JR is in the bedroom. He'll be right out in a second. Do you want something to drink?"

"I'll just have a glass of water."

While Mrs. Hawkins waited for Rochelle to come back with the water, JR had entered the room. He sat down on the couch opposite of her, with a twisted look on his face. The moment was awkward. Sitting in front of his grandmother for the first time in years set off a rush of emotions that he'd never experienced. When she wasn't around him, it was easier for him to shrug off how much he actually missed being around her. Now that he was finally forced to confront her face to face, he didn't know what to expect. He chose to just go with the flow and play the hard role like he was unfazed by her presence.

Rochelle returned to the living room with the glass of water and exited quickly so that they could be alone.

"So, what can I do for you?" JR asked nonchalantly.

"Well, JR, I want to first start off by saying that no matter how angry you are at me for putting you out of my house when I did, I am still your grandmother and I love you from the bottom of my heart. It hurt me so deeply to see you going down a path that I knew would only cause you harm."

"So, to show me your love you threw me out in the streets with no place to go?"

"I can't justify doing what I did at this point because I know you just won't understand. I didn't come here to argue with you. I came to make peace with you. I wanted more outta life for you than for you to be a drug dealer, but if that's what you want, then I have to accept it because it's your life." Mrs. Hawkins was wise enough to know that if she got into an argument with JR at this point, she would have no chance to mend their wounds. Consequently, she remained calm, despite his resistance, hoping that her love for him would tear down the wall he had built around his emotions.

"I hear you. I ain't done too bad for myself, as you can see. I got more money than I know what to do with in this lifetime. I got a beautiful woman and two healthy children. I guess God blesses us sinners too, huh?" JR grinned.

"JR, don't misuse the Lord's name as though He condones your drug-selling. You should be appreciative of His shielding you from harm, with the dangerous life that you live. God is not to be mocked."

"That's all good, Grandma, but did you come to talk about church, or was there a point to this visit?"

"Yes, there was a point to my visit. You don't have to be so sassy with your mouth, young man. I raised you better than that. First of all, I wanna know if we can begin to rebuild our relationship. I know it can never be like it once was, but I think we need to start somewhere. I wanna be a part of your children's lives. They are my flesh and blood. In spite of how you feel about me, don't deprive those babies of my love for the rest of the time that I have on this earth."

JR sat up from his slumped position on the couch, the hard exterior he initially displayed turning to a look of concern. "Are you sick or something?"

Mrs. Hawkins chuckled. "No, I'm not sick, but I ain't getting no younger."

"Oh, well then, I'm not gonna let you lead my kids on in believing that you love them so you can abandon them like you did me."

"Baby, I didn't abandon you. I prayed for you every day that you would be all right in these crazy streets. I gave you everything I could, and you know that's the truth. I showed favoritism for you over my other grandkids. Even when you were wrong, I still never stopped spoiling you and letting you have your way. That was my mistake, and I see that now. I should have been firmer with you from the beginning. JR, you are just too stubborn to see that I have swallowed my pride and came here to make peace with you because I love you. I am not your enemy. Let's put the past behind us to make a fresh start."

JR felt a lump in his throat. He couldn't hold back the love for her he'd tried to hide any longer. "Yeah, you can see the kids when you want. As far as me and you, I think we need to play that by ear."

"That's fine by me, baby," Mrs. Hawkins said excitedly. "I'm so glad that we had this talk." She got up from the couch to hug JR and kissed him on his cheek.

He cracked a slight smile and returned her embrace. "A'ight, that's enough of the mushy stuff. I gotta get outta here now. We've got somewhere to be." Then he yelled into the bedroom, "Rochelle, come on, it's time for us to go!"

As soon as he spoke, Rochelle came out of the bedroom, a

big smile on her face and Quentin and Savion by her side. She'd been eavesdropping by the door to the whole conversation and was happy to see them put their differences aside.

"Come on over here, you lil' cuties, and give your Mama Hawkins some sugar," she said to the boys, her arms outstretched. When they ran over to her, she planted wet kisses all over both of their cheeks.

"Mama Hawkins, I like you," Quentin said with youthful innocence.

"I like you too, Quentin. We'll be spending a lot more time together soon. Mama Hawkins has to run now. We can all walk out together."

JR grabbed the car seat, and Rochelle grabbed her car keys, and they all exited the apartment.

Mrs. Hawkins was happy to have JR back in her life and planned on reuniting father and son, once Nigel came home.

21

After fourteen long years, Nigel was successful, with Reverend Mitchell's help, in convincing the parole board, of his worthiness to be granted an early release from prison. He used every bit of his charm to convey to them how remorseful he was for his crimes committed against society. He'd made a strong argument to them, detailing his plans to become a productive member of society, and showing them how he used his time in prison constructively by getting his GED. He also provided them with documentation of his completing the Redeemed Souls Outreach drug treatment program and his regular attendance to NA meetings at the jail as evidence of his willingness to stay clean. He also mentioned how he attended church services every Sunday to add a spiritual foundation to his recovery process. Plus, Reverend Mitchell's passionate letter pledging to be a positive support system for Nigel by providing him with a job upon release was enough to sway the panel in favor of granting Nigel parole on his first attempt.

Nigel's transformation was nothing short of a miracle, something that not even he could have foreseen.

While in the Redeemed Souls program, he built a strong relationship with Reverend Mitchell that helped him to confront his own personal demons. Although he was only nine years his senior, Nigel looked at Reverend Mitchell as the positive male role model that his father should have been to him when he was a child. Reverend Mitchell instilled in him all of the necessary tools he would need to wrestle with his drug addiction when he returned to the outside world: self-esteem issues that played a major role in his wanting to live the fast lifestyle as a means of obtaining power and social acceptance; his internal defense mechanisms, which could pose a threat to his recovery; and how to recognize high-risk situations that could trigger him to use drugs, and ways to effectively deal with them.

He also instilled in Nigel his need to fellowship with other recovering addicts traveling the same road of self-discovery. Now a free man, Nigel planned to make good use of the wealth of knowledge imparted to him by Reverend Mitchell, the man he believed saved his life.

As he rode on the prison bus with the other inmates to the drop-off spot in Baltimore City, he took in his surroundings. It had been over a decade since he actually saw the streets. Nothing looked the same to him. It was like he'd stepped out of the twilight zone and into another dimension. He watched TV while he was incarcerated, but nothing that he saw on television could prepare him for the new world he was about to enter into as a reformed man. Areas of the city that he remembered as being well-kept were now littered with trash and debris. In fact, every block that the bus passed on its trek to the downtown bus station looked like a cemetery. All Nigel saw was a steady stream of drug addicts roaming the streets in search of their next fix. Long dope lines were on every corner. He closed his eyes and thanked God for delivering him from his self-destructive life course.

Although he felt relieved to be drug-free, a funny feeling came over him that he didn't expect. Watching all of the drug addicts on an endless chase for drugs gave him a burning feeling in the pit of his stomach. Thoughts of how he used to feel when he was high popped into his head out of the clear blue. A smile came across his face as he became enthralled in a daydream about the euphoric feeling that heroin and cocaine gave him so many times throughout his addiction. He had an urge to use again. He was confused because he'd never felt a craving for drugs this strong in the few years that he'd been clean. He tried to block the thought out of his head, but it grew stronger the closer he got to his destination.

When the prison bus reached the Greyhound bus station, he walked toward the front of the bus to exit and meet his ride.

When Nigel stepped off the bus, he was overwhelmed by the Baltimore summer heat. It was hotter than chicken grease on this particular July day. He walked away from the bus station to meet his ride, toward Lexington Market, a landmark in Baltimore City, where city residents would come to get fresh meats to cook, or individuals who worked in the downtown area came for lunch. Many of the city's heroin users hung out there too, drawn by several methadone clinics in the area.

As he walked through Lexington Market, Nigel saw a group of addicts high on their daily dose of "the juice." He saw other heroin users in the familiar dope nod that signified that they had some potent shit.

Although cocaine was his drug of choice when he left the streets, it was the heroin that called his name strongly today. The urge to use held his mind hostage at the moment. He wanted to feel that heroin high again. Just as he was about to ask a man where he could cop some dope with the thirty dollars in his pocket, he felt a strange hand grab him on his arm. He turned around and was stunned.

"Brother Nigel, I'm glad that you made it back to the city safely," Reverend Mitchell said with a worried look on his face. "My car is over here. Let's get a move on so we can rap a taste. I think I need to get you home." He knew what Nigel was about to do and felt relieved that he'd showed up at just the right moment to stop him from awakening the monster inside.

The man that was about to approach walked right past them. Nigel's desire to use instantly vanished. He felt like a kid that got caught with his hand in the cookie jar. "Hey, Reverend Mitchell, I was just looking for you," Nigel said, a guilty look on his face.

"Well, here I am, brother. It looks like I came along just in time, huh?"

"What do you mean by that, Reverend Mitchell?" Nigel asked, playing dumb.

"Nigel, you know exactly what I mean. I've been there before myself. You get clean in the joint and get all of this good information about recovery, but as soon as you hit the streets, that monkey jumps on ya back and erases all of those positive thoughts," Reverend Mitchell stated as they walked and talked.

"Yeah, I can't lie. You caught me. I was about to get me one. My mind was telling me that I deserved a blast for old times' sake. This drug thing is crazy how it plays games with ya mind."

"It's cunning, clever, baffling. It will come at you from all angles. It wants you to remember all of the good times you had gettin' high and not the bad side of things. That's why I kept telling you in all of my lectures at the jail that you gotta keep ya pain up front if you wanna stay focused. Remember being up in that cell locked away from ya family. Remember how it felt to be ill. That alone should bring you back to the reality that using is not an option if you want to truly be in recovery."

After walking for several more minutes, they finally reached the parking lot where Reverend Mitchell's car was parked.

When Nigel saw the silver luxury vehicle in front of him, he said, "Damn, Rev.! You're living the good life, ain't you? What kind of car is this?"

"It's called a Bentley Azure. It's one of the finest cars made by Rolls-Royce. It was a gift from my church members for all of my hard work redeeming souls. God's man is entitled to having all of the finer things in life," he said proudly. He pressed the button on his car remote and unlocked the doors.

Nigel opened his door and got inside, and was even more impressed with the navigation system and all of the sophisticated gadgetry on the dashboard. "God is certainly good to you, Reverend. I hope He blesses me in the same way."

"He will bless you, brother. Stick with me, trust my judgment, and you can't go wrong. Hey, before I get you home, I wanna take you by the church so that you can see our work for ya self. I want you to see all of my businesses that I have and some of the buildings that I've recently purchased that I wanna turn into recovery houses. A little AC and a relaxed ride in luxury is what you need to take ya mind off of that narcotic."

"Okay, that's cool, but I wanna get to my mother's house soon. I'm anxious to see her and to get with my son. I need to find him so I can rap to him about a few things."

As they cruised the streets of East Baltimore, Reverend Mitchell showed him the multiple businesses that he owned on Greenmount Avenue, a cellular telephone store, a shoe store, dry cleaners, and several carry-out restaurants. Nigel knew that Rev. Mitchell was an important man, but after seeing all of his assets, he was even more impressed. He was ready to follow this man into hell with a gasoline suit on.

The Redeemed Souls Holy Temple and its connecting primary education school was a sight for sore eyes, with its majestic beauty and excellent structure. Nigel thought, *This brother is paid out the ass!*

Reverend Mitchell parked his car in his reserved spot in front of the church and walked inside to introduce Nigel to his staff.

His secretary, Muriel, greeted them at the front door. "Hello, Reverend Mitchell. How are you this fine day?"

Muriel was one of those beautiful sistas that would go unnoticed because of her humble schoolteacher-like demeanor. Only a trained eye could catch the magnanimous curves that were hidden underneath her conservative attire.

Nigel found himself staring at her for several seconds too long. All of those years without being with a woman made him view her as a mere sexual object and not his sister in Christ.

"I'm fine, Muriel. This is Nigel. He just came home from prison. You'll be seeing him around a lot more. He'll be working around the church—Nigel, put ya tongue back in ya mouth. Sister Muriel is a married woman," Rev. Mitchell joked, to the embarrassment of Nigel.

Muriel laughed. "That's not nice, Reverend. It's okay if the brother admires my beauty. He's harmless. Hello, Nigel. I'm the minister's administrative assistant," she said flirtatiously.

"Hello, Muriel. It's nice to meet you," Nigel responded in his most mellow and seductive voice. He extended his hand out to meet hers. It had been so long since he felt hands so soft and gentle.

"Are you leaving for the day?" Reverend Mitchell asked.

"Yes, I have to pick my son up from daycare. I'll be in bright and early tomorrow."

"Okay, I'll see you tomorrow," Rev. Mitchell said as he waved good-bye.

Nigel turned his head to get a glance at her backside. "That sista was fine, Reverend. I didn't mean to stare so hard."

"Yes, Muriel is fine with her tight little body. Oh, excuse me, brother. You got me over here backsliding. I'm supposed to be the good reverend. I shouldn't be thinking those sinful thoughts."

"That's cool. You're still a man, no matter what you do. You ain't like no reverend I've ever seen before. You're cooler than a fan. You're not a 'tight suit' like them old-time ministers. I like your style." Nigel felt relaxed around Rev. Mitchell and was glad to have someone down-to-earth to confide in.

"Thank you, brother," Rev. Mitchell said, attempting to save face, "but what I meant to say was when you come to church on Sunday there will be so many beautiful sistas in the crowd that you might just lose ya mind. If I weren't a married man, I would feel privileged to have so many beautiful women to choose from to be my future wife. All of God's men need a helpmate."

"I agree."

"We're cut from the same cloth, you and I. That's why I took to you the way that I did. I want you to feel comfortable in telling me anything that's on ya mind."

Nigel shook his head in agreement and appreciation for the minister's openness with him and offer of support.

As they were about to enter the church, a young brother with cornrows in his head ran over to get the minister's attention. He was dressed in pair of baggy jeans that hung off his waist, and an oversized white T-shirt.

"Hey, Reverend Mitchell, I need to holla at you for a second.

I got a problem, or *we* have a problem that needs to be taken care of right away," the young man stated in an agitated voice.

"Not right now, son. I have business to take care of with this brother. I will get with you at a later time," Reverend Mitchell replied coldly.

"Well, this can't wait. I'm losing money as we speak. Or should I say that *we* are losing money," the young man said with a bit more urgency.

Reverend Mitchell walked over and yanked the young man up by his neck. He pinned him up against his Bentley and whispered something in his ear. Whatever he said to the young man got through and terrified him to death because, once the Reverend released his grip, the young man ran, as fast as lightning, away from the scene without looking back.

Nigel stood there not believing his eyes. He'd heard Rev. Mitchell talk about his thug side, but to actually see him in action stunned him.

"Sorry about that, brother Nigel. That was a young brother who was doing some work for me. He wanted me to pay him before he finished the job, but I already told him that wasn't gonna happen. I told him that three times already. These young kids have no respect for their elders. Sometimes you have to put them in their place, ya know what I mean?" Rev. Mitchell straightened up his suit jacket.

"Yeah, I know. I got a feeling I'ma go through the same thing when I see my son."

"Let's go inside so I can show you around."

They went inside of the church to continue their tour.

"Man, this place is nice!" Nigel exclaimed after viewing the huge auditorium where the church services where held. He was amazed to see an ex-addict capable of being as successful a leader of so many people. It gave him a shot of hope about his own future success if he stayed under his wing.

"This is God's house. We can't have God's work being

done in a rundown shack with raggedy furniture. God's house deserves the best of everything. You're one of his children, and He wants you to have the best. You definitely have a place in this temple for the rest of ya life, Nigel."

"Thank you, Reverend."

"This is where you'll be working for now, Nigel. I'm gonna have you doing odd jobs for me at the church just to get ya feet wet before I move you up to doing bigger and better things within my organization. I want you to learn to appreciate hard work."

After they finished the tour of the church and school facility, Rev. Mitchell took Nigel over to his mother's house. Reverend Mitchell parked his car and walked up to the front door with him.

Nigel was nervous as he approached the front door. It had been years since he last saw his mother. He knew that she would be surprised to see how good he looked.

Mrs. Hawkins answered the door with a look of shock and pride when she laid eyes on him. "Come on in here, boy. Now that's my son! That's my son!" she yelled proudly as she looked at him up and down.

Nigel and Reverend Mitchell entered the house.

"Hey, Mama, I'm so happy to see you," Nigel said as he took her into his arms and gave her a big hug. She kissed him on his cheek. "This is Rev. Mitchell, the man that I've told you so much about."

"Hello, Reverend Mitchell. It's nice to finally meet you. I just wanna thank you for the wonderful job you've done helping my boy get himself together and gettin' him into the church," Mrs. Hawkins stated happily. She couldn't believe the miracle that stood before her eyes. Nigel was as handsome as his father in his heyday.

"The pleasure is all mines, Mrs. Hawkins. You have a fine son. He just fell down into the pit of the unrighteous." Rev. Mitchell started to go into his sermon voice. "God brought me along to help him work out some of his kinks and character defects."

"Praise the Lord. It's good to see that you're so humble about your work. Albert and Franklin, come on out here and greet ya brother!" she shouted into the kitchen.

When they entered the room, there was a thick air of tension. They weren't as optimistic as their mother was about Nigel's change of heart and were only there to see him because their mother begged them to come.

Nigel decided to be the one to break the ice. He walked over and gave both of them a hug, and they both hugged him back halfheartedly.

"Albert, Franklin, this is Reverend Mitchell, my mentor and minister in Christ. He's helped me to see that we have— I have a lot of mending to do to build a real relationship with you two. He knows everything about our battles in the past," Nigel stated humbly.

Albert and Franklin were caught off guard.

"Reverend Mitchell, it's nice to meet you," Albert said first and extended his hand. Franklin did the same thing.

"Yes, it's nice to meet you gentlemen. I worked hard with your brother while he was in jail to get him to understand the value in having a strong family around him in this most crucial time. I can honestly say that despite whatever has happened between you in the past, your brother is committed to being a better person today. He's not the same man he used to be. If I could, I would like to have you all join me in a prayer in asking God to make this family whole."

Rev. Mitchell's words moved both Albert and Franklin. They all joined hands in the center of the living room as Reverend Mitchell prayed.

Dear Lord, I am calling on You this blessed day to ask that You spread Your wings of love around the Hawkins family and wrap them up in Your bosom. Watch over this family. Open up their minds and their hearts so that they are able to heal the scars that have kept them divided throughout the years. I pray that You keep Brother Nigel on the straight and narrow path. He's come a long way, but has much farther to go. Keep him safe from harm. It is only by Your mercy that he has this second chance. Please, Lord, bring this family together as living testimony to Your beneficence and grace. Amen.

"That was a beautiful prayer, Reverend," Mrs. Hawkins said. "Why don't you join us for dinner?"

"I would love to, but I have many things to do. I would like to extend an invitation to the entire family to come out to my church on Sunday to hear the Word and for a hearty Sunday dinner."

"We'll all be there bright and early, Reverend," Mrs. Hawkins promised. Albert and Franklin acknowledged that they would be in attendance as well.

Nigel walked Reverend Mitchell to the door. "Thanks, Rev. Mitch. I appreciate what you just did. I don't know how I could ever repay you for all that you've done for me."

"You'll have more than enough chances to return the favor. Make sure you're up early so that you're on time for your first day at work. You need to be at the church by eight-thirty."

"I know. I'll be up at six in the morning so that I am guaranteed to be on time. I'm gonna handle my business, Rev."

They embraced as the minister exited the house.

Nigel returned to the living room to face his family. He had his work cut out for him to convince his brothers that he was sincere, but with God in the equation, anything was possible.

22

Getting up at six in the morning was no sweat for Nigel. Morning wake-up calls from the correctional officers at that time had become a normal part of his daily routine in prison. He got up from out of his bed and went into the bathroom to take a shower. It felt good to be free to take a shower all alone after having to share shower time with a herd of other grown men for so many years. It was refreshing the night before to be able to sit down at a dinner table and eat a meal without having to rush to eat like he did at chow time in jail. Just to be able to breathe fresh clean air instead of the stale smell of prison funk was a blessing. He truly cherished his newfound freedom. He wouldn't give it up for anything in the world. He thought to himself that he must have been a fool to think for so many years that jail was a cool place to be. He was glad to be rid of that insane thinking, thanks to Reverend Mitchell.

The first week of work was rough for Nigel because he'd never done hard labor in his life. Nonetheless, it didn't take him long to get the hang of things. He made it to the church on time every day and completed every assignment given to him by the minister—cutting grass, trimming weeds, emptying garbage, making sure that the grounds of the church facility were as clean as possible.

Nigel worked with a crew of three other parolees that the minister had hired as his landscaping crew. One of his co-workers, Charlie, grew up in the same neighborhood as Nigel and knew his reputation from the streets. Nigel got along well with the rest of his coworkers, and they had no problems respecting each other's space while on the job.

It felt rewarding for him to get his first paycheck at the end of the week. After taxes, he made close to three hundred and fifty dollars. The hard work that he put in to earn his money made him appreciate every penny. It wasn't the kind of money he was used to making when he was hustling or robbing somebody, but it was enough for him to take care of his current personal needs. He didn't have to pay his mother rent, so he was free to do whatever he wanted with his check.

The first thing that he did on payday was hit the mall and go shopping for some new clothes. The minister also talked him into opening up a savings account so that he could build up enough cash to be able to get his own place in the near future. He planned to save at least a hundred dollars every week.

As the warm water from the shower beat up against his skin, he thought about his son. His mother had filled him in on some of the details of JR's life at dinner the night before. She told him that he had two handsome grandsons. Nigel was overjoyed to know that his lineage would be carried on through them and was anxious to meet them. In fact, knowing that he was a grandfather made him more determined to try and get JR out of the drug game. He wanted him to be the responsible father to his children that he never was to JR. He didn't want to see another generation of Hawkins men brainwashed into thinking that the thug life was the way to live.

After he finished his shower, Nigel shaved off his scraggly beard. The fresh shave made him look ten years younger than his forty-five years. Now free of drugs, his skin was clear, and he had regained most of the weight that he had lost due to his drug use. Nigel admired himself in the mirror for a brief spell and felt his swagger about to come back. In no time at all, he knew that he would find him a beautiful woman to be by his side.

He threw on the royal blue Sean John jeans and matching polo shirt that his mother had bought him. When he went to jail, men wore straight-legged pants and tucked their shirts in neatly. He'd come from a generation of hustlers that prided itself on being clean-cut and well-groomed. It would take him a while to get used to the new style of dress. He grabbed his wallet and jail ID off the dresser and headed downstairs to make a cup of coffee before he hit the road.

When he reached the kitchen, his mother was seated at the kitchen table with a pot of coffee brewing. "Ma, what are you doing up so early?" he asked. He bent down and kissed her on the cheek.

"I heard you moving around up there and decided to make you some coffee before you got out the door. Here's twenty dollars for you to catch a cab over there to see your parole officer." Mrs. Hawkins placed the money on the counter.

"Ma, I appreciate what you want to do for me, but I can catch the bus. You have spoiled me my whole life. I wanna know what it's like to get around like normal people do who don't have a car. My brothers might not believe that I have changed, but give me some time and you all will see how much I've grown up." Nigel stopped to sip his coffee. He reminisced about his first night home when Albert and Franklin rode him so hard in thinking that he would return back to his old lifestyle. It was like they had bets on him that he would fail in life. It hurt him that they thought of him in that manner, but he remembered what Reverend Mitchell taught him about how his positive strides in his recovery would force other people to reassess their faulty thinking about his being reformed.

"I'm proud of you, son. I'm glad that you want to show me that you want to be an independent man, but you better take this money and get ya butt in a cab. Those are my final words on that subject. Your brothers might not see the change in you, but I see it already. God spoke to me and told me before you came home that He was gonna send my son back to me before I die as a whole man and He did. God will remove the hardness in their hearts because it's by His will that you have been saved. That's something that neither one of them can run away from or fight forever." Mrs. Hawkins had a smile on her face. She truly believed that God answered the prayers of the righteous.

Nigel felt good to know that Rev. Mitchell and his mother gave him the same stern advice. With the two of them in his corner, he had a strong support system at his disposal when he felt any moments of weakness. It was up to him to utilize them *before* he made an irrational decision to use drugs again as opposed to *afterwards*.

Reluctantly, he took the twenty-dollar bill from his mother. When he called the cab company, they said that it would be thirty minutes before his cab arrived.

"Thank you, Ma, for believing in me so much. I'm gonna go over to Parole and Probation to meet with my parole officer. Once that's over with, I plan to make my rounds about town to get up with JR and have a man-to-man talk with him."

"You let JR be for right now. You need to focus on getting you together before you talk to him. That boy has a lot of rage toward you, but I know that deep down inside he really loves you dearly. Just like his father, he doesn't know how to put his male ego aside. Since he and I have begun talking again, he calls me at least twice a week to check up on me. I haven't told him anything about you coming home yet. I wanted to regain his trust first, and I think we're almost there. If you go over there and try to confront him now, he will do nothing but explode and Lord knows what will happen. Let me handle this my way."

"I hear what you're saying, Ma, but this is my mess that I created and I have to clean it up. My son is my responsibility. His mother disappeared years ago and has never been heard from again. It was horrible, all of the things me and his mother forced him to see so young. He at least needs to know that one of us still loves him."

"Boy, with all of your change, ya head is still hard as a brick about some things. You do whatever you wanna do, but don't say I didn't warn you." Mrs. Hawkins shook her head from side to side. She knew that a confrontation between the two Hawkins men would wind up being nothing but trouble.

"I gotta get outta here, Ma," Nigel said as he heard the cab driver blow his horn. "I'll see you later on today." He raced out the front door and hopped in the back seat of the cab. He told the cab driver what his destination was and they were on their way.

The whole ride over to the probation spot, he thought about his mother's suggestion that he not reach out to JR just yet. His natural impulse made him want to brush aside the suggestion, but then he remembered the lessons he'd learned from the program in jail about exercising patience and perseverance and decided to wait before he reached out to JR.

When the cab reached the Guilford Avenue Parole and Probation office, the front steps were littered with other offenders just like Nigel, who were there to meet with their agents and submit to urine testing. He got out of the cab and walked toward the front door. He ran into several individuals that he knew from his past life. Nigel exchanged greetings with them and made his way up to the receptionist's window to ask for his parole agent. The receptionist was a short, stout woman with braids in her hair. She had a gold tooth in the front of her mouth and popped her bubble gum so loudly that you would have sworn that she was out on the corner hanging out with her friends.

"Can I help you?"

Nigel responded, "Yes, this is my first day here. I was told that I have an appointment for intake today."

"Well, just sign ya name on this sheet and take a seat with the rest of the other convicts. I'll call ya name when the intake person is ready to see you."

Nigel felt disrespected and wanted to pull her card but decided to remain humble. He kept in mind that he was there for a specific reason and refused to let her ignorance deter him from his purpose. He took a seat in the overcrowded waiting room.

It took over an hour before the rude receptionist called his name.

"Nigel Hawkins, report to the window!"

Nigel walked over the window and received instructions on how to get to the intake office. He took the elevator up to the third floor and searched for office 305, where he was greeted by Mrs. Spencer, a middle-aged Black woman dressed in a black ankle-length skirt and white blouse. She shook his hand and took a seat behind her desk.

Nigel sat across from her and answered a host of questions about his family background, mental state, criminal history, and drug use. Once Mrs. Spencer completed her assessment, she walked Nigel down the hall to meet with the agent who would supervise his parole.

When Nigel saw her seated behind her desk, he was instantly

mesmerized. She looked to be in her early-to-mid-thirties and had an onyx skin tone with shoulder-length hair. Even though she was seated behind her desk, Nigel could tell that her body was a winner, just by her upper structure.

"Hello, Mr. Hawkins. My name is Agent Nicole Cooper, and I will be your agent for the course of your parole. It's nice to meet you." She extended her hand out to him, and Nigel shook her hand firmly and took a seat.

Once they finished their introductions, Mrs. Spencer exited and went back to her office.

"It's nice to meet you as well, Agent Cooper. I just want to start off by telling you that you won't have any problems with me. I just wanna complete my parole and move on with my life," Nigel told her.

"Well, that's good to hear. I wish all of my clients were like you. Then, I wouldn't have to work so hard," she joked.

"I certainly wouldn't want to work you too hard. I wanna make this as easy as possible for the both of us," Nigel said flirtatiously. He knew that she was his parole agent, but his attraction to her made that a moot point. Besides, the look on her face suggested that she didn't seem to mind his flirting. Nigel glanced over at her hand and didn't notice a wedding ring.

"I have a few things to go over with you so that I can lay out the conditions of your early release from prison. First of all, you will be required to attend an aftercare treatment program for six months and to report here to do urinalysis testing twice a week initially. Once you have a series of negative specimens, we can talk about moving you down to once a week. You will also be required to meet with me once a week on Thursdays for a progress report, and to find a job as soon as possible. I'm gonna need to see pay stubs to verify your employment. Do you have any questions for me as to what is expected of you?"

"No, I have no questions. As for me getting a job, I work for my minister, Reverend Johnny Mitchell, at his church, The House of the Redeemed. It's not too far from here, off of Greenmount Avenue. I also want to let you know that using drugs and breaking the law is a thing of the past for me. I'm a different man today, and I want something positive for myself now. I'm not gonna burn your ears up with false promises of me doing the right thing, but I plan to be a living example of a model parolee. Do you have any other questions for me?"

"No, I don't have any more questions at this time, Mr. Hawkins. I hope that you do complete your parole success-fully. You're right, I do hear a lot of talk from my clients about how they're gonna do right, but most of them wind up falling short. However, your tone is very sincere, and I believe you when you say that you are ready to make a change in your life."

When Agent Cooper got up from behind her desk, Nigel saw that his forecast was right on point. She had a thin waist and plump rear end that made a bulge develop in his jeans. He tried not to stare too hard, but Agent Cooper caught him gazing at her backside.

"I apologize for staring so hard," Nigel said frankly. "It's just that you are truly a beautiful woman." At this point, there was no sense in him denying his attraction to her, because it was so evident.

"Thank you for the compliment. I'm not the kind of woman that gets bent out of shape when a man admires me, as long as he is respectful. I appreciate the attention. Once you get to know me, you'll find out that I'm easy to work with and here to assist you in any way possible throughout this process. I'm not one of those uptight agents who lives to send another brother back to jail for the slightest thing. I like to keep an open-door policy for my clients who do every-thing that is required of them. If you're having a problem, come in to the office and talk to me, or call me on the phone before things get out of hand. Here is my business card. My cell phone number is on there as well, in case I'm not in the office when you call," Agent Cooper said in an empathetic and suggestive tone.

"Thank you, Agent Cooper. It's good to know that you will be there for me when I need support." Nigel felt at ease and relieved that he had such a laid-back and down-to-earth agent. The fact that she was drop-dead gorgeous was an added bonus.

"I'm just doing my job the best that I can. Now, if you would just follow me down the hall, I'll take you downstairs and show you where you'll be doing your urinalysis test for me today. I already have you in the system. Oh, and lose the Agent Cooper thing. You can call me Nicole. Calling me by my last name makes me feel old," she said in her raspy, but sexy voice.

"Okay, Nicole," he shot back, "now that we're being so informal, you can call me Nigel."

"Agreed. Oh, one last thing. You'll get a letter in the mail as to when you are to report to the aftercare program for treatment."

"I'll be looking out for it," Nigel stated, a sly smile on his face.

Nigel followed his parole agent down the hall and did his best not to peek at her derriere, but he couldn't resist. She caught him peeking again, but said nothing. Nigel picked up the vibe that she might be attracted to him as well. When they reached the urinalysis lab, Agent Cooper shook his hand and went on her way.

Nigel went inside of the lab and waited for his name to be called. Once he gave his urine specimen, he was out the door.

As he walked down the front steps on his way to catch a cab, he heard someone yell his name. He turned around to see who it was, and was surprised to see Pretty Ricky and Fats running behind him. They both looked worse for the wear. Their physical appearance and unkempt clothing suggested that they were still in active addiction.

He remembered Reverend Mitchell telling him to avoid associating with his old crew if he wanted to stay clean, but Nigel's love for his old homeys made him linger around to kick with them, despite the possible danger of him relapsing. The three of them had too much history together for him to not show them some love. Despite their raggedy appearance, he embraced both of them in a brotherly hug, and they stood in front of the building to do some catching up.

"Nigel Hawkins, I thought that was you. What's up, blood? My ace boon coon is home. How long have you been out?"

Although he was in his mid-forties, Pretty Ricky could easily pass for a senior citizen, with all of the wear and tear his drug use had imposed on him. His hair, which was once a stream of waves, was now shaven completely bald.

"I just got out a couple of days ago. It feels good to be free. I see you're still on paper too, Ricky. What's up with you, Fats? What you doin' down here at Guilford Avenue?"

"Man, I'm on paper too. I got five years probation for a CDS possession charge. All I had on me was three crack vials. For that, a nigga got all of that time hanging over my head. Ain't nothing changed out here since you went away. I'm still the same nigga. I'ma get high till I die, but my PO will never know. As long as I keep giving her clean urine tests, that's all that matters," Fats shot back, the twenty-five pounds of blubber that he'd put on over the years making his name more fitting for him now. Fats bought clean urine samples for twenty dollars from any of a number of individuals who sold them outside of the Guilford Avenue office in order to pass his urinalysis tests.

"Nigel, what's up with you, man? You look good, bro. Prison

served you well. Look at our homeboy, Fats. He's all clean-cut and what not. You ain't getting high no more?" Pretty Ricky asked.

"Nah, man, I've been clean going on three years now. I'm done with the streets. I've traded in my card. I'm on a different kinda time now, fellas. I've got God in my life," Nigel said proudly.

"You found God? Nigel Hawkins, stop playing with me. You're the most anti-religious cat that I know. Hell has a spot waiting for you for all the devilish shit we all done did in our lives. You're just saying all of the righteous shit because you just came home. I'ma give you about a month before you're right back out here with us smoking that ready."

"Nah, this is for real. While I was locked up, I got a chance to do some soul-searching. I met this real cool dude, Reverend Mitchell. His church is up off of Greenmount Avenue. He used be a thug like us, but he turned his life around and inspired me to wanna do the same. Drugs have caused me to waste a ton of years in my life. I wanna walk a different walk today. I gotta get with my son to get him outta these streets before they kill him. Why don't you brothers go to church with me on Sunday?" Nigel asked.

Pretty Ricky and Fats both laughed. Asking them to go to church was like asking a stripper to not give lap dances in a strip club. It wasn't gonna happen. The only God that they worshipped came in a glass vial.

"Go to church? Man, if they ain't giving out testers at the front door, I ain't got time for that shit. Yeah, you need to get with ya son. He's a disrespectful lil' muthafucka. I had a run-in with him a few years ago. He tried to act like he didn't know who I was. The nigga even had the nerve to put his hands on me. I shoulda kicked his lil' ass," Fats said about JR.

"Watch ya mouth, Fats. Right or wrong, that's still my son.

I ain't having nobody talk greasy about him or even thinking about doing him any harm." Even though he had changed in a lot of ways, when it came down to his son, Nigel would smack the taste out of anybody who spoke ill of him or threatened him with harm.

"Calm down, preacher man. Fats ain't mean nothing by what he said. He was just trying to pull ya coat to how these youngstas today ain't got no respect for us OG's out in the streets. Your son is a big player in the game today. His name is ringing out in the streets. He got a crew not too far from here that's moving serious weight. He works for that nigga Polo," Pretty Ricky said.

Fats ran down to Nigel what went down between them. After hearing his explanation, Nigel calmed down a bit.

"My son is working for Polo?" Nigel asked. "That clown is still around?"

"Yeah, Polo is doing his thing," Pretty Ricky informed him. "That cat got money up the ass, man. He ain't no lil' square like he used to be. He has much juice in this city. The streets fear that nigga,"

"Man, he's a pussy. That nigga has been scared of me all of his life," Nigel bragged. "You see he ain't do shit when I took Lorraine from his ass back in the day and I ripped him off for a few packages."

"Yeah, but that was the old days. Polo got the city on lock now, homes. You don't want any problems with that dude," Fats added.

Nigel's fatherly instincts took over. "Well, if he's got my son out here hustlin' we already have a problem with each other. You know where my son be slingin' at?" Nigel asked, totally forgetting that he'd decided a little while ago not to approach JR yet.

"Yeah, he's got a spot off of Old York Road that's pumpin'

twenty-four seven. He and Polo's son, Raynard, are best friends. You want us to show you where he's at?" Fats asked. "If you do, my car is around the corner. I can shoot you through there."

"Let's go."

The three compadres bolted around the corner and jumped into Fats's beat-up Chevy Impala. It was a hooptie, but it was good enough for them to get from point A to point B.

Nigel jumped in the back seat, and Pretty Ricky rode up front with Fats.

As they rode through the city streets, they reminisced on old times.

"Man, it's good to see you, Nigel," Pretty Ricky said. "I missed ya crazy ass, dog. You know I was pissed at your ass for a long time when we got knocked off because I saw you take that money out the register before you took me to the hospital that night. Over time, I got over that shit. I just charged that off to the game because that was straight a dope fiend move. Besides, we like family and been through too much for me to hold a grudge. Let's celebrate your coming home. You've been down for a long stretch. Fuck that clean and sober shit. If you've been clean for as long as you claim, hittin' this pipe one time ain't gonna hurt you. You owe yaself one." Pretty Ricky pulled out a fat, chunky crack rock outta his pocket and held a stem in his other hand.

Nigel's eyes got wide, and his mouth began to water. As much as he wanted to take the rock outta Ricky's hand and blaze it up in a crack pipe, he knew that once he hit that pipe one time, he would be off to the races. Reverend Mitchell had warned him repeatedly about being in the company of people that were actively using. As mad as he was at Ricky, he was even madder at himself for not exercising better judgment in getting in the car with them.

"Fats, let me outta this fucking car. Ricky, I told ya ass I don't want that shit! How the fuck are you gonna offer me drugs if you are a true friend?" Nigel slapped the rock and the pipe outta Ricky's hand. Then he grabbed him around the neck and almost choked him to death. Ricky tried to loosen Nigel's grip around his neck but wasn't strong enough.

Fats pulled the car off to the side to break them up. "Don't kill him, Nigel. He ain't mean nothing by it. We are your friends, man!"

Nigel came to his senses and loosened his grip around Ricky's neck.

Ricky gasped, "I'm sorry, man. That was my bad, but you ain't have to try and kill a nigga. I see you're real about this recovery thing. I shouldn't have tried to tempt you."

"No, you shouldn't have. You should've also told me that you cats were ridin' dirty. I'm on fucking parole. If I get violated, my ass is going up the river for the rest of my time left on parole. I ain't got shit else to say about the situation. Take me to where my son is at."

Fats and Pretty Ricky didn't say another word. They knew Nigel could do serious damage to both of them at the same time. Fats turned on his left blinker light and waited for a break in traffic. Once he found one, he proceeded a few more blocks before he parked his car across the street from JR's dope spot.

"There's ya son right there, Nigel" Fats said, pointing to a tall, stockily built young brother across the street.

JR had a group of teenage boys huddled around him and was decked out in jewelry and posted up in front of a cream-colored Benz.

Nigel gazed at his offspring, dumbfounded. *Well, I'll be damned. JR looks just like me.* With all of the things that he wanted to say to JR since he got clean, he couldn't muster up the nerve to get out of the car and walk across the street to approach him. He was clueless as to what to say or do. He just sat in the car and watched his son command his drug strip the same way he used to in his heyday. JR had definitely inherited his leadership skills and his love of the street grind.

"Nigel, you ain't gonna get out and holla at ya son?" Fats asked.

"Nah, just take my ass home." Nigel opted to listen to his gut instinct instead of acting out on his emotions. He knew that if he confronted JR in his element out in the streets about changing his life, it would get ugly. JR held resentment against him and seeing him now would only add fuel to the fire. His mother was right. He would let her be the catalyst for them mending their relationship.

As they rode down the road, Nigel was caught up in his own thoughts. He began to understand what the reverend meant when he said that getting high was an easy life, as opposed to living life on life's terms without drugs as a buffer. Nigel held his hands over his head in frustration as he thought about the mammoth task he had in front of him to stay clean and live a productive life. For the first time in his recovery, he began to have doubts as to whether he was prepared for it all.

23

Rochelle heard a knock at her front door. She walked to the front door dressed in a sexy, pink negligee. It was a new getup that she'd just bought from Victoria's Secret the other day to wear specially for tonight to entice JR. She'd sent the kids over to her mother's house for the night. JR had been outta town for a week on business and had called earlier in the day to say that he would be home tonight.

JR had been spending less and less time at home with her and the kids recently. Lately, he would be gone for days without calling her. Sometimes, not even Raynard knew where he was. When he was home, he was usually asleep from being out partying and getting high so much. Whenever, she tried to talk to him about them not spending time together, JR's short temper would take over. Several of their arguments wound up with his open hand slapping her across the face. She fought back as best she could, but JR's brute strength overpowered her.

Rochelle loved JR with all of her heart, but his drug use and hustlin' had begun to turn him into a different person.

She hoped that her powers of persuasion could bring the man she loved back into her life.

When she looked through the peephole of the door, she expected to see JR, but it wasn't him. It was Polo. She opened the door, keeping the chain attached. "Polo, what are you doing here? How did you get in the building without somebody buzzing you in?"

"I walked in with one of your neighbors. I was just in the neighborhood, and I thought that I would stop by. JR's gonna be outta town for a couple more days handling some things for me, and I just figured I would check up on you and the kids," Polo said in a mellow tone.

"He didn't say anything to me about him not coming home tonight. The kids are over my mother's house. I'm home alone," Rochelle replied, a hint of disappointment in her voice.

"Can I come in, or are you gonna make me stand out here in the hallway?"

"You can come in, but only for a minute. Let me throw on my robe." Rochelle closed the door and ran into her bedroom to throw on her robe. Once she covered herself, she opened the front door to let Polo in.

Polo took a seat on the couch. "It's a damn shame that boy got a fine thing like you at home by yaself. If you were my woman, I would make sure I gave you all the attention you deserved."

"Well, it is what it is. You gotta take the good with the bad. I love him, so I guess I gotta put up with his mess. I know things are gonna get better." Rochelle sat down on the couch next to Polo.

"So, what have you been doing with yaself while he's been gone?" Polo attempted to open her robe, and she playfully pushed his hand away. Then he rested his hand on her thigh, his touch warming her lonely soul.

"Come on, Polo, be nice. Don't start nothing that you can't finish. This is my house now. The house that JR and I share, remember?"

"I know, I know, but sometimes you gotta break the rules," Polo said nonchalantly, unhooking the belt to her robe and throwing it open.

Rochelle began to breathe heavily as he ran his hand down the center of her chest. "Polo, we swore that we wouldn't do this again. It's just not right. It's a mistake. We shoulda never started messing with each other from the beginning. You're supposed to be like a godfather to my man."

The moisture between Rochelle's thighs started flowing as Polo kissed her passionately on the neck, and she bit down on her bottom lip and closed her eyes momentarily.

Rochelle and Polo had been messing around off and on for the past year. It all started one day after she and JR had an argument and she went to Polo for advice on how to deal with JR's bad temper. At the time, Rochelle felt weak and vulnerable, and Polo's comforting shoulder wound up turning into an invitation to the king-sized bedroom in his estate. The sex with Polo was so off da chain, she had to have it again and again. He was attentive to her body in every way that JR stopped being.

Rochelle's sex life was virtually nonexistent over the last few months. Anytime she and JR did have sex, it was a short and brief encounter, with JR ejaculating before she got her chance to cum. Rochelle's heart belonged to JR, but her body was on loan to Polo to use at his discretion. Since that night, they'd slept together several more times.

On several occasions, she lied to JR, telling him that she was in class when she was really out with Polo. JR was none the wiser. He was too busy caught up in his own world to suspect anything.

The last time she and Polo were together was about a

month ago, and Rochelle swore that was gonna be the last time. Now she sat in her living room with a burning desire to sex the one man she knew was more dangerous than JR.

"Fuck that, lil' nigga. He works for me. Rochelle, you need a real man in ya life that knows how to handle a beautiful woman like yaself. You don't need no fool that wants to use ya face for a punching bag. Relax, baby," Polo said, smoothly sliding his hand inside her thong, "and let me do what I do."

Rochelle moaned, "Oooh, yes, that feels so good!"

"Let Daddy take you on a ride on his pogo stick." Polo undid his belt, unzipped his pants, and exposed all of his hardness for her to see. He pulled Rochelle over to him, and she plopped down on his lap.

Polo slid his naked manhood inside of her.

"Ooh, you make me wet, but we need to stop. We need to use some protection. I can't afford to get pregnant. JR would kill me." Rochelle wanted to do the responsible thing, but her body couldn't stop riding hard 'n' heavy on Polo's stiffness.

"Nah, forget that. This pussy is too good. I wanna feel this hot, young, tender pussy raw. I wanna see them juices rain down on this dick!" Polo cupped both of her ass cheeks in his hands, squeezed them tightly and wolfed on her nipples.

"Oooh, this just ain't right! It ain't right! You shouldn't be able to make my body feel this good!" Rochelle dug her nails into his neck then yelled. "I'm cummin', Polo! I'm cummin', baby!"

"I ain't ready to bust yet. I wanna hit it from behind." Polo held her in his arms and stood to his feet.

Rochelle climbed down out of his grasp and placed her hands at the top of the couch, hoisting her ass in the air. Polo then got behind her and proceeded to pound her pussy till it became dry.

"Hurry up, baby. I want you to cum for me. I wanna feel ya juices all over my ass."

"Here it is, baby. I'm cummin' all over ya phat ass!" Polo pulled himself out of her and released semen all over her backside, some of it spilling onto the couch. He closed his eyes and exhaled calmly.

"Damn, Polo! You got it all over the couch. I gotta clean this shit up."

Polo just sat back and smiled as she went into the hall closet to get a towel to clean up the mess.

"It's all good, sweetie. It's all good, true indeed. That nigga ain't gonna do shit to me. He's scared of my shadow," Polo said confidently.

"Yeah, but he would fuck my ass up. I think you need to go. I shouldn't have let this happen. I can't see you anymore. Please leave," Rochelle pleaded. She used the wet towel to wipe Polo's cum stains off of the couch and the carpet.

"I'm telling you, baby, that lil' nigga is not a problem. Besides, he ain't gonna be around much longer." Polo's facial expression turned to being more serious.

"What the hell is that supposed to mean?"

"Your boyfriend has been dipping in the cookie jar. His ass has been getting greedy. I've been watching him closely. The muthafucka's been stealing from me. I can't have that in my organization."

"Polo, you can't be serious. JR would never steal from you. He looks at you like a father. You must be mistaken." Rochelle knew that Polo was sending a veiled threat through her to JR, and she became afraid for his life.

"Nah, I wish I was, baby girl. I know what I know, and I gotta do what I gotta do about the situation."

"Well, I can't have that kinda talk around my house. That's my man ya talking about. You need to go."

"If that's how you want it, I can't argue with you, baby girl. You'll be back for more of this good dick. That nigga smokes too much weed to keep your sexy ass satisfied in the bedroom. You know the number when you get that itch you want me to scratch." Polo pulled his pants up and attempted to kiss her on the cheek.

Rochelle put her hand in the way of his lips touching her skin. "I mean it, Polo. This is it. I don't want this anymore," Rochelle said, tears forming in her eyes.

Polo threw his hands in the air and walked outta the front door without saying another word.

Rochelle was filled with feelings of guilt and shame about what she'd just done. She wished that she'd never slept with Polo from the beginning. She knew that her actions would be worthy of death if JR found out.

No matter how many times he'd cheated on her with other females, JR would never forgive her for fucking Polo, or any other man.

In a state of panic, she sprayed the couch and the living room with Febreze air freshener, to try and kill the stench of sex in the air.

Next, she went into the bathroom to take a hot shower in hopes that she could wash away her sins. As the hot water scorched her skin, she cried tears of regret for her actions. Once she finished showering, she grabbed her towel and went into the bedroom to dry off. After she dried herself off, she grabbed the remote control and plopped down on the bed to watch television.

After about ten minutes, the phone rang. It was JR. Her heart raced a thousand beats per minute.

"What's up, baby? You miss me?"

"Yeah, I miss you, JR," Rochelle replied.

"Well, I'ma be home in about an hour," JR said. "Then you can show daddy just how much you missed him."

"Okay, baby. I'll see you when you get here."

They talked for a few minutes before she hung up the

phone. JR would be home soon, and she would be forced to satisfy him sexually after just allowing Polo to screw her brains out. That meant that her sore insides would endure more pounding and thrusting.

She wanted to tell JR about Polo's plans, but couldn't figure out how to bring it up without him finding out about her cheating on him. The reality was, she was playing a dangerous game involving two dangerous men. There was no way that she could win. She buried her head in the pillow, wishing it was all just a dream.

24

Extreme with his cockiness, JR was playing the role of a drug kingpin to the hilt. The money and the fame started to go to his head. The more purple haze he smoked, the more irrational his thoughts and actions became. It was nothing for him to get into a beef with a rival drug dealer at a club over some bullshit and for the police to be called in to diffuse the situation.

He boasted loudly in public about being Polo's main man and dared any of his rivals to bring him a move. In the streets being so brazen and bold made you a target for any young thug looking to make a name for himself and was akin to signing your own death warrant. Nonetheless, JR didn't care about how many enemies he made because, as far as he was concerned, he would kill any muthafucka that dared to challenge him.

Raynard and JR recently started to grow apart because Raynard wasn't for the drama. At first, he used to party with JR and join him in his public tirades, but once he recognized the dangers in his actions, he fell back. He tried to caution JR about being so flamboyant, but his warnings were ignored. Raynard was contented with keeping a low profile and, like his father, stacking his money. He relayed his concerns to Polo in hopes that he could talk some sense into JR, but all Polo cared about was JR bringing him his money on time.

It wasn't enough for JR to be one of Polo's top earners. His mind began to churn and had him plotting to become the top dog in the game. He wanted Polo's spot. He wanted to be the head nigga in charge. As far as he was concerned, nothing was beyond his grasp in the drug game.

To increase his profits, he stepped on his coke a few more times than usual. That way he would be able to still pay Polo what he owed him without drawing any suspicion to his actions. JR planned to save up enough money to be able to go into business on his own.

On his many trips out of town to cop work for Polo, he'd made his own connections with some Colombian dudes that he planned set up shop with in the near future once his money was right. Polo would be none the wiser when he vanished with Rochelle and the kids like a thief in the night.

Outside of getting tweaked on purple haze, he also started smoking weed laced with cocaine. He didn't realize that he was hooked on the cocaine more so than the weed.

To make matters worse, a girl that he'd met in Atlantic City while he was gambling turned him onto ecstasy pills. Once he'd tried them, he was hooked after he'd had his first sexual experience under the influence of the drug. Now, he couldn't fuck unless he at least one *E* pill up in his system, because sex without it became boring.

More and more, getting high became more of his focus than getting money. His physical appearance also began to change. His complexion was darker, and his teeth became stained from smoking so much. He needed a haircut and a shave badly.

He had lost close to ten pounds over the past two months because getting high took away his urge to eat. Despite all of the negative side effects of his drug abuse, in his mind, he was still that nigga.

JR had just finished smoking a "coolie" as he drove down the road. He was on his way to stop by his grandmother's house unannounced. Since they'd reconciled, he went to her house a few times to have dinner with her, and for her to spend some time with the kids. But over the past few weeks, he'd only spoken to her over the phone, because he had been so preoccupied. He'd just dropped one of his lil' ghetto hotties off that lived around the corner from his grandmother, when he figured that no time was better than the present to see how she was doing.

JR parked his car in front of her house and sat there for a few minutes to let his high die down some. Once he was composed, he got outta the car and walked to the front door. From a distance he noticed a man in the front yard doing some work and initially paid him no mind. He figured that his grandmother must have paid somebody to do the work for her. As he got closer, however, the man looked more familiar to him.

The man was bent down raking up the grass that he'd just cut when JR approached the front of the house. "Who the hell are you?" JR asked the man.

The man stood upright and turned around. When their eyes met, it was like an explosion took place. JR got the answer to his question without the man saying a word. He looked just like him. The man was Nigel. This was the first time that father and son had laid eyes on each other in years.

As Nigel eyed his offspring from head to toe, all he could muster was, "Hey, son." He wanted to say so much more but was tongue-tied. He was totally caught off guard.

"I ain't ya muthafuckin son, and you ain't my father. You

just shot the sperm into my no-good mother that produced me. When the hell did they let ya no-good ass out the joint?" JR was hoping to provoke his father into trying to swing on him so that he could unleash all of the resentment he'd been harboring against him all of these years.

"I've been home for about two months now. You need to watch ya mouth, son, and show me some respect. Like it or not, I'm the one that brought you into this world." Nigel's recovery hadn't stripped him totally of his street bravado. Every now and then it would rear its head. He wanted to haul off and slap JR, but he remembered what Reverend Mitchell had taught him about being humble and choosing his battles in life.

"Man, whatever. I ain't gotta do nothing that you say. You ain't been here all of these years. I'm a grown-ass man."

The two stood face to face at the moment of truth.

"You're right, JR, I haven't been a father to you, and I'm sorry. I feel terrible about all of the pain that you had to endure all these years because of me and your mother's addictions. I can't change my mistakes of the past, but I can promise to be a better man today. I wanna be a part of ya life now, not as ya father, but a friend." Nigel extended his hand for JR to shake.

"Later for you, old man. I gots no love for you. I'm here to see my grandmother." JR brushed past Nigel's extended hand and walked up the steps and into the house.

Nigel just stood there dejected. He went back to his yard work, shaking his head in disgust.

Mrs. Hawkins was in the kitchen cooking when JR entered the house.

"Grandma, why you ain't tell me you had that bum staying here with you? I thought that we were building a new relationship based on honesty and trust."

Mrs. Hawkins was startled to see him. She stopped what she was doing and took a seat at the kitchen table.

"Calm down, boy. I didn't tell you that your father was home because I wanted to wait until I felt the time was right."

"The time ain't gonna never be right for me and him to be around each other. He had a chance to be a father to me, and he blew it."

"I understand your anger, but at least hear me out. Your father is not the man that he used to be, JR. He's changed for the better. I've seen it for myself. He's left the drugs alone, he goes to church now, he has a job, he goes to NA meetings, and he's in a treatment program. He wants to build a relationship with you. The first thing that he wanted to do when he got out was see you, but I told him to let me be the one to bring the two of you together. Give him a chance, baby," Mrs. Hawkins pleaded. "Do it for me."

"Grandma, us street dudes don't change. We are who we are, especially a junkie. He's running game on you. He might not be getting high right now, but give him a few months, he'll be up to his old tricks again. I got so many dudes like him working for me. Trust me, I know firsthand how this story goes. I've blocked him outta my life, and that's where I want him to stay."

Mrs. Hawkins prayed with her hands raised toward heaven as she sat across from JR at the kitchen table. "Lord, please lift the blinders of hatred off of this child's eyes and make him see the light. Take him, Lord, and fill his heart with love. Bring my grandson and my son together. Make them have the kinda relationship that a father and son should have. This family needs to be healed, Lord. Please, Lord, do this for me. I ask you in Jesus's humble name. Amen." Tears filled her eyes.

"Come on now, Grandma. Don't be crying on me now." JR reached out to embrace Mrs. Hawkins.

As they hugged, Nigel entered the room and stood behind them. "What's wrong, Mama?" he asked. "Are you okay?"

"She's fine, no thanks to you," JR answered.

"Look, boy, I ain't gonna take too much more of ya smart mouth. I let you get away with it outside. Don't push ya luck." Nigel clenched his fists so tightly that you could see the veins form in his muscular arms.

"So, what you gonna do if I get smart with you again, old man? You don't want it with me." JR smirked as he rose to his feet and stood right in front of Nigel. They were so close, their noses touched.

"Both of you, calm down," Mrs. Hawkins yelled. "Ain't gonna be no fighting in this house." She attempted to get to her feet to get between them but didn't move fast enough.

"Nah, Mama, if the boy thinks he's a man, then he needs to be treated like one." As soon as the words left his mouth, Nigel grabbed JR around the neck and twisted him into a headlock.

JR grabbed a hold of Nigel's waist and lifted him off the ground. The two fell to the ground and tussled back and forth.

Nigel was in good shape but was no match for the younger, stronger, and more agile JR, who quickly found himself on top of Nigel.

"You thought you was gonna steal me, old man? You shoulda known better," JR laughed as he began to let his hands fly. He connected repeatedly with Nigel's face.

Nigel attempted to cover up, but more than enough blows got through. Somehow, he summoned up the strength to flip JR over, and JR fell backward into a glass table in the living room, glass splattering everywhere.

Nigel got up and charged toward JR. Before JR could gather himself together and stand up, he was met with a right cross that sent him back to the ground. He was so staggered by the blow that when he tried to stand up, he fell back down flat on his ass.

"Don't underestimate ya elders, young man," Nigel said with a slight grin on his face. His clothes were disheveled, but he appeared unfazed. In fact, he was a little excited to be in a fight. It had been long time since he got some recreation in.

As he tried to pounce on JR one more time, Mrs. Hawkins stood in his way. "That is enough! I mean it. I will not have this in my house! If you two don't stop now, I'm calling the police to lock both of you up.

Hearing the mention of the authorities made Nigel come back to his senses. He remembered that he was on parole.

JR sat on the floor still dazed.

"I'm sorry, Ma. I should know better than to behave this way. I'm sorry too, JR. You're my son, I should never have put my hands on you. Let me help you up."

JR slapped his hand away. "I don't need shit from you. You got one off this time, but just remember that payback is mother." JR rose to his feet and staggered out the front door. He dragged his wounded pride and ego out to his vehicle and drove off.

"I am so disappointed in you. You acted just like an animal. You should have let me handle that boy. Now you may have pushed him away for good. May the Lord help both of you heathens," she stated, as she walked up the stairs.

"You're right, Ma. You are so right." Nigel sat down on the sofa to reflect on his impulsive actions. He let his machismo get the best of him, instead of handling the situation more intelligently.

In the past, getting high would have allowed him to escape the whole situation without a second thought. Now clean and sober, he was forced to deal with himself honestly and bluntly on life's terms. He didn't like where his anger just took him and wanted desperately to change. He knew that Reverend Mitchell would be disappointed in him for not acting more maturely and planned to have a talk with him tomorrow after work. He knew that if anybody could come up with a solution to help him get back with JR it would be the good reverend.

25

"Damn, baby, you need to slow down! Don't kill us up in here!" Latrice said as Raynard weaved wildly through traffic. They were on their way home from seeing a movie and having dinner at Fisherman's Wharf in downtown Baltimore, and their three-year-old son, Ray-Ray, was in the back seat fast asleep.

"Girl, stop playing, you know I got this thing here. Just sit back, relax, and enjoy the ride," Raynard responded calmly with a smirk on his face.

He reached across the seat to massage Latrice's thighs playfully, and she blushed sensually in response to his touch.

"You heard from JR lately?"

"Nah, we don't really talk that much no more. I saw him the other day at my father's spot. He said what's up and just bounced. He on some wild shit that I don't understand. I don't know what done got into my boy. He be smoking too much of that purple, if you ask me."

"Yeah, that nigga is crazy. I talked to Rochelle the other day. He's hardly ever at home with her and the kids. She also

said the nigga be hittin' on her too when he all highed-up. I
wish you would ever try that shit with me. You better never
go to sleep around me if you ever think about putting ya
hands on me. I'm a slice ya ass up like that bitch did niggas in
Basic Instinct," Latrice joked.

"You ain't never gotta worry about that with me, you my
boo. I don't get down like that. Besides, my pops would kick
my ass if he ever found out that I put my hands on you, the
mother of his grandchild."

"I know you wouldn't, baby. It's just crazy to me that he
done flipped on you like that. Y'all used to be so tight."

"Yeah, I know. Money changes niggas in the streets every
time. You also gotta understand that the nigga ain't never got
no real love at home with his moms and pops gone. I ain't
mad at him though. He still my nigga. He'll come up outta
this phase one day."

"That nigga don't deserve to have no best friend like you.
Shit, if Rochelle ever carried me like that, I would forget her
ass faster than you could bat an eye."

"I know you would, wit ya heartless ass. I hope our son
takes after me and has a big heart," Raynard joked.

"Whatever, nigga. That's why you love my heartless ass."
Latrice punched him lightly on his arm. Then she leaned up
outta her seat and kissed him on his cheek.

About fifteen minutes later, they pulled up at their four-
bedroom home in the Rosedale section of the city. Raynard
stepped outta his Lexus to open the back door to get Ray-
Ray outta his car seat. As he was unbuckling the seat belt
from around the car seat, a black Cadillac with tinted win-
dows pulled up beside him and screeched on the brakes. It
startled him so much that he jumped up to see who it was.
He hit his head on the rear window frame in the process.

The passenger in the Cadillac rolled down the window
slowly and asked, "Hey, yo, ya name Raynard?"

"Why? Who wanna know?"

"I got a message for him from Shakim. You him?"

"Yeah that's me, but I don't know no Shakim."

"I know you don't know Shakim, but he knows you. Remember his cousin Mark that you and ya boy murked down in Cherry Hill? Well, it's payback time, muthafucka!" The passenger began to unload shells from the 9 mm he held in hand, the shots ripping through Raynard's flesh and knocking him to the ground, and killing him instantly as his blood stained the concrete.

Latrice screamed in a state of shock. She couldn't move.

The passenger in the Cadillac, dressed in all black with a stocking cap over his face, got out, walked toward her, and pointed the gun at her head. "Bitch, shut that fucking noise up!"

She became silent. Her eyes glanced into the car at Ray-Ray, who was awakened by the gunfire to see his father laid out on the street in a pool of blood. He attempted as best he could to open the car door, but was unable to do so.

"Please, don't kill me! Not in front of my son! Please don't do this!" Latrice begged.

"We ain't gonna kill you, so relax. I want you to get a message to Polo. Tell him that Shakim and them New York boys is coming for him next. You got that?"

Latrice nodded.

The assailant then jumped back into the car, and the driver sped off.

Latrice ran over to the driver's side of the car to check on Raynard. He took one shot to the dome, and several other shots landed all over his body. She shook him in an attempt to wake him up, but his body didn't respond.

"Come on, baby. You're gonna be all right. We gotta get you a doctor." Latrice held Raynard's lifeless body in her arms and cried violently. The reality sunk in that he was gone forever.

By now, Ray-Ray had managed to get the car door open and stood in front of his mother, tears in his eyes. "Mommy, who were those people that did this to Daddy?" he asked hysterically.

"Some bad people just shot ya daddy! Come here, baby!" she yelled as she extended her arms out to hug him.

He jumped into her arms. "I don't understand, Mommy. Is Daddy gonna be all right?" He'd seen people on television get shot and get up like it was nothing and he thought that his father would do the same thing.

"No, Daddy is gone, baby. I'ma make sure them bastards pay for this!" Latrice lay up against the car for several more minutes, holding Ray-Ray in her arms in utter disbelief as to what had just transpired. She was drawn outta her trance by the flashing ambulance lights and the sounds of police sirens. One of her neighbors had heard the gunshots and called the police.

"Ms., are you okay?" a police officer asked.

"We need to get this woman into an ambulance. She's in a state of shock," another officer shouted. Two paramedics carted her and Ray-Ray off in an ambulance en route to the hospital.

Latrice didn't put up any resistance. Her life was just turned upside down by Raynard's death. She knew that once she got with Polo, there would be a war on the streets of B'more.

26

Nigel had just finished putting in another hard eight hours of labor keeping the grounds of the church clean. His body was sweaty, his back ached, and mentally he was just as worn out. His mind was still caught up thinking about the altercation that he had with JR the other day. The day after it happened, he wanted to approach Reverend Mitchell to seek his counsel, but he was busy with other church business. He decided to bring it up to his counselor, Frank Mackie, at AACC, with whom he'd developed a decent relationship. (AACC, Addict Assistance Counseling Center, was the drug treatment program his parole agent sent him to as a condition of his parole.)

Frank Mackie was a thirty-something-year-old, tall, dark-skinned brother with over ten years of experience in the counseling field. He wasn't a recovering addict, but he possessed a wealth of street knowledge that made him effective at his job treating drug addicts. He used to be a small-time hustler who sold weed while he attended school at Coppin State College. He also had a sincere desire to help others, which made it easy for him to establish a good rapport with brothers like Nigel looking to start a new life.

As Nigel rode the bus to his six o'clock group therapy session, he thought about JR constantly. His mind drifted back to when he and Lorraine first brought him home from the hospital after he was born. He reminisced about how proud he was to have a son. He thought about the few good memories he had of spending time with JR when he was in active addiction.

A feeling of sadness came over him when he thought about all of the years that he'd robbed JR of while he was in prison. He reasoned to himself that JR's life would've been so much different today, had he been a more responsible father. He thought about JR's children and how he wanted more than anything in the world to meet them and become a part of their lives. Nigel was so engrossed that he almost missed his bus stop. He realized it at the last second and was able to get off the bus and make it on time for his meeting.

When he approached the building, he saw a congregation of his fellow group members in front of the center. Some of them were taking a smoke break before group started, while others conversed about the latest gossip going on in the hood. As he walked up the steps to the front door, one of his group members, JB, called out to him.

JB, short for John Bryant, was a stone-cold crack fiend who was now clean and just as serious about chasing NA meetings today as he was about chasing the pipe back in active addiction. JB was dressed in a pair of baggy jeans with an oversized white T-shirt on. He wore a fitted Yankees baseball cap on his head that was turned around backward. He had a thick white gold chain with a Jesus piece draped around his neck. His fingers were covered with several diamond rings. If you didn't know any better, you would swear that he was a drug dealer by his appearance, his flashiness being just one of

his character defects that he carried over from his days in the
street. Today, he was a barber hustling his trade the same way
he used to sell drugs in the street.

Nigel had gone with him on several occasions to different
NA meetings across the city, but he wasn't as fanatical about it
as JB.

"What's shaking wit ya, Hawkins?" JB asked in his usual
slick tone.

Nigel walked back down the steps to greet JB, and the two
gave each other a pound. "Ain't nothing, man. I'm just trying
to take it easy. What's good with you?"

"You know me, going at this recovery thing hard. I'm just
chasing meetings and working hard." JB glanced at the bruise
above Nigel's right eye. "What happened to ya face?"

Nigel hung his head low. "I got into a scrape with my son.
We finally ran into each other. It got kinda ugly."

"Yeah, you looked like something was weighing you down
when I called out to you. Share what's going on in ya life
with the group tonight, bro. It'll help you take a load off."

"I think I will because I don't know what I'm gonna do
now. The boy hates my guts, and he shows no signs of forgiv-
ing me." Nigel pulled out a cigarette and lit up. He put the
cancer stick to his mouth, took a deep pull, and exhaled.

"He will. You just have to give him time. Remember, in recovery we can't expect people to change overnight how they
feel about us when it took us many years of irrational behavior to make them feel that way," JB reminded him.

"Yeah, you right." Nigel looked at his watch. "It's time to
go in. It's six o'clock now."

The two went inside the building and signed their registration cards at the front desk before they entered the group room.

About five minutes later, Frank Mackie came into the room
to convene the meeting. He sat in the front of the group—
about fifteen males and seven female clients—and began to

speak. "What's going on tonight, people? How is every-body?"

The group members replied with a variety of responses from, "Fine," to "I don't wanna be here today."

Frank took the negative responses in stride as good as he did the positive ones.

JB asked. "What's the topic for tonight, Mr. Frank?"

"Whatever you guys want it to be," Frank told them. "Does anybody have any issues that they're struggling with in this recovery process that they wanna share with the group?"

The room got quiet. Getting clients to open in a group setting about personal things was always a difficult task. All the same, Nigel boldly raised his hand to have his turn to speak. Frank nodded his head in acknowledgement that it was okay for him to address the group.

"Yeah, I got something to share with the group," Nigel said. "I know you all have heard me talk in several meetings about my wanting to build a relationship with my son after being gone for so long. Well, I finally got a chance to see him face to face, and it didn't go too well. We got into a fistfight. He hates me with a passion."

"Thank you for sharing with the group, brother," Frank said. That took a lot of courage. Now let's process your last statement. You say that he hates you? Do you really think that he hates you or that he just has some serious feelings about you being gone from his life for so long?"

"I don't know," Nigel replied, "but what I do know is that when a son puts his hands on his father, that's a sign to me that there's no love there."

One of the group members interjected, "I say you kick his ass and make him respect you. You his father and he need to remember that. Shit! If my son ever raised his hand up to me, I would stretch his ass out in a heartbeat!"

"Fighting is not the answer to solving ya problems. You need to come at him humbly and kill him with love!" one of the female group members advised.

"I hear what y'all are saying, but this is my son. I don't want to fight with him. I wanna get him outta these streets before it's too late for him. I don't want him to give the state fifteen to twenty of the best years of his life. I made that sacrifice for him already."

Several of the other group members expressed their personal opinions on the issue, and Nigel took it all in.

"Okay, I'm glad all of you offered the brother some support. Now I have one final suggestion for this issue. Nigel, you have to be the bigger man in this situation and not let ya pride get in the way of getting ya son back in ya life. Go at him again with no one else around. Apologize for fighting with him and take full responsibility for everything. That will throw him off guard. He won't have a choice but to respond positively to you because you've shown him no aggression like he expected. You see, ya son has seen the gangsta side of you. Now it's time for him to get acquainted with the new, more mature you."

Nigel nodded his head in agreement. "I'm feeling that, Frank. You're right. That's what I'ma do," Nigel said eagerly, his burden seemingly lifted somewhat off his shoulders.

After they finished addressing Nigel's issue, a few other group members worked up the courage to get some things off of their chest. The meeting went on for another thirty minutes before it was over.

After the meeting, Nigel had a one-on-one counseling session with Frank. He waited in the lobby for about ten minutes before the receptionist told him it was okay to go up to Frank's office.

"What's going on, Mr. Frank?" Nigel asked.

"Nothing much is going on with me, but I can tell by what you shared in the group that there's a lot going on in your life."

"Yeah, but I'ma be a'ight. As long as I trust in God, He'll help me to find a way to reach my son. I gotta admit that I was a little confused for a minute."

"It's only natural when you've been using chemicals to mask ya true feelings for so long that you would have a hard time dealing with these difficult life situations. It's good that you didn't keep this bottled up inside and decided to share it with the group. Opening up is one of the hardest things I've found for most of my clients to do. This shows me that you're serious about ya recovery."

"Yeah, I'm serious about staying clean, Mr. Frank. My son is my heart and soul. I want him to share in the joy I feel being drug-free." Nigel scratched his head.

"Just keep up the good work and he'll come around. On another subject, have you been keeping up with your appointments at P&P?"

"Yeah, I go to see Ms. Cooper once a week and do my urinalysis testing on Mondays and Thursdays. I got them bases covered. I don't mess around with my freedom."

"Good, good. Do you have anything else on ya chest?" Frank asked.

"Nah, I'm straight."

"Well, I guess I'll see you next week. Again, Nigel, if you ever have a problem and need someone to talk to, please feel free to call me." Frank extended his hand to Nigel, and they shook hands.

After leaving AACC, Nigel decided to stop by the church to talk with Reverend Mitchell. He wanted to share with him his current dilemma. The minister was very active in the community and usually on the run finding new philanthropists to donate to the church. He was so busy lately with church business that the two hadn't had much time to talk in detail. Nigel knew that he would be there because he had Bible study class and usually stayed afterwards to work late on his sermon for the upcoming Sunday. It was only a twenty minute walk from the treatment center to the church, so Nigel opted against taking the bus. Besides, he figured that a brisk stroll in the fresh air would help to clear his mind.

When he reached the church, he noticed Reverend Mitchell's BMW parked in his reserved spot in the otherwise empty parking lot. He used his key to enter the building. As he entered the building, he noticed that all of the lights were out except for the one coming from Reverend Mitchell's office.

As he got closer to office, he could hear Rev. Mitchell's in an intense conversation with someone, but he couldn't make out what they were talking about until he got closer to the door, which was cracked enough for him to see into the room. He was surprised to see Rev. Mitchell talking to the same young man that he saw him have a confrontation with in the parking lot of the church when he first came home.

"Mr. Mitch, I'm telling you, man, this new shipment that we got coming in from them Colombians is gonna make both of us some rich men," the young man stated.

"It sure will, as long as you keep them young boys out there grinding on them corners for me. I need to get all of that money. I'm getting tired of this church racket. These fucking church people can be a nuisance."

Rev. Mitchell inhaled several lines of cocaine up each nostril from the pile that was situated on his desk, and his associate did the same. Nigel couldn't believe his eyes or ears.

"I feel you on that, unc, but you gotta admit that you done got rich in the God business. I don't know how you did it for so long. It would have driven me crazy."

"Shit, it was easy. Saving souls ain't no different than us

selling drugs. It's all about selling a dream. Niggas wanna get high to escape the real world. Niggas come to church so that God can give them a fantasy image of life in Heaven. Me, I'm a hustler in every sense of the word. I saw an opportunity to make some easy money standing up in the pulpit, and I took it."

"You going to hell, nigga," the young man joked.

"That's cool, but I'ma go there a rich man."

The two men continued inhaling cocaine as they conversed.

The man got up from outta his chair and reached into a briefcase. He pulled four kilos of cocaine and placed them on Rev. Mitchell's desk. "Here you go, Rev. That's four birds for us. I wanna see how fast my young troops can get rid of this work."

Rev. Mitchell's eyes lit up when he saw the packages of cocaine. "This will be gone in no time the way ya crew be out there grinding. Ya know what, young blood, this church is the best front in the world for our little business arrangement. The law would never expect us to be doing this kinda business out of a church." Rev. Mitchell took the packages of cocaine and placed them in the safe behind his desk. The church was his stash house before putting the drugs out on the streets.

As he looked on, Nigel accidentally brushed up against the door, and it swung open.

The young man stood up and drew his revolver. He pointed it directly at Nigel. "Who the hell is this?" he asked. The cocaine had him wired and eager to pull the trigger.

"Calm down, brother. Put that thing away. He's cool. That's just Nigel. He works here. He's a part of the family."

The man lowered his weapon.

"Rev. Mitchell, what's going on here, man? What are you doing? Tell me this ain't what I think it is."

"Calm down, brother, calm down," Rev. Mitchell stated. "This is my business partner, Paul. I was gonna bring you into the fold eventually after I tested you out for a while to make sure you were reliable."

"Bring me into the fold? What happened to all of that talk about you not selling or using drugs no more? What happened to all that talk about God's soldiers not needing artificial stimulants to survive in this world? Explain this shit to me, Rev.? Tell me that you ain't another one of them fake preachers ripping people off."

"Look, brother, I'ma break this down to you real quick. What I kicked to you was real about God's men not living off of scraps. Sometimes even God's soldiers have to get their hands dirty. Do you think I could have amassed all that I have without God's permission?"

"You tryin' ta tell me that God condones you selling drugs in the community?"

"I'm telling you this bluntly, brother—I do what I do to get what I want. Right or wrong, ain't no nigga out here gonna be my judge when they ain't paying my bills. I want the finer things in life, and if it means that selling this white shit and spittin' a bunch of religious talk is gonna get it for me, then I'm all for it. Now you know everything. I like you, Nigel, and I want you to be a part of my empire. Are you trying to get down with the program or what?"

"Man, I can't believe this. You are full of shit. I thought you was the real deal. You just like all these other preachers out here. I don't want no parts of what you about."

"Well, then we can't let you leave outta here alive after what you just saw, now can we?" The young man raised his weapon and pointed it at Nigel once again.

"Put that away, Paul. Brother Nigel is cool. He's from the streets. He ain't gonna say nothing about anything. Are you, Nigel?"

"Nah, I ain't never been a rat. Y'all secret is safe with me," Nigel told them.

"You trust this nigga not to talk? Fuck that. I say we dead him."

"If you don't get that gun outta my face without using it, I'ma make you eat that muthafucka." The old Nigel Hawkins that showed no fear in the heat of battle was alive and kicking.

"Put that gun down, Paul. Let's not do nothing stupid. We've go too much money involved here, partner."

"I'll put it down, but if this shit comes back on us, it's gonna cost you ya life." Paul looked in the minister's direction, lowering his weapon.

Rev. Mitchell nodded his head, signaling that he understood the consequences of giving Nigel a pass. "If the brother doesn't wanna get down with us, that's his choice. I was gonna make you a rich man, Nigel. Ain't you tired of working hard for scraps? Come on now, you told me that you used to be a hustler. Where's that hustler spirit?"

"That hustler spirit is dead and stinking, like I thought yours was. I see that you talk the talk but can't walk the walk."

"I'm sorry that you feel that way, brother. You know that means I can't have you working at the church anymore after what you just saw. Just know that it's because I like you that you're still alive. Young blood would put two to ya dome without a second thought. Make this your last day working here. I'll mail your final paycheck to your house. Oh, yeah, I hope you're not foolish enough to show up for church on Sunday . . . because if you do then you will be dealt with severely."

Nigel walked outta the room with his head hung low. He was disillusioned as he exited the church. The man that he'd put so much faith in was a fraud. Did that make his belief in

God unreal? Were all of the good things that he'd taught him about staying clean from drugs unreal as well, if the man that taught him these things didn't live by the same principles? He was thoroughly confused. Not only was his spiritual foundation shaken, he was also now unemployed and back to square one.

The high that he felt after leaving the meeting at AACC was gone. *Fuck it*, he thought. The urge to use crept into his mind. He picked up his cell phone to make a call.

"Hey, Fats, what's happening, man?"

"Who dis? Nigel? Damn, blood, I'm just chilling. What's up?"

"I got a lot of shit on my mind right now that I don't feel like dealing with. Come pick me up, nigga. I'm at Greenmount and North."

"Me and Rick'll be there in fifteen minutes," Fats said. "Hold tight for me."

Throwing caution to the wind, Nigel sought out his old friends, Pretty Ricky and Fats. Even though they were nothing more than two dope fiends, at least they were true to themselves, unlike Reverend Mitchell. Recovery was the last thing on his mind now. He needed to get away from the real world, and Pretty Ricky and Fats would have just what he needed to accomplish his goal.

27

Raynard's funeral was the saddest day in young JR's life. He had to bury his best friend. Even though they weren't as tight as they used to be, he still had mad love for him. They had been through a lot of things together through the years. They made money together, fucked bitches together, and caught many bodies standing side by side.

Now that Raynard was gone, he felt a sense of emptiness. All of his plans to break off from Polo's organization didn't matter at the moment. He wanted to find out who killed Raynard for sure, so he could make them pay.

Polo, who JR hadn't spoken with since the funeral, was tight-lipped about the circumstances surrounding Raymond's death. He thought that it was kinda strange for him to be outta the loop of things given their history together. He was even more thrown off when Polo called him earlier telling him to come down to the GQ Social Club to have a sitdown. Polo didn't sound like himself. Something big had to be up.

When JR entered the lounge, the place was packed with a bunch of Polo's other lieutenants and workers. JR shook hands and exchanged pounds with his comrades as he made his way to the back office to talk to Polo. When he knocked on the door, he was greeted by Polo's two top musclemen, Wayne and Lamar.

Polo was seated behind his desk, his grill broken down and looking stone-cold crazy. The half-filled bottle of Hennessy on his desk signified that he'd been drinking heavily, trying to cope with his son's death.

"Come on in here, nigga. It took you long enough to get here." Polo took another sip of his glass of Hennessy.

"Polo, I'm sorry I was late," JR said. "I got caught in traffic. What's the deal, boss? Did you find out who the niggas was that killed Raynard? I wanna take care of them myself,"

"Shut up, nigga. You don't tell me what you wanna do. I'm the one that calls the shots in this organization, or have you forgotten?" Polo asked, his speech slurred.

"Nah, I know you the man, Polo."

"Don't patronize me, muthafucka. I know you been making moves on the side without my permission. You didn't think that I would find out, did you?"

JR tried to play it as cool as possible. "What you talking about, Polo? I would never cross you." He knew Polo had the upper hand on him, with all of his soldiers mingling throughout the place. He had a choice to make, either continue his lie or fess up to Polo about his plans. Neither choice would turn out good for him.

"You sure you wanna say that? Think before you answer that question because if you give me the wrong response, then that's your ass."

"A'ight," JR confessed, "I ain't gonna front. I do wanna break off and do my own thing, but I would never make a move without getting with you first to let you know what was up."

"Is that right? Then why the fuck was you snuggling up to

them Colombian muthafuckas up in New York when I sent you up there to handle business for me?"

Before JR could respond, Wayne and Lamar swooped in from behind him and lifted him off his feet and slammed him down on the couch across from Polo's desk.

"Calm down, Polo. It's not what you think. Yeah, I was trying to make a move of my own, but I wouldn't have done nothing officially until I got ya blessing. I put that on my seeds."

"It's funny that you mentioned your seeds," Polo said. "Lamar, go in the back and bring out my lil' surprise."

Lamar left and returned from the back room with Rochelle and JR's two kids, who were bound with rope and their eyes covered with blindfolds, and stood them against the wall.

"What the fuck is going on here, Polo?" JR asked nervously. "Why you got my family here?"

"Shut up. Don't speak until I tell you to, you lil' lying piece of shit. I've been in this game much longer than you and that's not by accident. Nothing goes down in this city without my permission. As far as the drug game goes, you're done in this city. I'm turning your crew over to Lamar here. You won't make another red cent off of my name in these streets. As far as your family, they're here for me to use as leverage to get you to do exactly what I want you to do." Polo chuckled.

"Please don't hurt my kids, Polo. I'll do anything you want, I swear."

"Relax, I wouldn't harm a hair on Rochelle's head. She's too precious to me. Ain't that right, baby?" Polo asked jokingly.

Lamar and Wayne laughed as well.

Polo walked over to Rochelle and planted a kiss on her cheek as his hands caressed her ass.

"Come on, Polo, you ain't even gotta disrespect me like

that. That's my girl. She ain't just some bitch on the street," JR said, seething with anger, but helpless.

"She's a bitch to me, but she does have some good pussy. We've become very close lately, while you've been out running the streets. While the cat's away, the mouse will always play."

"You been fuckin' my girl? Polo, how could you do this to me? You said I was like a son to you."

"Nigga, please . . . you ain't no son to me. I was playing you like a flute. I fucked ya bitch, just like ya father stole ya mother away from me. All the love I showed her and she turned her back on me for that bastard Nigel. I loved her dumb ass. She was a disloyal bitch, and that's why I killed her."

"You killed my mother?" JR asked, a look of disbelief on his face.

"Yeah, I had the bitch killed and had her buried somewhere she'll never be found. She didn't just disappear, I made her disappear." Polo laughed sadistically.

"I'ma kill ya ass, Polo!" JR charged toward Polo, but the clicking sound of Lamar's and Wayne's guns stopped him dead in his tracks. While it was true that he didn't have much love for his mother because of the way that she'd treated him, it still infuriated him to see the man responsible for her death be so bold as to brag in his face about killing her.

"Sit ya five-dollar ass back down on that couch, nigga!" Polo commanded.

"What you want from me, man?" JR asked angrily.

"I'm glad you asked. First of all, you're gonna take care of that New York nigga, Shakim. He's the one that killed Raynard. Y'all got me caught up in y'all lil' beef. I'm holding you responsible for Raynard's death because I never gave either one of y'all permission to go to war with them cats. You get no help from none of my people to do the job. You're on ya own. I don't care how you do it, but I want it done."

"You went through all of this for me kill that nigga, Shakim? Polo, I would have done that shit for you for pleasure."

"That ain't all I want. I also want ya father dead. That nigga has to go. I'll have ya family here as my security blanket. Once I see that both of them fools is six feet deep, I'll let ya bitch and ya lil' bastards go. I'm a fair man. You've got one week to make this happen. Now, get the fuck outta here," Polo shouted. "and don't come back until the job's done."

JR looked at Rochelle and his kids as Wayne led them into the back room at gunpoint. He was filled with mixed emotions. On the one hand, he hated Rochelle for fucking Polo; on the other, he loved her and his kids and didn't want to see them die. He knew Polo was crazy enough to kill them if he didn't do what he said.

His biggest problem in getting rid of Shakim was that he didn't have Polo's muscle to help him. And he had to think quickly, because time wasn't on his side.

28

Agent Cooper cruised in her graphite pearl Honda Accord coupe listening to the soulful stylings of India Arie on her stereo. She was on her way to make her monthly home visit to Nigel Hawkins, her favorite client. As she cruised down the road, she bobbed her head to the music. Since the first day she'd met Nigel, she was instantly attracted to him. She tried her best to fight her raging hormones and to keep their relationship strictly personal. However, after every visit he made to her office, it became more difficult. Nigel's charm and good sense of humor had her laughing endlessly whenever he came to see her on his report day. She loved the compliments that he bestowed upon her about how beautiful she was.

As a single, divorced mother of a ten-year-old daughter, and with no current love interest in her life, Nigel's flirtation with her was the closest thing she had in her life to male companionship. She was tempted on several occasions to cross the line with him when they were alone in her office with the door shut.

Nicole Cooper had been a parole agent for ten years. It was her first job after graduating from Howard University with a bachelor's degree in criminal justice. She married her high-school sweetheart, Leonard, in her sophomore year in college. They'd helped each other through school and had the perfect relationship, until Leonard lost his job with the government due to an altercation with his supervisor. Unemployed with no desire to find a new job, he became a couch potato and occupied his days drinking beer and watching soap operas. Whenever he drank, Leonard became physically abusive toward Nicole and their daughter, Leanna. The abuse went on for about two years before Nicole decided that she had enough.

Since their divorce, she'd only dated a few times and basically just spent most of her time with her daughter. Most of the men that she came across didn't spark any desire in her to get to know them better. When Nigel Hawkins came along, he reminded her most of the man that she loved the most in this world, her father. Nigel had a lot of the same ways and mannerisms.

Nicole's father, Darwin, was the most important man in her life until he died in her last year of high school. He died from cirrhosis of the liver after many years of drinking heavily. Even though, he was an alcoholic, he went to work every day and always made sure that the bills were paid. He could do no wrong in Nicole's eyes. She was daddy's little girl. He spoiled her to no one end.

She took care of him when he would come home from work too drunk to make it to bed. He tried to stop drinking several times, only to fall off the wagon after a few weeks. Nicole even went so far as to attend AA meetings with him as a means of support, but nothing helped. Alcohol was something that he couldn't live without for too long.

Darwin Cooper was an easy-going guy until he was intoxicated. Once he had a buzz on, he turned into an entirely different person. He and Nicole's mother would battle constantly, both verbally and physically, whenever he came home drunk. When he sobered up in the morning, he didn't remember anything that he did or said the night before. He would bring home flowers to Nicole's mother and a toy for Nicole as a way to make amends. Nicole's mother grew tired of him and eventually divorced him after being married for twenty years. Despite the divorce and his drinking problem, he and Nicole remained close until his death.

Nicole parked her car in front of Mrs. Hawkins house and exited the vehicle. When she got out of the car, the above-the-knee skirt she had on, along with her low-cut blouse, elicited hisses and howls from Mrs. Hawkins's neighbors as she walked toward the front door.

After she knocked four times hard on the front door, Mrs. Hawkins finally answered.

Mrs. Hawkins answered the door with a worried look on her face. "Hello, Ms. Cooper. Come on in." Mrs. Hawkins invited her to join her for a cup of tea, and Nicole accepted, following her into the kitchen.

"Thank you for the tea. Is your son around? I was concerned because he missed his appointment with me today. That's not like him. Whenever he's running late, he usually calls me. Today he didn't leave a message or anything. I hope that he is all right."

"Child, I don't know where my son is at right now. He hasn't been home in two days. He hasn't called me either. I don't know what to think. I'm just glad that I haven't received a call from the police department asking me to come identify his body."

"I'll you tell where he is," Franklin said as he walked down the stairs. He'd overheard their conversation from the top of the stairs and decided to add his two cents into the mix. "He's in some crackhouse gettin' high. I told you, Mama, that he would be right back to his old tricks in no time."

"Shut up, boy. This young lady here is Nigel's parole officer, Ms. Cooper. You need to mind ya business. You don't know what happened to Nigel. You always wanna think the worst of ya brother. Since he's been home, he's been in church every Sunday. That's more than I can say about you for the past two weeks."

"I'm sorry, Mama. I didn't mean to be disrespectful, but I'm just telling you the truth. They say that once somebody is an addict, they're always an addict, and Nigel is no different."

"I don't mean to interrupt you, but you should understand that statement before you speak on it. It's true that an addict will always be an addict, but that doesn't mean that he can't recover from his disease. As long as Nigel's alive and willing to try, I would like to think that there is hope for him to beat his disease as well."

"Well, I've said my piece on the subject. Y'all two can believe in that fool if you want. He ain't nothing but a junkie in my eyes, and I'm sick of him having my mother up all night worrying about him. I wish he would just go away." Franklin went back upstairs to finish hanging draperies in his mother's bedroom.

"Ms. Cooper, please forgive my son. He and Nigel have never gotten along since they were kids," Mrs. Hawkins explained. "He and his other brother have always been jealous of Nigel because he was their father's favorite. I'm sure glad that my son has someone understanding like yourself as his agent."

"Well, I don't believe that any of my clients are bad people. I just think that they make bad decisions. It's my job to help them see the error in their decision-making. Sometimes individuals like your son come along who make me believe that change is possible."

"Thank you for believing in him. Maybe between me, you, and his minister, Rev. Mitchell, we can keep him on the straight and narrow path. Would you like for me to have him call you once he shows up?" Mrs. Hawkins asked as Nicole finished her tea.

"Yes, that would be fine. Well, I have to be on my way."

Nicole stood up to make her way to the door when a key began to turn in the lock. Nigel appeared from behind the door looking disarrayed. He had on the same clothes from two days ago. His hair was uncombed and he was in a need of shave. When he saw Nicole, his eyes opened wide. He was nervous. He knew he couldn't hide that the fact that he had been using from her because his appearance gave him away.

"Agent Cooper, what are you doing here?" Nigel asked with a worried tone.

"Nigel, you missed your appointment today. I was concerned about you. Judging by the way that you look, I see that I had every reason to be." Ms. Cooper looked Nigel up and down.

"I'm sorry I missed my appointment. It's not what you think. I went to a party with an old friend and wound up spending the night there. I know that I was irresponsible. You're not gonna violate me for missing one meeting, are you?"

"No, I'm not gonna violate you, but we need to have a talk. Today is not a good time. You need to get yaself together. I wanna see you tomorrow morning in my office. I want you to be there at nine o'clock sharp." Then Nicole asked sharply, "Is that clear?"

"Crystal clear," Nigel responded as Nicole left the house.

Nigel knew he was gonna get an earful from his mother. Before he could sit down on the couch, Mrs. Hakwins came up beside him and bopped him upside the head. "Where the hell have you been, boy? And don't you lie to me."

"Mama, I messed up. I was feeling down and I hooked up

with Fats and Ricky. I know that was a mistake. I just wasn't thinking clearly at the moment. I learned from my mistake, and it will never happen again. I can promise you that."

"You can't promise me anything. You look a mess. Son, you were doing so well. What made you mess that up?"

"I just had a lot on my mind. I was upset about the fight I had with JR. I lost my job. I just felt worthless. I guess you could say I resorted to doing what I know best," Nigel said, honestly assessing his feelings.

"You lost ya job? I can't believe that Rev. Mitchell let you go for no reason. What happened?"

"Let's just say that Rev. Mitchell ain't who he claims to be. He's a fraud. Seeing that for myself, it made me question my faith in the church. Now that I've had time to think, I see that it's not the church that's the problem, it's just people like him who abuse their position that make people think that all church people are unreal."

"I don't understand. What did he do to make you doubt him so much?"

"I don't wanna go into that, Mama. Let's just say that he will have a lot to answer for on Judgment Day. Let's leave it at that. The most important thing I'm worried about is what's gonna happen to me when I go to Ms. Cooper's office to-morrow. She might send me back to jail," Nigel said, dreading the idea of returning to the joint.

"I don't think you have to worry about that. She has your best interest at heart. If you ask me, that woman is sweet on you." Mrs. Hakwins smiled.

"Why you say that, Ma?"

"A woman knows these things, son. Never mind that. I'm just glad that you made it home safely. Go on upstairs and get yaself some rest."

"Okay, Ma."

As Nigel walked upstairs to his room, he saw Franklin in his mother's room working. When their eyes met, Franklin just shook his head and said, "It's a damn shame," under his breath.

In the past, Nigel would have seized the moment as an opportunity to get into a confrontation with Franklin, but the new Nigel chose to respond differently. He simply walked into his room and shut the door to be alone. He knew that his using and disappearing for two days did nothing but give Albert and Franklin ammunition to make him look bad in front of their mother. All they would do was feed her the notion that he was always gonna be a no-good crackhead. It was now up to him to prove them wrong by picking himself up from his relapse and starting his recovery process all over. Nigel was determined to do just that. With no job, he was forced to pound the pavement to find employment.

He sprawled across the bed and thought about the task that lay before him until he dozed off to sleep. Tomorrow would be a new day and a chance to re-establish his sobriety. Unless Nicole changed her mind and decided to violate his parole and send him back to prison.

29

Nigel arrived at the Guilford Avenue office the next morning a half-hour early for his appointment with Nicole. He went up to the desk and spoke with the receptionist, in her usual rude tone, told him to have a seat until Nicole said it was okay for him to come up to her office. The whole time that he sat in the lobby, his palms were sweaty, and his stomach was in knots. He'd never been so nervous before in his life. He did have a good relationship with Nicole, but she was still his parole agent. Her first obligation was to her job. Even though she said she wouldn't violate him, Nigel was open to the possibility that she might change her mind. Nigel was willing to accept responsibility for his actions even if it meant going back to jail.

The old Nigel Hawkins would have never come in to see his PO if he even thought that there was chance he would be going to the pen. He would have stayed on the run until the law caught up with him. His humbleness in the situation let him know that he had matured greatly, and even though he'd slipped up and used again, he didn't think it was too late for him to get back on track with his recovery.

Caught up in his thoughts, Nigel almost missed his name being called by the receptionist. He made his way to the elevator and up the stairs to Nicole's office to face the music. When he entered her office, he wasn't greeted by her warm smile and bubbly personality. He closed the door behind him and took a seat across from Nicole, who sat behind her desk with a serious, all-business look on her face..

"Hello, Nicole, or should I call you Agent Cooper today?" Nigel said, sounding on edge.

"Nicole is fine. Nigel Hawkins, I am so upset with you that I don't know what to say. How many times have we talked and I told you to contact me if you were having problems? How many times have I told you that my door was always open if you needed some added support? I thought that we had a good enough relationship that you would come to me before you did something stupid. What happened?" she asked without taking a breath between her words. None of her other clients got her worked up like Nigel did.

"I know I disappointed you, Nicole. Hell, I disappointed myself. I really can't justify my actions. I did what I did, and I'm willing to accept whatever you do to me," Nigel said honestly.

"Is that all you have to say?" Nicole sat back in her chair and let out a loud sigh of disgust.

"I don't know what else to say. I was having a bad week. Me and my son got into a fistfight. I lost my job because I saw some things that I shouldn't have seen. The man that I thought was holier than thou turned out to be a fraud. None of that is a good excuse. It just happened."

"Well, how do I know that this was a one-time thing and won't happen again?"

"Because I recognize my mistakes and I realize that I have to be more intelligent with the way I handle things. I have a lotta time hanging over my head. I ain't trying to go back behind them steel bars."

"I just don't know what to do with you. I swear I don't know whether to kill you or hug you," she stated, giving Nigel the confirmation he needed to verify that the attraction was mutual, and opening the door for him to turn on the charm with her Freudian slip.

"Don't kill me. A hug of support would be nice. Can I get one?" Nigel asked boldly.

"I know I shouldn't do this, but bring your trifling behind over here." Nicole stood up from behind her desk to reveal a hip-hugging, form-fitting skirt that accented her curvaceous derriere.

Nigel walked over to her and took her into his arms. When they pulled apart from each other, their eyes met. Nigel leaned forward to kiss her, but Nicole put her hand over her mouth to stop him.

"That's not a good idea," she told him. "We shouldn't start something that could get us both in trouble. It's just not right."

"Nicole, I've been in trouble all of my life. I ain't scared. I like to walk on the wild side. I know you're not scared. We've both been wanting this since we first met. It's time for us to stop playing around," Nigel said boldly. His concern about her violating his parole had flown out the window. Instead, he planned to violate her in the most erotic fashion.

"Oh, you talking trash, huh? Well, Mr. Hawkins, I don't know if you're ready for a woman like me. You need to get yourself together first. You're my client. We can't do this. It's just not ri—"

Suddenly Nigel took her in his arms and planted a knee-knocking, nipple-raising kiss on her lips. Her body melted into his arms as their tongues wrapped around each other's. Then he grabbed her around her waist and hoisted her up onto her desk.

As his hands explored her body, Nicole closed her eyes and enjoyed the feeling. It had been over six months since she felt the touch of a man.

Nigel planted short passionate kisses on her neck. His hot breath made her nipples become harder.

Unable to resist the temptation, Nicole forgot she was at work. She unbuttoned her blouse to reveal her succulent breasts.

Nigel lifted up her bra and took them into his mouth one at a time.

"Nigel Hawkins, what are you doing to me, you nasty man?" she whispered in his ear and gently nibbled on his ear lobe.

"Making you feel like the beautiful queen that you are," Nigel replied. His words made her body convulse.

Since her abusive relationship with her husband ended, no man said anything to her that sounded so sincere and sweet. She pulled his shirt over his head to reveal his bare chest and ran her hands across his flesh as they gazed into each other's eyes.

"I've wanted you since the first time that we met. I need a woman like you in my life to keep me on track. I wanna feel what it's like to be inside you." Nigel ran his hand between her thighs until it reached up under her skirt. When he felt the moisture that dripped from her private parts, he knew there was no turning back.

"Ooh, Nigel . . . give it to me. Make me feel good," Nicole commanded in her gentle, sexy voice. She stood up long enough to slide her skirt and thong off then sat back on the desk.

Nigel obliged Nicole by dropping his pants to the floor and inserting himself inside of her slowly. This was the first time he'd been with a woman since coming home from prison, so he was overly excited. The tightness of her opening let him know that it had been a while since she'd had intercourse as well. Her facial expressions of discomfort turned into a smile of joy once he was securely inside of her love canal.

As Nicole lay back on her desk to enjoy his penetration, Nigel moved slowly so that their lovemaking wasn't loud enough for her coworkers who may have passed by her office to hear.

Nigel spread her legs wide as he pounded her vagina ferociously like a wild animal, his rhythmic strokes filling her up with sheer delight.

They went at it for twenty minutes before they both climaxed.

"Damn, that was good. It's been a long time." Nicole ran her hands across her breasts and squeezed her nipples.

"I'm speechless."

"I can't believe that I let this happen. I'm at work sexing a client. I have truly lost my mind. We can't do this again. At least, not here."

"I agree. So does this mean that I have a get-out-of-jail-free card with you?" Nigel asked playfully. He grabbed his pants and pulled them up as he fixed his clothes.

"If you keep giving me loving like that you just might," Nicole joked.

"Nicole, I was serious when I said that I'm done getting high. I'ma be up bright and early in the morning looking for a new job. Just give me some time, and my actions will speak louder than my words," Nigel said confidently.

"For some reason, I believe you even when common sense

tells me that I shouldn't. You've had that effect on me from the first time you came into my office. It's something about your aura that just turns me on. Your personality just disarms me. I can't fight it anymore. I want you, but I think we need to take it slow and play it smart," Nicole suggested, thinking about her job. She fixed her clothing and sprayed Febreze in the air to block out the scent of sex in the room.

"That's cool with me."

"Enough of the personal stuff. Let's talk business. I'm bumping you back up to doing urine testing twice a week. You don't have to do one today because I know it's gonna be dirty, but I want you to come in on Thursday for testing. By then, your system should be clean. I want you to bring me in some job applications to show me that you're looking for work. I also want you to attend one NA meeting every day and bring me in a signed NA slip from the meeting secretary. I'm putting my neck on the line for you. Don't make me regret it."

Nigel walked over to her and kissed her on the cheek. "You won't, Nicole. I'ma show you better than I can tell you."

Nigel exited the office with a big smile on his face. He was in a zone. *I still got it. That Hawkins charm is back in full effect.* When he exited the front door to the building, he noticed Fats and Pretty Ricky sitting on the front steps.

"Nigel, what's up, man?" Fats asked.

"Ain't much," Nigel said as he brushed past them. "I gotta run. I can't talk right now."

"Damn, Nigel! You ain't got a minute to kick it with ya boys? It was all good the other day when we were all together. Why you acting different now?" Pretty Ricky asked.

Nigel didn't respond. He just kept walking. He knew that if he stood there long enough with Pretty Ricky and Fats, he would wind up using again. The NA saying about "changing people, places, and things" in recovery was for real. He knew if he wanted to stay clean, he couldn't hang out with them. The last time they were together, it almost cost him his freedom, and he wasn't about to make the same mistake again.

30

JR sat in his car contemplating his next move. He had to get his family back. Even if Rochelle did do him dirty fucking around with Polo, he didn't wanna see her die. He loved her too much. She was a good girl for the most part. He started to feel partially responsible for pushing her into another man's arms. He was so caught up chasing new pussy out in the streets that he neglected home. He neglected spending time with his kids. They were growing right in front of his eyes without him being a part of the process. The thought of losing them made him a desperate and dangerous man.

He had been in the same spot on the corner of North and Greenmount Avenue for almost two hours waiting for Nigel to walk to the bus stop. He hoped that he would be walking down the street any minute from Parole and Probation. Having been on probation several times himself, he knew the urinalysis days of the week by heart. The bus line was the only one that went near where his grandmother lived, so he figured that this would be a surefire place to catch up with him. A bundle of nerves, he gripped tightly on the burner in his lap. He wanted Nigel dead for so many years. Now he would finally get a chance to carry out the execution.

JR was filled with mixed emotions about his father. He wanted to hate him for not being there for him, and at the same time, he felt love for him for reasons he couldn't fully understand. He had gone to bed many nights as a child wishing death upon Nigel. When he finally got a chance to see him face to face the other day, their fight allowed him to release some of his frustration, even though he felt bad about the whole situation later on. Deep down inside, he still wanted his father to be a father to him.

As he sat in his truck smoking on a blunt, he thought about the crazy stories his father used to tell him when he was younger. He thought about his father always coming to his defense whenever his mother abused. He wanted that protective person back in his life for so long but just never knew how to say it in words.

Once he met Polo, he thought he had found that father figure. Now that Polo's motives for bringing him into the fold had been fully exposed, he realized that was a big mistake on his part. It was too late for regrets. He had to act now. It was Nigel's life for Rochelle and the kids. There was no negotiating this fact.

After waiting another half-hour filled with uncontrollable anxiety, JR finally saw Nigel walking toward the bus stop. When he looked at Nigel, JR realized that he was looking at himself in the future. Physically, they shared a similar build and the same cocky, gangster stride. When Nigel got close enough for him to say something, JR rolled down the window to speak.

"Hey, can I holla at you for a second?" JR shouted.

Nigel looked into the window to see who it was. When he saw that it was JR, he was stunned. "What you got to say to me? I thought you spoke your mind the other day. You made it clear that you wanted no parts of me." Nigel puffed on his cigarette as he stood right in front of JR's truck.

"Look, Nigel, never mind that bullshit. I need to talk to you about something important. It involves ya grandkids that you wanted to get to know so bad."

"What about my grandkids? Did something happen to them?" Nigel asked with a look of concern on his face.

"Yeah, now if you wanna know more, I need you to get in so we can take a ride," JR said.

Nigel hesitated for a second before hopping in the truck. Once he was in, JR pulled off.

"So, what's wrong with my grandchildren?"

"Hold tight, I'ma explain it all to you in a minute. First, I need to rap to you for a minute. I got some things that I need to get off my chest. Let's go somewhere to talk."

Nigel got a funny feeling that something wasn't right. Nonetheless, he went along because he wanted to find out what was wrong with the children.

They rode along in the truck with neither one of them speaking a word. The silence was deafening until JR pulled into Druid Hill Park, where they both got out of the truck and walked over to a bench about ten feet away. Nigel took a seat on the bench, and JR stood in front of him.

"So, what's up? What did you bring me out here to the park for?"

"You know, when you first went to jail I used to cry myself to sleep every night. I felt like you and my so-called mother deserted me. It's because of the two of you that my life is so fucked-up right now. I hold you responsible for everything that's gone wrong with me," JR said reflectively.

"What does the past have to do with your kids?"

JR reached into the small of his back and pulled out his burner. He pointed it at Nigel.

"You're the one that taught me when I was little that this

drug shit was the life to live. Now look at you. You're a washed-up junkie. I'ma drug dealer just like you used to be. It's because of what you taught me that I chose to live this life. Now because of you, my girl and my kids are about to die unless I kill you," JR said, tears in his eyes.

Nigel's heart began to race. "Son, you don't want to do this. Calm down, please. How do I have anything to do with whatever has happened to your girl and your kids? Help me to understand what's going on."

"That muthafucka Polo wants you dead. He got a thing for you that he won't let go of because of the past. He's the one that killed Lorraine. She didn't just disappear. He made her disappear. He says that if I don't kill you, then he's gonna kill my girl and my children. So you got any last words, muthafucka? Speak now because you're about to meet the Grim Reaper," JR said coldly.

"JR, stop and think a minute. You kill me and you're going to jail for a long time. I know I did you wrong, but I swear to you I've changed. Let me show you by helping you deal with that punk muthafucka Polo. I know just how to get to his ass. It might have been a long time since we've dealt with each other, but I know that nigga like the back of my hand. A bitch nigga never changes, no matter how much money he got. He's still a sucker at heart. Put that gun down, and let's talk like men. I swear on my life I can get you out of this jam."

"That's some bullshit. How the fuck are you gonna help me?"

"I'ma come up with a plan to get rid of that nigga. I hear he's sitting fat right now. That means that he ain't on his p's and q's like he should be. That's the easiest time to catch a nigga slippin'. I say we turn the tables on him. Let's bring the drama to his doorstep, instead of letting him think that he holds all of the cards. You kill me and the only person that wins is Polo. He'll still kill ya girl and ya kids with me out of the picture. Think about it, JR. I know I taught you better than that."

JR lowered his gun. "You better be coming correct, old man. If anything happens to my family, then I'ma kill you without a second thought."

"I know just what to do to get to him, trust me, son. I know we have our differences, but I'm still your father. I would never let any harm come to you or your seeds. I would give my life for you or my grandchildren. It's because of me that you're in this mess. I taught you about this lifestyle, and now I gotta get you out of it. If anything happens to your family—hell, my family—I'll kill myself for you."

"That ain't all. He also wants me to kill this NY dude named Shakim that killed his son Raynard."

"This dude Shakim, is he a major player in the streets? Does he have a lot of soldiers?" Nigel's mind was clicking at full speed. This was the type of shit that he used to live for when he was in active addiction.

"Yeah, he's gettin' money, and his team is strong. What does that have to do with anything?"

"Everything is related, son. Leave it up to me, and Polo will be a distant memory once I'm done with him."

Nigel ran his plan down to JR.

JR was a little skeptical about it, but he had little room to bargain. He was desperate and needed all of the help he could get.

31

Since the day that he'd decided to help JR get his family back from Polo, Nigel went about his daily routine for the next few days as though nothing was wrong. He reported to see Nicole as she'd instructed him. His urine test was negative, and he'd supplied her with several job applications from businesses where he had sought employment.

The two of them went out to dinner and enjoyed a relaxing evening together. They went to a restaurant in a clandestine section of the city, where it was less likely that Nicole might run into one of her co-workers or other clients. If that were to happen, it would spell sheer disaster for her career. The chemistry between them was undeniable despite the dual relationship they shared as lovers and parole agent to parolee. They weren't sure how they were gonna make the relationship work, but they were both willing to give a try and let the chips fall where they may.

Although he'd stopped going to Rev. Mitchell's services, Nigel hadn't given up on the church totally. He started attending Sunday morning services with his mother at her home church. He refused to let Rev. Mitchell's hypocritical ways shake his faith. He began to realize how hard he had worked to make himself into a respectable man. He couldn't deny the miracle that God had worked in his life, getting him clean from drugs. Thanks to his mother and their long talks, he began to see that it was God and not Rev. Mitchell who had the power of transformation.

On the surface, his life seemed to be going along smoothly. No one would've suspected that he was up to something sinister. In fact, today his mother thought that he was out looking for a job. He hated lying to her, but given the situation, it was the best option for him to take. The less she knew about what he was involved in, the better it would be for her if anything went wrong. The police couldn't get information out of her that she didn't have.

Today was the day for everything to go down. Nigel and JR plotted out their strategy inside of an abandoned row house in Northwest Baltimore. JR pooled his financial resources to get the firepower that they needed, and Nigel agreed to put together a crew to carry out his mission.

Nigel came up with a killer scheme to get even with Polo and for JR to get his kids back. Once that was done, he was sure that JR would trust him. *What better way for him to demonstrate his love for his son than to help him get his family back?* Doing him this solid was sure to open the door for them to establish the kind of relationship he'd dreamed of having with him since he came home from prison. If everything went right.

Nigel had sworn that he was done with street life when he left prison, but if dealing with the demons from his past was going to bring him closer to his son, then he was willing to make that sacrifice.

"Man, I don't know if this plan of yours is gonna work. What do we need these bum niggas for?" JR glanced at Pretty Ricky and Fats and took a long toke on a blunt.

Pretty Ricky and Fats both looked like death warmed over from their years of abuse. Nonetheless, Nigel enlisted their help with his plan. He needed people with him that he knew were some thorough niggas when it involved gunplay. When he explained the situation to them, they couldn't refuse Nigel's request for help. With all of the shit they all had been through together in the streets, they would always be family.

"Because I can trust these so-called bum niggas here. They might look burnt out to you, but these two rode shotgun with me on many occasions. They're both serious with their shit. Neither one of them will hesitate to lay a muthafucka down if I say so. I trust them with my life. Let ya old man handle this, son. You have to trust me. And you ain't one to talk about somebody being a junkie the way you've been smoking weed. That's your third blunt tonight. You need to take it easy with that shit."

"I ain't ya son, Nigel. We ain't that cool, so don't try and tell me what to do."

Nigel raised his hands in submission, as if to say he didn't want to argue with JR. Inside, he knew that JR was putting up a front with his tough-guy demeanor.

Pretty Ricky said, "Cool it, young blood. We ain't gonna fuck this up. We're gonna get ya family back."

"Shut up, nigga," JR shouted. "Only speak when you're spoken to."

Pretty Ricky raised up outta his seat and charged toward JR, but Nigel stood between them. "Both of y'all, calm down. This ain't the time for y'all to be beefin'. My grandkids lives are on the line, or have you both forgotten?"

JR nodded his head in agreement and sat back down in his seat, and Pretty Ricky did the same.

"Now that's what I thought," Nigel said. "We gotta be on point for this mission here. No mistakes are allowed."

"Well, I'm ready to get busy. That nigga Polo is going down." JR loaded the clip into his 9 mm Beretta and placed it in his dip.

Pretty Ricky and Fats were armed with .40 caliber Glock 27 handguns to do some serious damage.

Nigel chose to pack the smaller snub-nosed Colt .38 revolver. It didn't have as much kick as the other artillery, but it suited him just fine to do what he needed it to do—put a hole in a muthafucka.

"So, how many niggas you think Polo got posted up in the spot?" Nigel asked.

"I know for sure that he's gonna have Lamar and Wayne up in there because those are his two main enforcers. Then he'll probably have one or two other cats up in there to back them up," JR replied.

"Well, that'll be at least four dead bodies outlined in chalk that the coroner is gonna have to clean up," Fats chimed in.

Pretty Ricky laughed.

"This is just like old times, fellas, but it's a one-time thing. We get in and get out with no mistakes. Are y'all ready to do this?" Nigel asked. It had been a long time since he'd held a gun in his hand. The cold steel in his palm brought back fond memories of his former life. The beast inside of him was thirsty for some "get back" on Polo.

"Hell yeah!" was the united response of his three comrades.

"Well, then let's roll," Nigel said.

They all exited the house and jumped into the beat-up Chevy Blazer that JR had copped from a fiend for an eight ball of crack rock. As they rode in the hooptie headed to Polo's lounge, 50 Cent's song, "Back Down," blasted out of the radio.

When they were in the vicinity of the club, JR turned the

music down to a whisper. He parked the car around the corner from the lounge.

It was a little after two o'clock in the morning, and the streets were empty. The club was now closed, but JR was sure that Polo had left Lamar and Wayne in the club to watch over Rochelle and the kids until he carried out Polo's mission. The only other persons in the club should have been the bartender and maybe one or two waitresses. The bright security light was on in the front of the lounge.

The four men exited the vehicle. Nigel and Pretty Ricky headed to the back of the club, and Fats stood behind the front door, while JR banged on it hard several times.

Lamar peeked through the peephole to see who it was. When he saw JR, he cracked a smile and opened the door. "Nigga, what the hell are you doing here? You must have some good news for Polo," Lamar said cockily. The bulge in his jacket let JR know that he was packing as he stood in the doorway.

"Yeah, I took care of my pops and that nigga Shakim, just like he wanted. I just wanna get my family now, man. Come on, Lamar, let me in," JR said humbly.

Before Lamar could respond or react, Fats popped out of nowhere and got the drop on him. He had his pistol locked and loaded, and was ready to squeeze.

Terrified, Lamar put his hands in the air.

"Lamar, who is it?" Wayne asked from inside the club.

Fats put the barrel of his gun up against Lamar's head. "Be careful what you say, or I'll blow your fuckin' brains out!"

"It ain't nobody," Lamar lied. "It's just some crackhead bitch. I'm about to go and get me a blowjob out in the car. I'll be right back."

Fats motioned for Lamar to come outside, and he stepped out of the lounge and closed the door gradually behind him.

"Who else is in there with you, besides Rochelle and the kids?" JR asked.

"It's just me, Wayne, Skeet, Trini, and Myron the bartender. Everybody else is gone. The club is closed. Polo ain't here. Come on, dog, you know me and you ain't never have no problems before this here situation. I was just doing my job the other day. Why don't you cut a brother some slack and lower that gun."

"Fuck that shit you talking. Is my family all right? Where y'all got them stashed at?"

"Yeah, they're fine. We got 'em down in the basement. We ain't harm a hair on their heads. Come on, man. Tell ya boy to put that piece away. You don't want them kinda problems with Polo, trust me."

"Fuck Polo and fuck you," Fats yelled. "Open that fucking door and let us in."

Lamar did as he was told and opened the door. As soon as they were inside, Fats emptied three rounds into his back, and he immediately slumped over onto the floor, his eyes slammed shut.

They trampled over the dead body and ran into the main area of the lounge.

When Wayne saw the two intruders, he reached for his gun, but before he could get it out of the holster, JR let off a round and shot him in the hand, knocking his gun to the floor. As soon as JR's gun went off, a loud thumping noise came from the rear of the club. Nigel had blown the lock off the back door with his gun. When Myron heard the commotion, he stopped counting money and slumped down behind the bar.

Trini and Skeet tried to run toward the back exit but were thwarted in their path by Nigel and Pretty Ricky, who walked them back into the lounge at gunpoint, their hands in the air.

"I want all of you muthafuckas on your knees, now!" Nigel demanded forcefully. Myron came from behind the counter and got down on the ground.

"Hey, Nigel," Pretty Ricky yelled, "I want that money out of the cash register."

Nigel stopped him in tracks as he walked over to the bar. "Nah, Rick, that ain't what we came for."

"Shit, man. That's free money right there. I know it's a couple of grand at least. If you don't want none, I know what I can do with it, ain't that right, Fats?" Ricky asked. There was no way the two crack fiends were going to leave a drawer full of money.

"Later, man," Fats told him. "You heard Nigel."

"Take me to my kids," JR demanded.

Wayne got up off of the floor and led JR to the basement, who stayed right behind him, with his gun off safety the whole time. If Wayne made one wrong move, his life would be over in an instant.

"They're back here, JR," Wayne said. "We made sure that they ate. Man, I hope that counts for something."

When JR saw Rochelle and the kids tied up in a dimly lit room like a bunch of savages, he was pissed.

Rochelle's eyes lit up at the sight of JR, a sense of relief overcoming her.

"Untie them, fool," JR demanded.

Wayne swiftly undid the ropes that were tied around their arms.

Once they were all free, they ran over to JR to hug him.

Quentin yelled, "Daddy, I'm glad you're here. I was so scared!" He ran over to grab a hold of JR's right leg, and Savion grabbed a hold of his left.

"Baby, I'm sorry for everything. I swear I am. I will never betray you again." Rochelle hugged JR tightly.

"This ain't the time, Rochelle. Take the kids upstairs. Me and Wayne got some business to handle."

Rochelle gathered up the kids and ran up the steps. She

saw the look in JR's eyes and knew it all too well. She didn't want the children to witness what was about to go down.

"A'ight, we alone now, nigga," JR asked. "Where's ya boss?"

"He's at one of his lady friend's house. I think he's with Maria. She lives on the East side," Wayne said nervously.

"He got any muscle with him?" JR asked.

"Nah, he's alone. He never takes anybody with him when he's getting some pussy."

"What's the address?" JR asked.

Wayne read Maria's address off to JR, who stored it in his memory bank. "I gave you what you wanted, JR. Come on, man, show a brother some love."

"I ain't got no love for you, clown. It's time to say good night." JR pulled the trigger four times, killing Wayne before he hit the ground. Then he ran up the steps, gun in hand.

"Is everything good?" Nigel asked.

"Hell yeah, it is," JR said nonchalantly. "I put that sucker to sleep. Now let's get rid of these other three so we can bounce."

"You is cold, nigga. I can see you got my blood in you, boy."

"You da one that taught me that a dead muthafucka can't tell the police shit," JR said, quoting Nigel to the letter about one of his many childhood lessons.

"Fats, take Rochelle and the kids outside to the truck now," JR demanded.

Fats hurried Rochelle and the kids out the front door. "Okay, come on y'all, let's go."

Two minutes later, he returned to the lounge out of breath from running.

"Rock-a-bye, baby," JR said. Without a second thought, he shot Skeet in the head twice. Then Fats emptied his clip into Trini, his blood splattering all over the floor.

Pretty Ricky shot Myron three times in the chest and

watched as he took his last breath. Then he went behind the
counter and snatched the money out of the cash register.

Nigel shot him an evil stare. "Man, how can you be thinking about money at time like this?"

"Consider this as payment for our services tonight, Nigel,"
Pretty Ricky responded. "I'ma need me a blast after this."

"I'm wit ya on that, blood," Fats added.

"Let's get outta here before the police come," Nigel stated.

The four men exited the lounge, leaving a bloodbath for
the police to handle. The murders would definitely make the
morning news.

Nigel had his plan thought out carefully. He wanted to hurt
Polo in more one ways than one, and since it was his club, Polo
would have some serious explaining to do to the police.

32

Polo got a call from Leonard, one of his top lieutenants, informing him about the murders that took place at his club. Leonard saw it on the morning news and instantly contacted his boss. Polo jetted outta Maria's house like a bat outta hell en route to the lounge. He was a bundle of nerves the whole ride there, knowing that he had Rochelle and the kids stashed there and that whoever hit up his club had to discover them at some point. It crossed his mind that this attack may have come from Shakim and his boys. That thought faded from his mind and turned to JR as being the most likely culprit. He would know for sure if this was true if Rochelle and the kids were gone when he reached the club. If they weren't gone and the police found them, he would be in for some serious shit. All Rochelle had to do was explain how Polo kidnapped her, and he would be guaranteed a long prison bid for the kidnapping charges alone.

Polo knew that the police would be on his ass for sure to see what he knew about the situation. With all of the media attention and the brutality of the murders, they would want answers and wouldn't rest until they got them. Along the way to the lounge, he called his attorney, Joel Goldenbaum, and instructed him to meet him at the police station in about an hour. He filled him in as best as he possibly could with what he knew about the shooting.

When he pulled up in front of the club, there were squad cars everywhere. The press was all over the scene. He was bombarded by reporters as soon as he stepped outta his car. They shoved microphones in his face to get a statement, but Polo made no comment. He briskly rushed past them into the lounge. There were several plainclothes detectives waiting for him inside. He did his best to remain calm.

"Polo, my man, it looks like you really did it this time, huh?" Officer Bradkowski said with a wide grin on his face.

Peter Bradkowski was a medium-built, White male with hairy arms. He had been on the force for over ten years in the homicide division. He and Polo had crossed paths several times throughout the years for several murders that took place involving Polo's crew. He was never able to make a case stick to Polo or anyone in his crew. That made him a bitter muthafucka, eager for a chance to stick it to Polo whenever the situation arose. This was the kind of opportunity that he'd been waiting for since forever. He hoped that today was his lucky day to finally nail Polo and send him to the pen for a long time.

"Man, I don't know what the hell went down here. I wasn't here. I was with a lady friend of mine. She can testify to that. Ain't no way in hell you gonna connect me to these bodies, pig," Polo replied boldly. His outward confidence was just a mask for his inner peace. Seeing his top muscle stretched out in a pool of blood had him feeling vulnerable to attack.

"Yeah, right, Polo. All of the deceased worked for you,

didn't they?" Bradkowski knew the answer to his question because he had butted heads several times with Lamar and Wayne in the past throughout the course of his many investigations of Polo's crew.

"So what? That might be true. But like I said, I wasn't here, and I don't know what went down."

"It looks like somebody was trying to send you a message. They killed your top bodyguards in a ruthless manner. The drug business must not be good to you right now, I surmise. I hear the word on the streets is that those New York boys are trying to take over the whole city. My guess is that they'll be gunning for you next. This would be a good time to tell us what you know."

"First of all, I don't sell drugs, I'm a nightclub owner. Allegations like that are scandalous, and I might have to sue you pigs. Second of all, I can't tell you a damn thing about this whole ordeal. If somebody is after me, ain't nothing I can do about that. I tell 'em all to bring it on. Polo ain't never ran from nobody."

"Well, if you have nothing to hide, then you wouldn't mind coming down to the station and answering a few questions, would you?" Officer Sam Johnson, Bradkowski's partner asked.

"That ain't a problem at all. I kind of figured that you would try something like this. I'm innocent. My attorney is already on his way to the precinct. Let's go, so I can get this over with as soon as possible. I need to grieve over my lost comrades," Polo said calmly.

"After you, sir," Officer Johnson said, and Polo walked in front of them out of the lounge into the streets.

They dodged the media and hopped into a squad car. Polo took the back seat. Since he came in voluntarily and wasn't placed under arrest, he didn't have to wear handcuffs.

In less than five minutes, they were at the police station. When they went inside, Joel was seated on a bench, waiting for Polo to arrive. The two men greeted each other with a friendly hug. Joel shot the two detectives a cold stare. They all walked toward the interrogation room.

Once inside the room, the two officers threw every question in the book at Polo. Joel was there to make sure they wouldn't try to entrap him or force some type of confession out of his client.

After being drilled for about an hour about every drug-related crime under the sun, Polo was allowed to leave. Since they had no cold hard facts to tie him to anything, they had no choice but to set him free. On their way out of the precinct, Joel and Polo engaged in small talk.

"Damn, Polo, what the hell happened last night? Somebody has it in for you bad. Do you know who could have done this?"

"Nah, I'm not sure, but I have a few ideas."

"Well, you better be careful, my friend. You need a lift?"

"Nah, I'ma catch a cab. I'll be fine. I'll be in touch," Polo replied. Joel shook his hand and was on his way. Polo had him on retainer for situations like this. Polo then walked up a few blocks from the police station to hail down a cab.

As he stood out on the curb, a man dressed casually in a pair of khaki pants, a polo shirt, and a light spring jacket walked up beside him. The man grabbed his arm firmly. Polo felt the butt of a gun piercing through the pocket of the man's jacket up against his back. When Polo turned slightly to see who it was, he was surprised to see Nigel. They hadn't been face to face in almost twenty years, but the sight of him still instilled fear in Polo.

"It's been a long time, huh, Polo? Don't get excited. We

don't wanna make a scene out here. Walk with me," Nigel said calmly.

Polo had no choice but to comply or otherwise have his brains spilled out all over the sidewalk. The old Nigel Hawkins that he knew would have had no problem committing such a heinous act. "N-n-n-nigel, where the hell did you come from? You had something to do with this?"

"Ha-ha, that's right, my old friend. I guess you're not as sharp as you thought you were. You always did think you could outsmart me. Just like in the old days, I always get the last laugh. That's enough with the small talk. Keep it moving," Nigel ordered.

Polo's body shook like limbs on a tree in the heart of spring on a windy day.

When they reached Fats's car, Nigel shoved him into the back seat and climbed in the car behind him.

"So this is how it's going down, Nigel?" Polo asked.

"You made it this way, partner. You killed my wife. You tried to send my son to kill me. You put my grandkids' life in danger? How did you think this was gonna play out?" Nigel asked.

Polo had no response. He couldn't even put up his best poker face because Nigel had him by the balls.

"Hey, Nigel, that fool always did wish he was you when we was kids," Fats joked.

"Fats, shut ya mouth," Polo barked. "You ain't nothing but a no-good crackhead."

"Yeah, but he's a crackhead that's gonna live to see another day. You, your time is just about up," Pretty Ricky said, adding his two cents.

Minutes later, they arrived at their destination. It was the same abandoned row house they had used as a meeting place in the beginning of the mission. The three assassins got out with their guns in hand and led Polo into the house to meet his fate.

Once inside the house, Nigel struck him on the back of the head and he fell to his knees. He stood in front of him and aimed his gun at his temple.

"You want me to beg for my life? Well, that ain't gonna happen. If y'all gonna kill me, then let's get it over with. Fuck all you bastards," Polo shouted.

"You got a lot to say for a nigga that's about to die," Fats said.

"That's right, I'm talking shit. I hear old Nigel here is all up in the church now. He's supposed to be reformed. He ain't got the heart to pull that trigger no more."

"Is that what you think? Well, once again you're wrong," Nigel said with a hint of doubt in his voice. Truthfully, he had changed from the cold-hearted man he used to be. The old Nigel inside of him wanted Polo dead. The new reformed Nigel now had a conscience about taking another man's life. Thinking back to when he'd left prison, this wasn't where he wanted his life to be at this point. He had visions of starting a new life with his son and family and wanted to be a productive member of society.

As he stood with the gun in his hand about to administer street justice once again, he was at war with himself. His hand shook feverishly.

"Well, kill me then, Nigel. Get it over with. I see ya hand shaking. You scare, nigga?" Polo asked, calling his bluff.

"Nigel Hawkins ain't never scared," Nigel replied coldly and pulled the trigger. He was at war with himself no more. He let off multiple rounds into Polo and slowly watched him bleed to death. When he was done, he picked up the prepaid cell phone that JR gave him and placed a call.

"Hello, officer, I wanna give you some information on a bunch of murders that done took place in the last few days. It involves that gangsta dude Polo and his crew. I heard that some New York boys led by this dude name Shakim was warring with dem. Word on the street is that Shakim sent some hitmen down here to kill Polo and his boys. I hear that they're responsible for them murders at Polo's club. I also hear that they killed Polo, and his body is up in an abandoned house off of Fulton Avenue in the 1500 block. I think the address is 1523 to be exact. Yeah, that's it, 1523 Fulton Avenue," Nigel said, disguising his voice.

"Okay, sir, we will certainly look into that information. Would you care to give us your name?" the operator asked.

"No, ma'am, I ain't crazy. Dem drug boys ain't killing me like they did them fools. I don't want no parts of that crap. I'm just a concerned citizen that lives in the neighborhood. I'm sick of all the drugs and killing that these boys do out here. It's your job as the police to lock them up, not mine," Nigel said before he hung up the phone.

"Nigel, you are a fool," Fats said as he laughed.

"Yeah, I am, but I get the job done. Did I sound like an old man?" Nigel asked.

"You sounded like somebody's grandfather," Pretty Ricky answered.

"Forget you, fool. Let's get outta here. The police should be here any minute," Nigel said.

His plan went down perfectly. The house that they'd used to kill Polo was located a few blocks away from one of Shakim's main drug strips. It was common knowledge in the streets that the two organizations were at war. The plan was to have the police think that Shakim was behind Polo's death as well as the bodies found at Polo's nightclub. With the heat on Shakim, the police would never give a second thought to the idea that anybody else committed the murder, and Nigel and his crew would be in the clear. This was a chapter in his life that was now closed. He just hoped that he could start a new one with JR without the turbulence of the past being a factor.

33

The murders of Polo and his top associates were all over the news. Television and newspaper reports described the killings as gangland executions carried out by professional assassins, a brutal turf war between two warring drug crews that turned deadly. Police reported issuing arrest warrants for Shakim and several of his top soldiers in connection with the murders. Their pictures were broadcast all over the news. They had yet to be brought in for questioning. The police were offering a reward for their capture. The news of all the murders made them look bad in the press, and they needed results fast.

Nigel figured that Shakim and his boys probably fled the city to go back to New York or somewhere else. Either way, there was no heat on him, and the police were occupied hunting for their suspects. He was relieved that it was all over. Now he could focus on building a relationship with his son.

Since the ordeal was resolved, Nigel and JR had hooked up several times over the following weeks to hash out their differences. JR got a chance to vent out all of his frustrations toward Nigel that he'd held inside for so many years, and Nigel accepted responsibility for his shortcomings as a father. They both agreed to take things slow in building a relationship, to start out as friends before they could work on being father and son.

Today, Nigel would finally get a chance to meet Rochelle and his grandkids officially. He'd been waiting for the past hour for JR and his family to arrive to meet him for dinner at TGI Friday's in Owings Mills. He drank two glasses of raspberry lemonade as he sat anxiously awaiting their arrival. The whole time, his mind was fixated on what it would feel like to be a grandfather. He wanted to know what kind of woman Rochelle was and if she was a positive influence on his son. He hoped that this experience had taught JR a valuable lesson and made him see the dead-end road that the streets had to offer. Caught up in a daydream, he didn't realize that his guests had arrived until he heard JR call his name several times.

"What you thinkin' about, man?" JR asked as he took a seat.

"I'm sorry about that, y'all. I wasn't thinking about much of nothing. I'm just glad to see you all. Are these my grandkids?" Nigel asked.

"Yeah, this is Quentin and Savion. Boys, this here is your grandfather. Say hello to him," JR instructed.

They both spoke to Nigel as they each held on to one of Rochelle's hands.

"Hello? Is that all you got to say? Come over here and give your Grandpa Nigel a big hug."

They both let go of Rochelle's hands and jumped into Nigel's arms. He scooted over to make room for them to sit next to him.

Rochelle took a seat next to JR. "Hello, Mr. Hawkins. It's nice to finally meet you under different circumstances. You two look just alike." Rochelle glanced back and forth at Nigel and JR.

"That Hawkins gene is a strong one," Nigel joked.

JR cracked a smile. "I'm starving. Are y'all ready to order some food? What you want to eat, Nigel?"

As though on cue, their waitress appeared, ready to take their orders.

"Well, let me get an order of baby back ribs and a side of French fries. I could also use a refill on this raspberry lemonade, if you don't mind," Nigel said.

The waitress then took the rest of their orders.

"You two make a lovely couple. When is the wedding?" Nigel asked.

JR almost choked on his glass of water, and Rochelle playfully slapped him on the arm.

"I don't know, Mr. Hawkins. I was just thinking about the same thing myself. Hint, hint."

"Nah, for real, we might tie the knot next year if all goes well," JR said. This was news to Rochelle. She and JR had talked a lot and promised to work things out since the Polo situation was over, but she had no idea that he was thinking about marriage just yet.

"Now that's what I'm talking about," Nigel said excitedly.

"So, Pops, what's ya next move?"

"Well, I got a job lined up. I'm supposed to start working at this warehouse downtown on Monday. It's in the evening from eleven to seven in the morning," Nigel replied. He tickled Quentin and Savion until they laughed uncontrollably. Seeing them filled him up with joy.

"That's good. You don't have worry about money ever. I got you on that end. After what you did for me, I owe you for life," JR said.

"You don't owe me nothing, son. I would do anything in the world for you."

JR nodded his head in gratitude. "You talking about me . . . when you gonna get a special lady up in your life?"

"Who said that I don't already have somebody special."

"Who is she?" JR asked.

"It's a sticky situation. I would rather not discuss it right now."

Rochelle butted in before JR could pry any further. "We understand. It's good to take things slow. When the time is right, I'm sure you'll let us meet her." She sensed that Nigel was caught up in complicated situation.

"Let me holla at you for a second in private. Baby, we'll be right back before the food comes." JR got up from the table to walk outside, and Nigel followed closely behind him.

"So, what's up, JR?" Nigel asked. "What you need to bend my ear about?" He took out a cigarette to smoke.

"Well, keeping real, I was thinking real heavy about something for the past couple of days. Well, before I got into it with Polo, I made this connection with these Colombian dudes in New York. They're gonna hit me with them bricks dirt-cheap. I was thinking that me and you should do this thing together Pops, just like you taught me when I was younger. What you think about that?" JR asked.

Nigel was so stunned that he dropped the cigarette in his hand. "Son, I can't believe that you would ask me something like that after all that just went down. You almost lost your family to this drug game. How can you possible wanna stay in that life and think that I'm gonna risk my freedom to join you?"

"Like you just said, it's something about that Hawkins blood. Grandpa was a hustler, you was a hustler, this is what I was born to do. I don't wanna do nothing else. Besides, with Polo and Shakim outta the way, this city is wide open for a new king to come along. I say that king should be me."

"I love you, JR. I think that I have proven that I would do

anything in the world for you, but I can't go along with you on this one. I see you still think you got another run in you. I know that feeling. I had it before. The difference between me and you is that I have hit my rock bottom. I don't want that life no more. All I can do right now is pray for you and hope you see the light before you wind up behind bars or in a casket."

"Shit, you can die walking out your front door. Selling drugs ain't the only way to die."

"No, but it sure as hell can speed up the process. What about Rochelle? What does she think about your plans?"

"My baby is down to ride with me in whatever I do," JR said proudly.

"I'm not gonna give up on you, JR. You're my son, you're my flesh and blood, I love you. My love for you is what kept me going all those years in jail. I know I can't make you change your mind. All I can do is pray for you."

"Yeah, my mind is made up. I just thought that I would throw that out to you. I still got that money stashed away for you. It's yours whenever you need it," JR said.

"Thanks, son, but I would rather work for what I need today. One thing I would like for you to do for me, if you don't mind."

"I can respect that. What you need me to do?"

"Would you mind going to NA meetings with me sometime? It would mean the world to me. I could use the support." Nigel was hoping JR would say yes to his request. He not only wanted him to come for support, he also wanted him to get a chance to hear some of the war stories of other addicts, in hopes that it might appeal to his conscience in making him see the destructiveness of selling drugs on the Black community.

"I can do that. I see you're serious about staying clean. That's good for you. Let's go back inside." JR put his arm over Nigel's shoulder as they went inside to rejoin the family.

Nigel knew what JR was going through because he'd been there himself in the past. It's called a hustler's ambition. When you get addicted not to the money but the rush of getting the money. It's the kinda thing where you can go through the adversity of near-death experiences, but if you're lucky enough to survive, that urge to get back in the game rises back up stronger than ever. It's as though your brains almost being blown out on the sidewalk didn't just happen to you but somebody else. Your mind will have you rationalizing all of the mistakes you made in the game and how you're gonna do it different this time. Nothing takes away this ambition of a hustler, but time and pain. JR was still young and hadn't experienced enough pain yet.

Nigel could preach to him until he was blue in the face, but it wouldn't matter. JR was bent on doing his thing. Nonetheless, Nigel swore to himself that he would be there with JR through his trials and tribulations that were sure to come down the road. Nobody in the game could escape the drama.

Nigel reasoned that the best thing he could do for JR was to stay drug-free and bend his ear with positive thoughts. He was committed to being a living testament and example to him that there is a good life outside of the streets. He wasn't gonna mess up his second opportunity for nothing in this world.

He sat through the rest of the evening with a fake smile as he played with his grandkids and got to know more about Rochelle, all the while, his mind fixated on how he could get JR to see the light before it was too late. He figured that now that the lines of communication were open between them, anything was possible as long as he maintained his faith in God and remained steadfast in his sobriety.

When they were done eating, they hopped into JR's truck to head home. Along the way, Nigel had dozed off. He was awakened from his slumber by the ringing sound of his cell phone. It was Nicole.

"Hey, Miss. How are you?" Nigel asked.

"Nigel, I'm not sure. We have a problem. Can you talk?" Nicole asked in a serious tone.

Nigel sat up in the seat to be more attentive to what she had to say. "Yeah. What's up?"

"I don't know how to say this except to come right out with it bluntly—I'm pregnant."

Almost in a state of shock, Nigel dropped the phone in his lap. Nicole could be still heard talking in the phone.

"Grandpa, are you okay?" Quentin asked Nigel after he saw the crazy look on his face.

"Nigel, what's wrong?" JR asked.

Nigel said nothing. His mind was frozen. He had just got JR back in his life, and now he had another child on the way. The drama never stopped for him, it seemed.

The End

Author's Commentary

Growing up in Baltimore City, I've seen the destructiveness of drugs and how it has affected virtually every Black family in my community. Almost everybody I know, including myself, has either an uncle, brother, sister, mother, father, or distant cousin strung out on crack or heroin, whether they want to admit it or not. It really doesn't matter if they want to admit it or not, because the facts are there in black and white. The drug problem in Black America is real and becoming more of a cancer to our society with each passing day. If something is not done soon, the future of our race is in serious jeopardy.

The ones that suffer the most from this epidemic are the offspring of addicted parents. Improper parenting and an environment of social dysfunction render most of these children powerless and ignorant to their true potential to achieve success in life. That is why today we see the corners of our inner cities filled with young Black men peddling death to one another instead of working toward a more progressive and productive future for themselves and their community. Instead of being the next generation of great thinkers and businessmen, they are on a course to become long-term residents of our nation's jails and penitentiaries.

I have worked for over ten years as a counselor in the addictions field, dealing with a wide of array of clients struggling with chemical dependency issues. I've seen how devastating addiction can be not only for the drug user, but also the individual's entire family. I've counseled mothers who have shared stories about selling their child to drug dealers for a ten-dollar crack rock, and grown men who have admitted to prostituting themselves on the streets for their next fix of "Harrison Ford" (heroin). I've counseled respected public figures and seen how drugs have destroyed their character and standing in the community. The one common thread that comes to mind with all of this insanity is that drug abuse will lead all of its afflicted individuals, no matter what their social or financial status, down one similar path. That path is one of humiliation, degradation, a loss of self-respect and self-worth, and nothing but a colossal waste of a human existence.

My last statement is not to suggest that a drug addict's life has no value, because it does. I'm suggesting that until the individual begins to believe within himself that he has infinite value and limitless potential, his time on this Earth will have been nothing more than a waste of his God-given talent. I don't believe that any of us was created to become addicted to a substance, but I do believe that some of us, utilizing our God-given right of free will and choice, made the unwise decision to indulge in drugs even after having some knowledge of its negative effects. My argument is that the same free will that was exercised to take that first blast is the same free will that the addict must recapture to become whole once again. This is not an impossible task because I've witnessed firsthand many success stories.

Although this novel was a work of fiction, the struggles of Nigel Hawkins parallel the plight of many Black men in our society today who at some time or another in their lives have allowed themselves to be sucked into the false dreams and promises offered by the world of drugs and crime. Nigel's battle with his own personal demons, while at the same time trying to right the wrongs that his actions have contributed to his own son's delinquent behavior, is only a microcosmic view of a larger cultural issue that continues to plague father-son relationships in the ghettoes of Black America. I've come across many Black men who come home from prison determined to change but, due to unforeseen circumstances, find themselves engaging in the wrong things (i.e. criminal behavior) for all of the right reasons like Nigel did in this story. The thug mentality that is pervasive in Black male youth today has been passed down from generation to generation within our community. Sadly, the drug culture and all that it entails has become a rite of passage of sorts for many young Black men who feel empowered by the fast money and the allure of notoriety associated with being a drug dealer.

After reading this book, I hope that the reader can take away several valuable lessons. First of all, for those who have no understanding of the multiple dynamics of drug addiction, it is my sincerest intention to have opened your eyes to seeing that drug addiction is truly a mental, physical, and spiritual disease, and not just something that happens to weak people incapable of just saying no to their drug of choice. Second of all, I pray that more Black men become accountable in their actions and decide for themselves that the street life is a dead-end road offering nothing but a surely catastrophic demise for anyone who chooses to indulge in such illicit activities. I hope that many more of my brothers take the time to maybe shed some light from their own experiences on a young brother who may be struggling with the same issues that led many of them into seeking a self-identity out in the streets, so that it may possibly dissuade him from falling into the same pitfalls as the hundreds of thousands of Black men now incarcerated across this nation.

Finally, for all of those individuals at war with themselves and their powerlessness over their drug of choice (heroin, cocaine, marijuana, etc.), I hope that you find a source of inspiration in the process that Nigel endured to achieve his sobriety. Please don't believe that drug addiction is a death sentence from which there is no escape. Know that once you have it in your mind to stop using drugs and disrespecting yourself, you'll find that there will be many people that will come into your life offering assistance in your journey. However, you must be just as diligent, persistent, and dedicated to staying clean as you were to getting high. Sobriety is a way of life that promises prosperity, but continuing to use will guarantee you nothing but pure hell for the rest of your days on Earth. Make the smart choice and make a change in your life!

Peace and Love,

Thomas Long

Be on the lookout for "A Thug's Life" the
movie
Entitled "4 Life"
Available on DVD in Spring 2007

For more information go to
www.watchmenowfilms.com or
www.athugslife.com